David Free is a critic and novelist based in Northern NSW.

GET POOR SLOW

DAVID FREE

PICADOR

Pan Macmillan Australia

First published 2017 in Picador by Pan Macmillan Australia Pty Ltd
1 Market Street, Sydney, New South Wales, Australia, 2000

Cataloguing-in-Publication entry is available
from the National Library of Australia
http://catalogue.nla.gov.au

Typeset in 12/17 pt Sabon by Post Pre-press Group, Australia
Printed by McPherson's Printing Group

MIX
Paper from
responsible sources
FSC
www.fsc.org   FSC® C001695

For my family,
and in memory of my mother

1

I'm starting to doubt this thing will end soon. Last night one of them came up to the house. I was inside, doing what I do these days when it gets dark. No lights on, no book, no TV, no sounds, just a glass in my fist with not much left in it. For some reason I was on my feet, walking past the big side window, when a whisper of movement beyond the pane made me halt and turn. And there the fucker was, standing out in the rain. At first I thought he was me. I thought I was looking at my own reflection: a trick of moonlight on glass. Then I raised my arm to take a drink and he didn't raise his. That was a worry, but I took the drink anyway. There was more light out there under the moon than there was in the house. We looked at each other for what seemed a while. I was drunk, which wasn't helping. If I'd said something to him he'd have heard it through the glass, but I could think of no quip equal to the occasion. One of us was in the wrong and I doubted for once it was me. He reached down for something near his waist. I thought: this is probably it.

I'm about to get shot. I had time to work out I wouldn't mind that very much. At least it would change things, one way or another. Then he brought the thing up to his face, and in the light of its flashes I saw what it was.

There's a way such scenes are meant to play out, in the age of the image. The infamous man is meant to stride towards the lens, hands raised into the storm of light, grimly primed to fuck up the other guy's camera or face or both. Out in the rain, the other guy seemed put out that I wasn't doing these things already. He'd got his shots, but he wasn't leaving. It was my turn to move, and movement has sort of stopped being my thing. I have this strange inertia these days. My tastebuds are all shorn off, and the world feels bleached-out, as if every day is the day after someone has died. But I wanted him gone. So I played my part, I drifted with the tide, which is another thing I seem to do now. I went for the front door. Beyond its stippled glass panes his volleys of light started up again, bursting like flak. He was moving back across the deck to the front steps. He looked washy and deformed through the glass, a lean nocturnal fiend supplying his own lightning. By the time I yanked the door open he was jogging down the dark steps, the tethered camera lolling around his waist. I didn't bother going after him. I walked out to the deck's edge and watched him trot away down the dirt drive. When he looked back through the weak wet moonlight and saw I wasn't coming, he stopped trotting and slowed to an insolent stroll. That bothered me. At last I mustered some outrage. The heavy tumbler in my hand was still half-full. I drained it in one go, as if biting the pin from a grenade, then hurled it high into the night. When it was somewhere near the peak of its arc I stopped hoping it would hit him. Maiming a journalist would be fun for about two minutes. Then it would start being one more thing I can't live down. Anyway it missed him. It hit my car instead. I heard the sound of glass bursting and hollow bodywork taking a deep dent: the sound of my life getting worse than it already was. Beyond the car, in the sheltering night, the photographer laughed. *Then* I wished I'd nailed him. He was down at the haven of the front gate now: out where all the vans are parked, with the logos of the TV networks stencilled expensively on their sides.

There are headaches so foul they pollute your sleep. I've forgotten what the other kinds are like. Even in my dreams I want to ram my skull through a sheet of plate glass to get relief. Bad tunes get stuck in my head and go round and round, their needle jammed deep in the melting shellac of my brain. I was dreaming she wasn't dead. We were talking. I couldn't hear what she was saying but that didn't matter. The point was that she was there. She had never gone away.

And then I had that moment of freefall when the dream is over but reality still hasn't kicked in. In that moment I still wasn't me and she still wasn't gone. And then I landed, and the truth lunged back into my head for another day, like a fat bandit vaulting the counter of a convenience store. I half-opened my eyes, and got a ruinous blast of morning light. I wasn't in my bed. I was on the couch. The phone was ringing. I shut my eyes again. You never know whether to open them or keep them closed. Each thing feels worse than the other while you're doing it. There was a coffee table to my left. I thought maybe there was something medicinal on it. Sometimes, the night before, I have the wit to lay out a care package for the morning after. I eased sideways to check. That made a fistful of small but solid objects slide off my chest and rain down on the hard wooden floor. Harmonicas. What a bad sign that was. Apparently I'd felt pretty good during the night. I had not acted in moderation. While my life burned, I'd lain there in the dark like Nero, playing the blues in multiple keys.

I sat up. The fire in my skull took a smudged moment to follow, slopping around in my wake like a shouldered sack of trash. Half-blind in the light, I squinted at the clock and hated what it said. I got up and made it to the sink by feel. The room isn't big, and there's not much to run into on the way. The phone was still ringing. At the sink I opened my eyes again, but not by much. Looking at things hurt. I reached for a bottle of what turned out to be olive oil. I didn't find that out by drinking it, but I got close. When I found the bottle I wanted I took a restrained lash of its heat. Restrained was the last thing I felt like being, but I had to go out in public today. I had to drive. I had to perform. From my uppermost cupboard I pulled down my war chest and dealt myself a wretched hand of blister packs: a pair of twos, a three, a five. I thumbed out pills. One pill I thumbed too keenly: it crumbled like plaster and sprayed to the floor. That put me down on my knees for a while, eating bitter white dust off the wood with a wet finger. I felt relatively okay down there. I wanted to rest my skull on the cold boards and stay there all day. But in ninety minutes I was due down in the vile city again, to assist Ted Lewin with his inquiries. I needed to be at my least bad for that. Nimbleness would be required. A line had to be trod. I didn't want to assist him too much. He was doing a solid enough job on his own. But assisting him too little was starting to be no good either. It was doing bad things to our relationship.

Back on my feet, I tried hard not to look again at that bottle of oil. Overnight, in the cold, the stuff inside it had gone all white and lardy. It reminded me of pornography, and pornography reminded me of her. There were ghosts everywhere, and she was all of them. I cracked a final pill from its cocoon and rolled it between my fingers and thumb. I was in two minds about putting it in my mouth. It was a gel cap, half-red, half-white. It was tubular and nasty, like a rifle slug. And it would work like a bullet too, if I took it. When it blew away the pain, it would blow away half my wits and motor skills with it. Going into Lewin's miked-up room in that state was semi-unthinkable, but so was going in there the way I felt now. For a while I got stuck on the paradox and just stood there at the sink, not moving. Tumbleweeds of razor wire clashed in my skull. Finally my hand got sick of waiting and made a rogue move to cram the pill into my mouth. It didn't work. My fingers twitched and botched the execution. The capsule hit my lip and dropped to the counter and rolled. I threw my other hand at it. That side-swiped it into the sink, which had been full of dirty water for exactly as long as she had been dead. The water was thick and oyster-grey. Pale blooms of scum or ice or lichen were floating on its surface. I plunged my hands through them. My forearms burned from the cold. The gel wouldn't last long down there. The longer it stayed under, the worse it was going to taste when it came up. If it was any other pill I'd have let it drown. But a box of red-and-whites costs more than I get paid for a book review. I frisked submerged steel.

My fingers were slick with grease. I pulled up a few things that weren't the pill. By the time I found the real thing it had the texture of a flagging hard-on. I swallowed it before I could decide not to. Tasting it gave me a solid excuse to take one more mouthful of bourbon. It tasted better than the sink water, but not by much. The day I start liking the taste of it will be the day I'm really in trouble.

I put on coffee. The phone was still ringing. I still didn't pick it up. I went to the front window and pulled back the edge of the curtain. The light lanced into my eyes and buried itself hilt-deep in my skull. Down at the front gate, where my dirt drive met the steep scrappy road, the big vans were still parked. They were from rival networks, but their crews stood together in one big chummy gang, breathing vapour into the dawn, a gaggle of drooling villagers waiting for the monstrous common enemy. Instead of pitchforks they had boom mikes on sticks. Instead of flaming torches they had steaming cardboard cups. The girl reporters wore big unsexy parkas. Sticking out from underneath was the stuff they would wear on camera: short skirts, dark stockings, high heels. One of them saw me at the window. She rapped the shoulder of the guy next to her and pointed. I let the curtain drop.

I sat there on the curtain's safe side and drank coffee till my breath tasted of that and not booze. I do not get head-aches because I drink. I drink because I get headaches. If you don't get the difference, leave now. On mornings like this one, the crack in my skull feels blazingly reborn. It feels as if it got put there overnight. I feel thick hot blood raging inside it like lava. The pain detaches me from the here and now. I rarely feel present in my own life. If it's not the pain, it's the stuff I take to get rid of it. And now there is the fog of the other thing too, her, hanging over the world like a sick scuzzy moonlight that won't go away.

The phone started ringing again. I hadn't noticed it had stopped. This time I decided to pick it up. It couldn't be worse than listening one more time to its endless bitter skirl.

'You dog,' a man's voice said. 'You sick, sick cunt. You're a dead man.'

'Come and do it,' I urged him.

He said a few more things. I hung up. I'd got his gist.

I poured more coffee. I have a mashed nose and a limited sense of smell, but even I can tell that the house is starting to stink of garbage. I've grown wary of putting things out at the kerb. I have become ashamed of my trash. A week ago I put out a crate of empty bottles. It wasn't even a big crate, as crates go. And the next day, down at the gate, I got questions about my drinking. I answered them with a fair bit of candour. I was a novice in those days. I still believed that the truth, or part of it, would set me free. I told them I drink so I can feel as good as everyone else feels when they don't drink. I told them my idea of fun would be never having to drink again. I tried hard to evoke my drinking's nuances. I told them about my accident, my head hitting the ground. I told them the details would bore them – the way they bore my expensive doctors, the way they bore me.

And that night the TV started saying I had a drinking problem. A psychologist came on and dropped dark hints about the lingering effects of head trauma. And I hadn't even told them the whole truth. Just a bit of it. And how sinister this fragment had made me seem, how abnormal. If you can't tell them everything, tell them nothing. Under a big enough spotlight, any life will start to look sordid. I'm still learning these things. My life used to be nobody's business except mine. Now it's everyone's except mine.

In the bathroom I ran water for a shave. I told myself that things weren't out of control yet. They just felt as if they were. I could still pull the ripcord whenever I liked. I am the author. I know things other people don't. Even Lewin. Especially Lewin. I know things he doesn't, and it would be rash to give up that edge too early. Then again, there is such a thing as waiting too long. Ripcords don't work after you hit the ground.

I got dressed. I wear what people expect a literary critic to wear: black jeans, black boots, a brown jacket over a grey shirt. It's the only respectable outfit I own, and I have reason to fear that it's starting to stink too, like everything else. In truth, literary critics don't dress like this. They stay home and write, wearing pyjamas. They don't shave. But suddenly I am a public man. I have an impression to make – or an impression to rectify, fast. People know who I am now, and I'm running out of time to make them think I'm someone else. When the first photo of me appeared in the newspaper, the headline said: *The Face of Evil?* You had to love that question mark.

I was running late. I filled a flask and slid it into the pocket against my heart. In the pocket on the other side I stashed a deck of foils and a small vessel of mouthwash. Everything I need to get through a day can still be discreetly carried on my person, as long as the day is only half a day long.

I locked the front door and went down to the car. In the slab of shadow cast by the house, the clumpy grass was still rimed with frost. The car still had shards of last night's tumbler on it. I swept them off and drove down to the gate. There I stopped the car but not the engine. I rolled my window down. And here they came, eclipsing the winter sun: the girl reporters losing the heavy jackets, the rolling scrum of branded mikes and lofted smart phones. Tedious as these scenes are, they must be played out. Not stopping for them feels good, until you see what it looks like on the news: your furtive car slinking past them, your smudged sinister form behind the glass. And them on their side of it, yelling the question at their own guiltless reflections. That looks bad. Even I can see that.

'Did you murder Jade Howe?' one of them now shouted.

'No,' I told her.

How many times do I have to say it? How many times do they have to *film* me saying it? Answer: one time a day for each different network. Every morning every last girl must ask it afresh, as if she's never asked it before – as if this time she will shock me into uttering the truth. If the camera doesn't get her the first time, she will ask again. And I must respond calmly, without boredom, every time – unless I want discourtesy added to the list of my sins.

'There've been reports,' said someone else, 'that your fingerprints were found in her bedroom.'

'I hadn't heard that,' I said.

'Mr Saint, did you murder Jade Howe?' another girl said.

'No I did not.'

The trick is to keep things flat, stripped of highs and lows. My worst moment of the morning will reliably feature as that night's money shot. All I can do is make sure the worst is not too bad.

'Why were your fingerprints in her house?' somebody else said.

'Because I was in there once,' I said, 'when she was alive.'

'In her bedroom?' someone said lewdly.

The guy from last night was back there on the fringe of the crowd, holding his camera over the pack like a priest lofting a censer. How many more shots of me does this guy need? Are there still people left who don't know what I look like?

'Wasn't she a bit young for you, Mr Saint?' said someone else.

I said, 'End of press conference.'

Detective Inspector Ted Lewin's eyeballs do not match. One of them is damaged or malformed. Violence has been done to the iris: the brown of it has oozed out beyond its natural circumference, like the broken yolk of an egg. When I have cause to look him square in the eye, I never know which eye to look square at. I don't have cause to all that often. When I get the chance, it would be nice to know the effect is not going to waste.

'I'm the last bloke on this case who thinks you didn't do it,' he told me this morning.

'Last week you were the second-last.'

'Well,' he said, 'this has been a bad week for you.'

The room in which I assist him with his inquiries is small. Nothing in it is designed to make you want to stay. There are no windows. Everything except the furniture is clinic-white: the floors, the walls, the panels of the ceiling, the strip lights. You can catch yourself thinking that nothing you say in there will matter in the world outside. You can catch yourself forgetting that there *is* a world outside. We sit on plastic chairs and face each other. For the first two sessions Lewin worked in tandem with some other guy, a mute sidekick. Now we convene alone – as if the other guy was the problem. I do my best to keep my body language open and relaxed. A laminated table stands to one side of us. On Lewin's end there is a stack of stuffed manila folders that gets closer to the ceiling each week. Above us, in the room's top corners, there are dark plastic bulbs housing digital cameras you can neither see nor hear. The air smells of nothing. It has a zero-gravity feel. In the sterile cube of that room, the nuanced answer goes down no better than it does at my press conferences. You are either one thing or the other in there: clean or dirty, guilty or innocent. You either have nothing to hide or everything to hide. Who are the people who meet this room's standards? They must have no secrets at all. They must be able to lay out their full life stories without hesitation or shame. Lewin seems like the kind of man who could do that. I've never heard him raise his voice. He doesn't swear. He keeps the temperature of things low. He talks about her dead body without passion. For him, her death is a given, a problem that can and will be solved. All he wants from me is the truth, pure and simple. Oscar Wilde had an answer for that. The truth is rarely pure and never simple. And look at what happened to him.

Lewin said, 'I've got blokes who think we've got enough to charge you now. Today.'

'The same blokes who keep leaking things to the press?'

'Things like what?'

'This morning I got told you found my prints in her bedroom.'

Lewin did a thing with his tongue that caused his cheek to bulge with displeasure. This is as upset as he ever gets.

'Who told you that?' he asked me.

'One of the people at my gate.'

His cheek whitened like a flexed knuckle.

'It's true?' I asked him.

'Would it surprise you?'

'No.'

'Why not?'

'Because I was in there. Once. When she was alive.'

Here was one of those times when I found it crucial to look him in the eye. His ravaged iris looked back at me, or seemed to. It didn't look happy, but it never does. His other eye, his good eye, gave nothing away.

'You never said this before,' he said.

'I'm saying it now.'

'Why were you in there?'

'It was her bedroom. Do I have to say it?'

Lewin waited for me to say something more, something better. He speaks only when necessary, and sometimes not even then. He prefers to listen, and watch, and let you blow your jittery load into the endless brutal silence. He is especially mute about the personal stuff, the dirty stuff. Boy did he land the wrong case.

'We were intimate,' I clarified.

'Okay. And when was this?'

'A couple – a few days before she died. I'd have to check the date.'

'I'll get you to do that, Ray. I'll get you to do that.'

The disapproving tongue rolled from the inside of his cheek to the inside of his lower lip. Sartorially Lewin does not occupy the cutting edge. He dresses like a maths teacher. A stick of white chalk would not look out of place in his hairy right hand. He wears old grey slacks with a crease down each leg. He wears abraded short-sleeved shirts and badly knotted RSL ties. Did he resolve, back in the mid-1980s, never to buy another shirt before retirement? Is he deliberately pushing them to the point of disintegration? His hips are narrow but he has a big old medicine ball of a gut. He has a formidable quiff of silver hair. His eyebrows have gone rogue: each bristle is as thick and stiff as a quill. There are further bushels of silvery growth on his forearms, in his nostrils, in the gulches of his ears. He wears white singlets under his shirts: their bulging rims swerve poignantly beneath his armpits, like the cables of a suspension bridge. I feel he has a stay-at-home wife who irons the trousers and shirts and mandates the wearing of the singlets. On his end of the desk, near his stack of folders, he keeps a grey felt hat, a fedora. It looks like Jack Ruby's. Unlike Ruby, Lewin does not commit the gaffe of wearing his indoors. I have never seen it on his head, because I have never seen him outside this room. To start with, but not for long, I let Lewin's bus-driver act lull and deceive me. I let his clueless threads give me a false sense of security. But what other sense of security is there, in the end, except the false one? I know now that I have to be on my toes for him. I went for years without needing to do that for anybody. My toes were badly out of practice. And then she came along. And now Lewin.

'It's time you started taking this seriously, Ray,' he said.

'I do. I will. I'm learning as we go, Ted. I used to think a few things were still my business.'

'Nothing's your business, mate. Not any more.'

'I'm starting to get that.'

'Got any more surprises for me?'

'No. And by the way, I wasn't just thinking about me. I was thinking about her too. I was thinking even a dead girl's entitled to her privacy.'

'Not a murdered one. Not in this room.'

'"This room"? The things I say in this room, Ted, have an eerie way of leaking out of it.' I seized this scrap of moral credit while it was handy, and threw it on my parched side of the scales. Who knew when the next crumb would fall my way?

'Let me worry about that.'

'Please do. So far it doesn't seem to be working. Who else listens to these tapes, Ted? Who's listening to us right now?'

'A lot of people who think they should be in here instead of me. A lot of people who think I'm not riding you hard enough. You're a hard man to stick up for, Ray. You keep lying to me about the small things. When that happens, people start wondering if you're lying about the big things too.'

He is good at making me feel I have let him down. And he seems to think I let her down too, when I do that. I feel I can decide that bit for myself, since I knew her and he didn't. Otherwise, I keep discovering in myself a dangerous urge to please him. Sometimes – this is an odd but recurrent thought – sometimes I suspect he knows everything that I know anyway, and more besides. Sometimes I think there's no point keeping the rest of my secrets from him. He knows most of the worst stuff already, and he still looks at me as if I'm human. Let's give him credit for that. Remember, he has raided and tossed my home. He knows about the booze and the prescriptions. His tech guys seized my laptop, and pulled a copy of its hard drive. There's stuff on there so bad that I choose not to remember it, but Lewin knows about it all. The images I look at late at night, all my aborted drafts: he has perused those maps of hell. After such knowledge, what forgiveness? He has sniffed the cadaver of my unpublished novel. Did he read it? Did he like it? One day he just handed the typescript back to me, silently. He knows nearly everything, and none of it perturbs him. No crime short of murder – her murder – vexes his great senatorial head.

'Let's go back to the start.' Lewin sighed through his nose. The silver hairs in there stirred. 'You first met her when?'

'At her place, a few nights before she died.'

'And then at your place, *one* night before she died?'

'One night before the night of her death, yes.'

'So you were intimate twice?'

'Not exactly.'

'Be exact,' he said without relish.

'On two separate nights – on two discrete occasions – we were intimate. Once at her place, once at mine. Not – or not necessarily – limited to once each time.'

'And before that first time you'd never met her?'

'Face to face, no. I *knew* her, because she sent me a letter once. As you know.'

'And you threw this letter out.'

'Yes. Eventually. Which at the time didn't strike me as an act I would subsequently have to explain, defend, read about in a newspaper, or think about ever again.'

'And she never sent you any emails?'

'No.'

'Never texted you?'

'No. We corresponded, the old-fashioned way. The way that doesn't leave a trace on a server. Which I know you don't like. But that's how it happened.'

'Do book reviewers normally get fan letters?' Lewin was not a literary man, but even he smelt the stink on this whopper. He kept coming back to it. Each week he made me say it again – to see if I could still pull it off with a straight face.

'Sometimes. Not often. But it happens.'

'The night you were at her place. How long did you stay?'

'All night.' Another lie, in theory. But when I said it, a strange thing happened in my head. I saw her bedroom at night: me on a bed and her on me. For a galvanic second she was alive in my skull again, as alive as any dead person can get, and more alive than many a living one, not excluding myself. It felt like an authentic flashback – as if my torn memory was now ready to convert fiction into fact. Or maybe it *was* a fact. I was in no position to rule that out.

'Other than that, you've never been inside her house?'

'No.' Something metallic ticked in the silence. A clock? Do clocks still tick? 'If you found my prints, that's when they got there.'

'So the night she died,' Lewin said. 'You never went inside then?'

'I've told you. I wasn't there.'

'But you were there the next morning.'

'Yes, but I didn't go inside.'

'I was wondering if your story had changed on that too.'

'It hasn't. It's not a story.'

He waited.

'The sun was up when I got there,' I said, not for the first time. 'I parked in her driveway. I knocked on her door. She didn't answer. I went home.'

'You didn't try the door?'

'No.'

'You gave up that easy?'

'If I'd known she was in there dead,' I said, 'I'd have kicked up more of a stink. I thought there'd be other chances.'

He waited. I considered letting him wait forever. Then I said, 'I know what your witness says. But your witness is wrong.'

He waited some more.

'What this person must have seen,' I said, 'was me leaving the doorstep. Not me walking out of the house. Me leaving the doorstep.'

'This is a large mistake to make, Ray.'

'I agree. Take it up with your witness. He's either blind or he's a fucking fool, and that's why we're sitting here. I knocked on the door and I left. That's all.'

'Looking agitated.'

'That part's possible.'

'Why?'

'Because I'd driven a long way to see her.'

'Why?'

That deserved either a flippant answer or no answer at all. I settled for silence. What we were talking about was not all that funny. Some things remain sacred, at least to me. Some things are too hallowed to be talked about in Lewin's room: her heat, the way her tongue fluttered, the blue veins on her chest. Her secrets are my secrets now. If I don't keep them, who will?

'Let's talk about the night she died.' Lewin pulled a folder from his stack.

'Didn't we just do that?'

'I mean you. Your movements.' The folder was fat with data. He kept it closed, for the moment. He tapped its edge against the desk.

'I *had* no movements.'

'I thought you didn't remember.'

'I remember that much.'

'You called her.' He put the folder on the desk. The cover fell open. I saw spreadsheets, columns of raw output, dates, times, colons, slashes, dashes, alphanumeric strings. A spew of ugly type, all of it bad for me, even the punctuation. It is not Lewin's style to produce documents that make me look good. He selected a stapled printout and started leafing through it. All this was taking a long time. Silence kept closing back in on us, lapping around the little islands of our words. Machinery vaguely hummed. His printout rustled. 'You talked to her for five minutes.'

'So you've told me. It sounds plausible.'

'Or rather six,' he said, when he'd found the page he wanted, the relevant column, the germane cell. 'Ten fifty-one to ten fifty-seven.'

'If you say so. Who am I to dispute the metadata?'

'You still don't remember?'

'No. Which happens, at least to me. I'd had a bad day. I'd

had a drink. I'd dropped a few pills. You've seen my medicine cabinet.'

'But you remember some things.'

Here we went again.

'You remember you weren't at her house,' he said.

'I don't forget things that big.'

'You say that, but I don't see how you can know it.'

I requested a break. In the toilets, in the stink left by some depraved colleague of Lewin's, I necked another red-and-white pill before I could think twice about it, or even once. You can't *have* thoughts when your head feels like that. Two red-and-whites in one day. I wouldn't be getting a hard-on for a while, but then again why would I be needing one? I took a small but not unwarranted swig from my flask. I made scrupulous use of the mouthwash. When I got back to Lewin's room I had a speech ready.

'The blackout angle is bullshit, Ted,' I told him. 'It's pulp fiction. You must know that. I remember what happened. I just don't remember it all that well. I took a few pills, I drank a bit, and I had a conversation I don't recall the finer points of. That's it. I didn't turn into Mr Hyde. I didn't go out for a midnight drive and cut up a girl I hardly knew. I fell asleep on the couch. Or I passed out, if you prefer. I was in no shape to get behind the wheel, I assure you.'

'But the morning after, you were in good enough shape to take a drive then?'

'I wouldn't say that. But I made it, apparently.'

'At six in the morning?'

He had a way of making it sound deeply implausible – getting up that early for her, driving all that way.

'To visit a girl you hardly knew,' he said.

'So I wanted to know her better. Why not? I haven't entirely retired from the human race.'

He laid down another one of his epic pauses. One day I'll just say nothing back, and see what he does about it. From the corridor outside, as if from a long way off, the buzz of workplace interplay washed in – banter, laughter. I remembered the feeling, but I remembered it less well all the time.

'Unless you want me to lie,' I told him, 'my story is never going to get any better. I've told you what happened. All I can do is sit here and keep saying it. I was at home, I was asleep, and there was nobody there to verify it. I know you don't like that. I don't either, much. But this is what every night of my life is like, barring the odd miracle.'

Lewin sighed. 'Would you call yourself an alcoholic?'

'No.' We were back at the usual dead ends.

'How much money did you make last year?'

I told him. But he already knew – I could tell from the way he didn't yodel in disbelief.

'You live on that?'

'I'm not sure how, but yeah.'

'And that's from reviewing books?'

'Right.'

'And that's the way you like it?'

'I didn't say that.'

He closed the file, and went back to tapping its spine on the table. His bad eye bulged. 'Anything you want to add, Ray?'

'No.'

'If there is, now's the time.'

The pills, if they're working too well, can make you lose your fear of reality's edge. Danger can sneak up on you. Suddenly Lewin was talking in a tone he'd never used before. His patience was starting to sound the way his shirts looked: eroded, frayed. For a bad moment I thought I had finally found the limits of his cool. I thought: today's the day. Then he tossed the folder back on the stack and said:

'You're still not in this too deep, Ray. But you're getting there. You're getting there. We're going round in circles. We can't do that forever. One day soon we might have to arrest you. Don't make me do that. If you do, I won't be able to help you any more.'

'That's what you're doing now, is it? Helping me?'

'Believe it or not, mate, yes. I'm trying to eliminate you from inquiries. I'm helping you and you're helping me. That's the theory. But you're making it harder than it has to be. Sometimes I think you're doing it on purpose.'

Still that tone. This was not ending well. He was letting me walk out again, but again I'd be walking out in worse shape than I'd turned up in. This couldn't keep happening. Pretty soon it would stop being logically possible. I had to throw him something more now, something fresh.

'I liked her, Ted.' I looked him in the eye again. I gave each eye equal time, just to be sure. 'Maybe I haven't made that clear. I liked her a lot. There's your answer, if you want to know why I got up at six in the morning to see her. You know what she looked like. You've seen the pictures. The whole country's in love with her now. Well, I knew her when she looked like that and there was still something you could do about it. Back before she was everyone's favourite dead person.'

'Are you saying you were in love with her?'

'No.' I'd walked straight into that one.

21

'So you're saying . . . What?'

'I'm saying put yourself in my shoes. I'm saying bear this in mind when you're wondering why I behaved a bit oddly. Not homicidally. Oddly.'

'I'm trying, Ray. But put yourself in mine. Let's say you were me. Wouldn't *you* be looking at you?'

'Probably. But I'd be wasting my time.'

'So where'd you be looking instead?'

'The guy stabbed her thirty times, right?'

'That's what they say in the papers,' Lewin said.

'I'd be looking for someone who knew her for more than a few days. Someone who either loved her or hated her.'

'Right. And you didn't love her, like you say.'

'I hardly knew her,' I said, as if that made a difference.

'And you didn't hate her.'

'I didn't know her long enough for that, either.'

I left the car in the basement of the justice precinct. The parking there is free. That much can be said for being a person of interest. A big salty wind boomed up from the harbour, funnelled by the cold stone buildings. I plunged into it with my face pointed at the pavement. Junk-food wrappers rattled along the gutters. Garments flapped around passing bodies like washing on a line. I hate the city at the best of times. Now that I'm an enemy of the people, I like it even less. Walking down a city street, I feel like a doomed man in a motorcade. My skull feels eggshell thin. Some people don't recognise me, which is good of them. Some half-do, but don't quite make the connection in time. But there are always the ones who know me right away, and want to tell me what they think of me – as if I don't know already. As if I can't have a rough guess.

Today I made it two blocks towards the water, head down, before I felt some hag on a crowded corner come at me from behind, craning her face into mine. Before she could get started I crossed against the light. Dodging angry cars, I heard her rain angrier slander on my spine. It was nothing new, but it was noisy enough to make people look my way. I made the mistake of looking up to see how many had. A guy coming past got a jolt of instant recognition and swerved back at me, getting ready to speak his mind. He changed it when he got close enough to see how tasty I look in the flesh: the bent nose, the network of white scars around it, the curl my mouth makes when I'm not on TV, putting on a show. Something about all that made him decide to shut his mouth and move on. I try to look as if I still care, when I'm on TV. I turn on the remnants of my charm. I play to the swinging voters. I act as if I still have a few things left to lose. On the street I feel freer to be myself.

I shouldn't have been out there at all. I should have been back in the car, halfway home to my intoxicants and my couch. That hour in Lewin's hard chair had ignited the ruined nerves along my spine. But my afternoon was only half-done. Now I had to sit down some more: with Jeremy Skeats, my boss, the literary editor who knows nothing about literature. It sounds like a good joke if you're not on the end of it. I looked at my watch and made my usual Skeats resolution. Whatever he wanted to say, I would sit there and behave myself while he said it. Whatever books he offered me I would take, because I was in no position to turn anything down. I never was, and he knew it. I hated him for that, but I hated him for a lot of other reasons too. Nevertheless, I would behave. And when I was done behaving I would drive home, get horizontal, and not get up again for a very long time.

He wanted to meet at a place called Diana's. It sounded like a funny name for a bar, and when I got there I saw why. It wasn't a bar. It was a coffee shop. Skeats was established at one of the outdoor tables. You couldn't miss him, and you weren't meant to. He wears suits but he doesn't wear ties. The suits look expensive and no doubt are. He wears white tailored shirts that hang open almost to his navel. The exposed area of his chest is tanned, ludicrously. No man worth knowing looks so healthy. No man even vaguely devoted to the life of the mind spends so much time in the sun. His head has a tangle of gelled golden curls on it, like the pelt of some pampered spoodle or six-year-old French king. His cheeks are darkened by a pointillist stubble that would make me want to hit him even if I didn't know him. He goes to the gym. He lifts weights. He looks like an off-duty musketeer. People call him a public intellectual. I agree with the public part.

I sat across from him. Inevitably, he was dicking around with his phone. Less inevitably, he stopped doing that as soon as he saw me. He put it on the table and stopped looking at it. This was ominously courteous of him.

'Raymondo,' he said, giving me the full radiance of his facial tan.

'Can't we sit inside?' I asked him.

'Why?'

'Because people keep looking at me like I stabbed a girl to death.'

He frowned a bit, trying to work out what that had to do with him. 'I won't keep you long,' he said. I noticed now that the wreckage of a prior meeting was sprawled between us on the table: two drained mugs, two saucers, a half-demolished muffin. Someone had been sitting in my chair before me. Someone he assigned better books to, and paid more money. I was the footnote, the afterthought. There was a newspaper on the table too – our newspaper, our emaciated broadsheet, stirring in the restless air, pinned to the wood by the puerile weight of Skeats's phone.

Hooking an arm over the frame of his chair, he lolled casually back and said, 'So how's it all going?'

'Not well,' I said. But he hadn't got me here to ask that. A surge of wind came up the steep street and throttled the shaft of the big umbrella that stood in the table's core. Golden Boy's gelled curls stirred at the fringes but not the roots. Our newspaper flapped and shifted. The phone shifted with it, caught in its undertow.

'It can't be easy,' Skeats said, trying hard not to look as if he was thinking about his phone. His spare hand – the one he wasn't lolling casually back with – reached down and covered it, tenderly, until the wind eased.

'It isn't.'

'The girl . . . Shit. She looked like a hell of a nice girl.'

'She was.' I had an odd sense that he was pretending not to know her name. How could anybody, even him, not know it by now? The TV repeats it every night like an incantation, like a byword for ravaged innocence.

'You want coffee?' He looked around for a waiter, but not all that hard. Often I get the feeling that Skeats is not a real person. He lives between air quotes, somehow.

25

His whole existence seems to be pitched at some unseen camera or crowd.

'No.' My head pulsed. I pulled out my flask and took a jolt.

Skeats looked at me as if I'd tied off a vein and jammed a rusty spike into it. When the flask was back in my pocket he said, 'So how long'd you know her for? Before she . . .'

'Not long.'

On the table his phone gave its little bird call. I waited for him to attend to it. He didn't. 'You know her all that well, or . . . ?'

'Is this an interrogation? You sound like Ted Lewin.'

'I'm just wondering how deep in this you are,' he said.

'I'll get out of it.'

Off behind my left shoulder, in the indoor part of the café, something was going on. I had a bad feeling it was about me. I heard a woman's voice half-raised in admonition. I heard a man's voice raised a bit louder. Skeats glanced back there but saw nothing that troubled him. Maybe he wasn't looking hard enough.

I said, 'They still haven't sent me that money, by the way.'

'What money?'

'The money for the Vagg review.' I watched him hard to see if he'd made the connection yet – to see if he knew that she'd still be alive, if it wasn't for his towering mediocrity. But he hadn't. You could tell by the way his face displayed no shame. If it was ever going to, this was the time. 'The least you can do,' I said, 'is pay me for it. Considering.'

'It's on its way,' he said smoothly. You had to salute the man's lack of wit. He had all the pieces. He was just too stupid and vain and lazy to put them together, and work out what he had done. If I got through the next ten minutes without lunging across the table for his tanned throat it would be even more of a miracle than usual.

'How can it still be on its way? They tie it to a carrier pigeon?'

His phone cheeped again. Again he didn't answer it. He didn't even look at it. That scene behind my shoulder, whatever it was, was still percolating.

'Speaking of money,' I said, 'how about slinging me a book or two?'

'Actually,' he said, 'that's what I wanted to talk about.'

That didn't sound good. And why was he looking at me and not his phone? This was an eerie reversal of form. Suddenly it occurred to me to worry a lot about what we were there for. My dazed head had let me down again. Once more it had failed to sniff out the dangers of the present. It was stuck on Jade, spinning its wheels in the past again, as if all the bad stuff had happened to me already. And meanwhile here Skeats was right now, in plain view, lubing up to fuck me again. I was about to get fired. Why else would he have wanted to meet me here, now, in public, in daylight, face to face? Who, these days, wanted that?

'As you know,' he said, 'I don't believe in keeping my writers in suspense.'

I should have left then. When Skeats hits you with one of his moronic homilies, it's not because something good is about to happen to you. But before he could follow through, something else happened. A chair hit the floor behind me. Skeats looked back there. *Now* he was troubled: the static had grown so flagrant that even he could feel it. I turned and saw it too, through the gauze of my aching eyes. This big puce-faced yokel in a business shirt was bowling towards us, pinballing off tables and chairs. He only had eyes for me. He looked as if he'd played rugby once, but not for a while. At a minimum he was about to denounce me. If he had something non-verbal in mind, he would find I was at least as up for it as he was. The afternoon could end in worse ways. It would be nice to get blood on Skeats's shirt, even if some of it turned out to be mine.

The guy arrived and slapped his meaty palms on the table. He leaned over me hard, till his fat red carbuncle of a face was about all I could see.

'You're not fooling anyone,' he said. '*Mate.*'

I waited. His breath stank of dead fish. His features boiled and quivered, like raw offal on a hot grill. But his heat had already peaked. I had come to know his type. He'd wanted to say his piece, and he'd pretty much said it. There would be no violence.

'I promise to try harder,' I told him.

His wife was beside him now, trying to yank him away by the elbow. The guy shook off her grip with a sulky lash of his arm. Yes, he was all spent now. He had struck his blow for justice, and in the aftermath of his big moment he looked clueless, even senile. The event had let him down somehow. He'd been expecting so much more from it. Improvising, he decided to sweep something off the table with the ruddy T-bone of his hand. A mug? No. He was too law-abiding for that. He went for the newspaper instead. Skeats, reacting in record time, intervened: to rescue his phone. His craven hand scuttled in and nabbed it to safety as the yokel's came down, yanking up the broadsheet and flinging it out to the wind. Then the yokel was out in the wind with it, the wife hustling him away. The paper flapped down to the stained pavement and lay there twitching.

Skeats watched it convulse for a while. It gave him a good excuse not to look at me while he said what he said next. 'I've been thinking it might be wise, Ray, if we dialled down your profile a bit.'

Out in the gutter the wind tugged at the fallen broadsheet. A big double page went surfing up the street. Nobody bothered dodging it. It was just a newspaper.

'Define "dial down",' I said. I wasn't about to make this easy for him. I wanted to watch him writhe.

'In the short term, I reckon it might be wise if we cooled it on your stuff altogether.'

'That's not dialling me down. That's switching me off.'

'Not permanently,' he said. 'Just for a while.'

'Define a while.'

'Until this thing blows over.'

'Who says it *will* blow over?'

'Well, Christ, it can't go on like this forever. Either they'll clear you or . . .'

'Or what? Arrest me? It won't come to that. It's under control. I'm handling it.'

'Ray, this isn't just me. This is coming from the men upstairs.'

'The wise men of the newspaper trade?' My eyes were still aimed at the gutter, at that flapping and twitching broadsheet. 'I like that. The whole place is giving out the death gargle, thanks to them. They think they can restore it to glory by sacking me?'

'I'm not sacking you, for Christ's sake. Take a month or two off. Clear your name. Let the stink of all this dissipate.

Come back when you can just be a critic again, as opposed to public enemy number one.'

He thought he could afford to smile again. He thought we were pretty much done. He thought he could walk away from the whole thing in a minute or two, just by walking away from me. I'd be a fool to set him straight about that now. Then again, I'd be an even bigger fool if I didn't do it soon, very soon. I couldn't wait to see his lipless fake grin just freeze and hang there, like a bird shot in flight, while the rest of him soaked up the news.

'This thing's my problem,' I said again. 'Let me deal with it.'

'I'll tell you something, Ray. From the outside, you don't seem to be dealing with it all that well.'

'Is that right?'

'Yes. It's right. From where I sit, it looks like it's getting worse all the time. Why don't you get yourself a lawyer, for Christ's sake?'

'They cost money, for a start. Also people with lawyers have a way of looking guilty.'

'People without them can look pretty guilty too.'

'You think I'm guilty?'

'I didn't say that.'

'You think firing me will make me look *less* guilty?'

'I'll say it again. I'm not firing you.'

'Right. I just won't be working or getting paid.'

'Temporarily, mate. Temporarily.'

Maybe it was true, or maybe he just wanted to get through the next five minutes without hearing the speech where I told him what I really thought of him. We both knew I had that speech in me. He was right to fear it. Even I did, in a way.

'I think this is the right move for you, Ray.' He was lolling back in his chair again.

'Yeah. Having no money will be ideal, on top of everything else.'

'I'd appreciate it if you didn't fight me on this.'

'And I'd appreciate it if you didn't talk in clichés, but you can't have everything.'

He didn't like that. 'While you're away' – he unyoked his arm from the chair's back and leaned testily forward – 'while you're clearing your name of murder, Ray, maybe you should think about a few other things too.'

'Such as?'

'Such as the big picture. Such as the way you approach things.'

'And what conclusions would you like me to reach, Jeremy?'

The afternoon was failing. Light was draining from the street like a beaten army. People were on their way home. The people on foot were moving faster than the people in cars.

'You know what I'm talking about,' he said.

'Remind me.'

Skeats sighed indulgently. He has this radically misguided view of our relations. He's so dumb he doesn't even know he's the dumb one. 'I've said it before, Ray. Maybe this time you'll take it in. You need to rethink the Dirty Harry routine. Times have changed. Books are in deep shit. They need all the help they can get. The way things are going, I don't have that much use for a hanging judge any more. I spend half my Monday mornings getting an earful from whoever the poor bastard is that published the book you kicked the shit out of the day before.'

'You want me to be an industry lapdog, like Barrett Lodge.'

'I prefer to think of him as an accentuator of the positive.'

'I believe I recently tried that. Accentuating the positive. It didn't work out that well, from memory.'

'You really want to talk about that episode, Ray?'

'Why shouldn't I?'

'Because it involved some odd behaviour.'

'From me or from you?'

I threw that out mainly for my own amusement. But I got an interesting result. Skeats's face made a comically bad attempt to look like the face of a man who had no idea, no idea at all, what I was talking about. I could see he was bluffing, but I was in no condition to sift the connotations. Maybe the lie had serious weight or maybe it was just recreational. With him it was always hard to tell. But it was strange that he was still so bad at dissembling, after all the practice.

'I'm not saying I don't value your stuff, Ray,' he said. 'You know I do. If I didn't I wouldn't print it. And I'm not saying you don't have a future. I'm just saying . . .'

'I know what you're saying,' I said, so he would stop saying it.

'Good. Excellent.' He slapped the table as if the ordeal was over. For him it was. I felt one last urge to drag him down neck-deep into her blood with me, where he belonged. But I rode it out and let him go. I watched him weave his way back up the hill through the crowd. He moved urgently and with purpose, outstriding the swarm of the less important. All those people, and none of them read books any more, or papers. Just screens, the smaller the better. Skeats's

32

was clamped to his ear already, like everyone else's. Maybe he was telling the men upstairs that the deed was done. I watched his bobbing curls vanish like froth into the human tide and I thought: You poor fool. Do you think I will ever forget this moment? When my memory works, it works forever.

A shadow fell over the table. I winced and looked up. What now? Just a waitress. She had red hair and a ring through her nose. She was around Jade's age, if not younger. She had a pleasant look on her face, which meant she had no idea who I was. Don't young people watch the news any more? Doesn't my infamy make the grade in their celeb feeds or selfie streams? She blushed a bit and looked down at her own fingers. They were pinching a folded piece of paper. I got the picture now. Skeats hadn't paid his bill. The girl could see that giving it to me was a bit rough, but she didn't know what else to do. Her hands were sort of stuck in the middle of the act. She was young and self-conscious and her movements of body and face had an exaggerated quality.

'What happened to the fancy guy?' she said.

I held my hand out. She blushed a bit more and slipped me the bad news: seventeen bucks for two coffees and a muffin. I pulled my wallet out, hoping there'd be something in it. There was a twenty and nothing else. I told her to keep the change. She wouldn't take it. She dug in her apron for coins. I decided I'd better wait for them, since she had a job and I didn't. I wondered who else I was paying for, apart from Skeats. Barrett Lodge?

'I hope he's going to pay you back,' the girl said, rummaging. I liked her tone. It dripped with Skeats-hatred. He must have done or said something, before I came, that gave her a correct impression of his personality. Or maybe she just hadn't liked the look of him, which would have been fair enough too. Either way I liked her more and more all the time. In my former life I might have had a crack at taking her home. In my current life there was a three-ring circus camped at my front gate. So even if I got her past the question of my face, we'd have that question to get past too. And there was no good answer to it, and if I told her even half the truth the evening might never recover. At a minimum she would stop looking happy and innocent for a while, and I didn't want to be responsible for that. Anyway, she wasn't Jade. All the women in the world have that defect now. Whoever they are, they're not her.

'Don't worry about the fancy guy,' I told her. 'The fancy guy's going to pay.'

2

I know a lot about the big half-hours that can make or break a life. When I was a kid, I took a swan dive off a garage roof and cracked my skull on a concrete slab. This is not a metaphor. Or maybe it is, but it happened. I got my hands down first. If I hadn't, I'd have died then and there. At the time I must have thought that would be a bad thing. A few of my fingers broke. Then the rest of me came down. I was spinning forwards, flipping over. My face bit the slab and skidded and my body went on over it and my neck arced to breaking point like a vaulter's pole. Bits of my face got left on the slab. Bits of the slab got left in my face. My bottom teeth bit clean through my lower lip. My nose got smeared across my face like a lump of butter chucked into a hot pan. My spine didn't break. It just felt as if it did. I still wonder what breaking your back must feel like, if not breaking it felt like that.

The only good thing about smacking your head that hard is that your stunned skull will never let you remember it.

The impact ripped a ragged permanent hole in my memory. Don't ask me what I was doing on that roof. Don't ask me why I went near the edge. According to my insulted brain, I was never even up there. The data never got laid down. There's just this messy jump-cut or splice and I'm waking up on my back, with a ring of blurred faces a long way above me. An ambulance was already present. For ten minutes my body had been lying there on the planet but the rest of me had been somewhere else. It had been down there under the slab, seeing what death felt like. It felt like nothing. I had no complaints. On bad days I wish I'd stayed down there for good. Instead I resurfaced. At the time it felt kind of pleasant. For the last time in my life, I felt no pain. I was just tired. I wanted to slip back under the slab and sleep. But this hunkered paramedic kept wanting to know if I could move my foot. I tried. I looked down to see if it was working. That was a mistake. I saw what had happened to my hand. I lurched onto my side and vomited a gutload of dirt and black blood.

I have learned not to think, much, about what my life would have been like if that afternoon had never happened. It would have been different. I know that much. Possibilities narrowed for me that day. Potential was belted out of me. I was never going to be a leading man after that. I would be a critic at best, but never a player. When you're in pain most of the day, there is only so much work you can get done. I would write better books than most of the books I review, if I had a different body. And I would look better than most of their authors, if I still had my old face. But I don't, and I have grown to like my new one. I no longer pine for a mint-condition look. My fake teeth are more plausible than some people's real ones. My fingers are gnarled but functional. My nose has been straightened out, sort of. A cobweb of fine white scars radiates from the big central gouge on its bridge. I don't get all the women I want, but who does? I get a few. Some of them dig the scars. They like touching them. I don't mind that, as long as they touch the rest of me too. When my skin gets tanned the scars don't. In the mornings, when I shave, the mirror looks as if it's been cracked by a pebble in the night. By forty you're meant to have the face you deserve. I got the face early. It took me a while to earn it. I believe I am finally there.

You get a short cut to the truth, when something like that happens to you early. It's not enough to say life is a lottery. Losing a lottery can't hurt or kill you. I made one mistake and I got half a life, or on a good day three-quarters of one. Then again I might have died that day, and had no life at all. Alternatively, I could have just stayed away from the edge and skipped the maiming altogether. That would have been nice. If things had gone that way I would be somebody else now. I wouldn't be me. I would be a nicer guy all round. It's hard to believe in an unchanging self or soul when your body has turned on you. Also it's hard to believe in free will, when you can't remember being present for the hinge moment of your life. The outer evidence says I was there: up on that roof, and conscious, and moving for some reason towards the edge. But since I don't remember doing it, it's hard to feel I had much choice in the matter. Things happen to you and you can't stop them. If you try to, other things will happen to you instead. Maybe they will be worse. There was a woman across the street who saw me drop. She had a hard time describing what she saw. She said it looked like a dive, but it looked like a fall too. It looked like both things at once. I have learned to live with that ambiguity. Maybe it *was* both things. Maybe it was a leap gone wrong. Maybe I caught a toe in the gutter. Maybe I thought I'd land on my feet.

The difference hardly matters now. It stopped mattering the moment I hit the earth. All that matters now is the damage, which has never stopped happening to me. Thirty years later, the thumped gong of my body is still shivering. The nerves along my spine still scream as if they got crushed yesterday. You'd think they'd chuck it in, you'd think they'd leave me alone, now that all my other nerves are dying – the nerves in my fingertips, the nerves in my dick. But they maintain the rage. They spit and arc like severed power-lines. If I sit in a chair for more than ten minutes my spine lights up like a vein of lava, and then my skull explodes like the Hindenburg. So I write standing up – like Hemingway, like Nabokov, like Philip Roth. Unlike them I do it on a computer. I stand a beer case on my desk and put an open laptop on the summit. I type on a plug-in keyboard positioned at cock height. It's a strange set-up to look at, but usually there's no one to look at it except me.

Thirteen days ago, at about four in the afternoon, I was standing at my prose rig doing my thing. I must have been having a good day, if I was still on my feet at that hour. Either I was writing something serious or I was emailing Skeats about money. But what's more serious than that? Beyond the laptop my front window showed me a slab of overcast sky. Back then I didn't close the curtains. I had no reason to. A storm was coming in. Under it, a small red car appeared at my gate, then swept its slow way up the steep dirty ribbon of the drive, throwing up dust like a magician's fistful of smoke. What was vanishing in that plume was my old life, although I didn't know it yet. I stood there behind my rig and watched the little car get bigger. Naturally I hoped it had come to the wrong place.

I stopped hoping that when the driver got out. Her hair was dark and she wore it long. Her body was little and ripe and packed with the promise of obscenity. I'm bad at ages but I put her somewhere between twenty-five and thirty. She wore jeans and a V-neck jumper the colour of charcoal. A lot went on inside it when she moved. She came up my front steps, squinting into the dropping sun. She hadn't seen me through the window yet. She moved without scruple, as if things generally went her way. When you looked like that they probably did. She stopped at the screen door and cupped a hand over the mesh to look in. When she saw me standing there, right on the other side of it, she jumped.

She said, 'Are you Raymond Saint?'

I told her I was.

She told me her name was Jade Howe. I looked at her and couldn't believe my luck. I was right not to, although I was wrong to think the luck was good.

'It isn't an easy place to find, this little shack of yours.'

Why she'd wanted to find it I didn't ask her, yet. I let her think I wasn't curious, as if girls like her dropped in on me every day. She was sitting on the couch that ran along my back wall. I stood with my spine against the cold side window and took my second good look at her. Her eyes were dark, maybe even black. A spray of little freckles dusted her nose like a flung pinch of sand.

'Was it worth finding?' I asked her.

She took a look around the little room. I could see that she'd been dying to. Things get squalid when I'm in the middle of writing something, and I'm always in the middle of writing something. The sink was stacked with unwashed plates. Books I had no room for on my shelves were heaped around the walls in random drifts. On my desk, and on the floor around it, were the magpie's scraps of paper I wrote my notes on: envelopes, torn bits of magazine. Some of them had been lying around for months, although she had no way of knowing that. Likewise, she had no way of knowing that the half-full bottle of booze beside the keyboard had not been half-full for very long.

Anyway, she didn't seem to care. She took in the scene, then she just looked at me and smiled. It had been a while since any girl had done that to me, except as a matter of store policy. But maybe she was selling something too. I had a feeling I'd like her anyway, even if she was. Outside, that storm was sliding in. Trees were limbering up for it in the high grey wind. The air had gone all staticky and cold.

'What's that you're drinking?' she asked.

I told her. I offered her some. She surprised me by saying yes. Not many women do. I put a glass of it on the low table near her knees, then went back to my place at the window.

'So what *is* that?' She was looking at the prose rig.

'I write on my feet.'

'Like Hemingway?'

'My God. You're a reader.'

'I'm in the business.'

'You don't say.'

'I love your stuff, by the way.'

'My stuff?' I pondered that claim. I turned it over in my head, like an archaeologist inspecting an implausibly large chunk of Troy. 'You mean my reviews?'

'Yeah,' she said. 'I wish I could write like that.'

'You'd be amazed by how often I don't hear that.'

'Somehow I thought you'd look scarier.'

I thought about telling her how she looked, but I had a feeling she already knew.

'You reviewing something now?' She turned her head, when she said that, to look out at the thrashing trees. There was something off about the way she did this. It seemed coy, and I had already worked out that coyness wasn't her thing.

'I'm always reviewing something,' I said. Did I sense even then what she was up to? I waited till she showed me her dark eyes again. 'So what part of the business,' I asked them, 'are you in?'

'I do publicity for Bennett and Bennett.'

Ah. That brought us a notch closer to business. Bennett and Bennett published bad books. They'd published good books once, back when publishers could still afford to do that. These days what they mainly printed were gimmick books: non-literature by non-writers. Novels by super-models. Cookbooks by wicketkeepers. Memoirs about crossing the Sahara by unicycle. I didn't hold this against them, much. Every publisher did it.

'And yet you like my reviews.' The light outside was dropping fast. Gumnuts rattled down on the tin roof. 'You must be the only marketing girl in the country who does.'

41

'I'm not,' she said with mock horror, 'a marketing girl.'
There was an ironic spark in her eyes I was starting to like.

'So what are you?'

'I handle writers.'

'Have you come here to handle me?'

It was poor stuff, but there was something about her
that encouraged bold speech. Plus I was fairly loaded. Let us
bear in mind that it was four in the afternoon. Anyway she
took it with a smile. She was used to hearing men say stupid
things. She knew we were all fools. Her legs were crossed
and her torso was tipped towards me, as if she wanted to
talk in whispers. Yes, her body set a tone of conspiracy from
the start. But who was going to overhear us? A gap had
opened between her jumper and her torso. I didn't look into
it yet.

'I don't do critics,' she said.

'What a pity. Who do you do?'

'Novelists, mainly.'

'I happen to be a novelist too.'

That one caught her out.

'You're writing a novel?'

'No, I wrote one.'

'Called what?'

'Called nothing. It never got published.'

'That sucks,' she said.

Yes. It did suck. She leant forward some more. It was
dark enough to turn on a light now, so I didn't turn one on.
A mood was building and I'd have been a fool to mess with
it. Any minute now the sky was going to crack and spill its
heavy load on us. It looked as if a filthy paintbrush had been
soaking in it. We both knew she couldn't leave under a sky

like that. Whatever was happening, we could afford to let it happen slowly.

'I was the wrong kind of novelist,' I said. 'I made the mistake of not getting famous for something else first.'

'Like hosting a game show,' she offered.

'Right. Or losing my limbs halfway up Everest.'

If she knew the business was a joke, why did she work in it? For that matter, why did I?

'Did you ever submit it to us? To Bennett and Bennett?'

'You turned it down, but so did everybody else. I hold no grudge.'

'Maybe you should try us again.'

'I don't think so. The world's had it with novels, don't you think?'

'Maybe it has. I don't know.' Again she felt a sudden need to avert her gaze. This time what she looked at instead of me was one of her own subtly chewed fingernails. 'The thing I'm working on now, it's a non-fiction thing. Kind of history for the common man.'

'And who wrote it?' I mechanically asked, although I had known the answer for a while.

'Liam Vagg,' she said. Then she defiantly looked back up at me: plump, sly little Jade, with her sleeves rolled halfway up to her elbows.

'You're handling Liam Vagg? I hope you've been wearing rubber gloves.'

'You know his stuff then?'

'As it happens, I'm reviewing that very book.' I gave her a moment, just in case she wanted to rig up a look of puzzlement or surprise. She didn't bother. 'But I have this strange feeling you already know that.'

She didn't stop looking at me, but this huge wave of guilty blood broke over her face, and washed down over the beach of flesh that ended at the V of her jumper.

'Who told you?' I asked her.

'Your editor.'

'Skeats?'

She nodded.

A rancid thought hit me. 'Christ, you're not a *friend* of his?'

'Jeremy Skeats? No. I've never met him. We've only talked on the phone . . .'

Outside, the treetops heaved in the wind, all rubbery and drunken. A frenzied palm lashed the sky like a switch. And now the loathed spectre of Skeats was in the room with us, dangerously messing with my mood.

'So you rang him up,' I said, 'and you asked him who he'd assigned Vagg's book to?'

'Yeah.'

'And he just told you?'

'Well, not straight away. First he asked me out to lunch.'

'What the fuck for?'

'He said he wanted to talk about books.'

'Horseshit. He's never read one.'

'I'm just telling you what he said.'

'And what did *you* say?'

'I said maybe.'

Here came the rain, and not subtly. It crashed down on the roof like applause on an old record. I thought about telling her Skeats was married, and had children, but the whole theme had to be ditched. It was warping my performance.

She tilted her empty glass at me. 'Do I get a refill?'

While I was pouring her one I turned on the light. It was so dark now that I had to, if I wanted to see her at all. Our reflection appeared in the rippling side window. Wind shook the glass and made the scene wobble. I sat down in the armchair across from her. It wouldn't do much for my back, but the rest of me wanted to close the gap between us.

'So you're doing the publicity for Vagg's new novel,' I summarised, lifting my voice over the rain. 'You call Skeats and ask him who's reviewing it. He tells you it's me. And now here you are.' It couldn't hurt to let her know that I smelt the vice in the room.

'Should I go?' she said.

'I didn't say that.'

'Should we forget it? Should we talk about something else?'

'No,' I said. 'I'm enjoying this.' If she was losing her nerve, I wanted her to get it back. 'Interesting things don't normally happen to literary critics. This thing's getting more interesting all the time.'

She said nothing. She was letting me run the show for a while, or letting me think I was.

'So what do you want to know?' Raising my voice some more, the foliage beyond the rain-blurred windows rolling and boiling like a crazy sea. 'You want to know if I've read the book yet?'

'Have you?'

'I have. What else? You want to know if I liked it?'

'I get the feeling you didn't.'

'Well, did *you*?'

'No.' A bit sadly. 'Not really.'

45

'So what made you think I would?' Me of all people, I nearly said.

'I guess I didn't.'

'And what made *Skeats* think I would, for that matter?' Here was something I might have asked myself before, in private, if my head worked properly. I looked away from her for a moment. I had to. It was hard to have abstract thoughts while looking at her. 'This isn't the sort of book he normally throws me,' I said.

'Why not?'

'Because it's local product, and it's no good.'

'And when something's no good, you piss on it.'

'Exactly, and pissing on the local stuff isn't Skeats's style. He likes going to the festivals. He likes getting photographed with his arm around the stars. Books like this he normally throws to Barrett Lodge.'

'Because Barrett Lodge likes everything?'

'Or *says* he likes everything, because he's too slothful to say anything else.'

No doubt there was more to be said on this theme. But a burst of lightning chose that moment to strobe the scene outside, all those treetops jiving in the rain, and then a startling crack of thunder shook the flimsy boards under our feet. '*Fuck*,' she said. I liked the way she said it. I'd have liked it any way she said it. Then she said something else that got half-lost in the antics of the big sky. I thought I heard it, but asked her to say it again.

'Come here,' she said, flattening a hand on the couch's other cushion.

It was what I thought she'd said, but it hadn't hurt to hear it twice. I took my drink over there and I sat. If I'd ever had the edge on her, I lost it then. The couch was not large, and she was making no big effort to stay on her side of it. Suddenly it wasn't all that easy to breathe.

She leaned in close and half-shouted: 'That's what I like about your stuff.' Her breath was all hot and nectary with booze. The look in her eyes had moved well beyond mischief now. They flashed with a heat so indecent that I almost had to look away from them. Almost, but not quite. 'You always say what you think.'

Outside the loaded gutter spilled ropes of water on the sizzling deck. Her nearest breast was all over my elbow. She wasn't taking it away.

'Want to know what I'm thinking now?' I said.

Maybe she heard that or maybe she didn't. Anyway what she said back was: 'It hasn't got you all that far, has it?'

'What hasn't?'

'Saying what you think of things.'

'Jesus. What does *that* mean?'

'I mean . . .'

She let her eyes do a lap of the room. It didn't take them long. You had to admire her style. She'd known me twenty minutes, and already she was telling me I'd squandered my life.

'I've got a hunch about you,' she said then.

'What hunch is that?'

'It's a weird feeling. I've read so much of your stuff, I feel like I know you.'

'Okay.'

'I feel like I could say anything to you and you wouldn't mind.'

'You may be right.'

'And I mean, if I say something you don't like, I feel like you'll just tell me to fuck off and that will be that.'

'Try it. Chance your arm.'

If we were still sitting there in five minutes my spine would be molten. But I had the feeling we wouldn't be. I looked at her brown or black eyes and tried to work out where the pupils stopped and the irises began. My breath gusted hard, as if driven by an iron lung. The storm drowned out the sound of it, but only just. A sharp animal scent drifted in from the drenched earth. If I was Norman Mailer I'd say that it drifted from her. For all I knew it did. My ruptured nose is not my keenest organ.

'Do you want me to say it for you?' I said.

She didn't tell me not to.

'You want me to whitewash the Vagg review. That part's not hard to work out. You want me to write a thousand words about that piece of shit without *mentioning* it's a piece of shit. Stop me when I start going wrong.'

'I will.'

'There's more? What more can there be? You want me to tell people – what? That he has talent? Style? Wit?'

'You're the writer.'

'This would be in return for what?'

'Money.'

'That's all?' I tried looking playfully disappointed, but I'm rusty at stuff like that.

'A lot of money.'

'From who?'

'From Vagg.'

'And how much is a lot?'

Her breast rose and fell against me. My elbow was

taking its full weight now. My other hand was on her thigh. We were past being polite about the small stuff. It was open season on the lesser crimes. I felt a radiant heat through her jeans. I had a hard-on of once-in-a-decade savagery. 'How much,' I asked her again, 'is a lot?'

'If you don't want to do it, I don't think I should tell you.'

'Who said I don't want to do it?'

'Do you?'

'Tell me how much money a lot is, and we'll see.'

'It's a lot. Take my word for it. Or don't you trust me?'

It was my move. She smiled, daring me to make it. We'd reached the point where more talking could only fuck things up. Even I could see that. I'm a word man, but silence has its place. I reached up and pushed the hair off her forehead. I flattened my palm against her face and moved it slowly down. When it got to her mouth she parted her lips and took in my thumb and bit into its first joint – not all that hard, but not all that softly either. She watched me over the top of it. Then she opened her teeth and took the whole thumb into her mouth and let me sample the wet heat of her tongue. The whole thing felt too easy, but good things always do. Her eyes blazed at me like two lights saying *Go. Don't stop. Go.* So I went.

Only a fool would write about the rest. After it we lay beached on the bed, stunned and speechless. Her curled body was half on top of mine and half not. The flesh between her ribcage and hip gathered in soft folds, piling up on itself like freshly cranked pasta. While I toyed with it, she plucked at the crimson scars on the back of my hand. My other hand wielded my uncapped bedside flask. The rain had stopped. The afternoon light had come back again, briefly, so it could fade back out in the proper way. Now and then we sipped lazily from the flask. We were in no rush to let reality back in the room. We were doing so well without it. But sooner or later the world had to be rejoined.

'How much money,' I finally asked her, 'is a lot?'

'Ten thousand dollars,' she said.

'No.'

'Yes.'

'Jesus.'

'I know.'

'This is out of Vagg's own pocket?'

'To him, that's not that much money.'

'What's he want me to say? That he's Thucydides?'

'Call him a master craftsman. He'd settle for that.'

'Why do all lousy writers want to be called master craftsmen? What do they think it *means*?'

'He just wants people to think he's a proper writer.'

Even that was asking too much, but I didn't want to spoil our party just yet. Liam Vagg was no good, as either a writer or a man. Until Skeats had sent me his new book, I'd done my best to stay hazy about the details of the Vagg career. For some reason I get no joy from reading up on the vast fiscal triumphs of my inferiors. I knew that he'd robbed banks once, in his mad-dog youth. Everybody knew that about him. Being an ex-con was his gimmick. In prison he got literate and wrote a crime memoir. It got published. It was a monster hit. They turned it into a movie. Maybe there was a sequel, and maybe they made a movie out of that too. Somewhere around then he had reinvented himself – as a pop historian. Who had given him permission to do this I didn't know. Judging from the one book of his I'd read – and I was fucked if I was ever going to read another one – Vagg was an historian the way I'm an opera singer when I whistle Puccini on the can. Reading him was like hearing a proper book get recounted from memory by a drunk.

These days Vagg played the ex-con stuff down, except when the publicity people got him to play it up. He was a reformed character now. He could afford to be. He dressed in designer clothes; he wore his long proletarian hair in a silver ponytail. But he still looked lean and pale and ugly, like a retired greyhound. He still had blurred tattoos hailing from the era when skin art was strictly for scum. On the jackets of his books he posed with a leashed pit bull, as if to let you know he could kill you twice if you gave him a bad review. Yet somehow the ageing villain had attained respectability, except in the eyes of people who still read proper books. Since nobody did, he was in the clear. He was foully rich. He lived on the harbour. He went on TV and gave his views about the national character, and world politics, and law reform. He was a hooligan seer, a hack tycoon. He had it all, except for merit. What the hell did he want with a good review from me?

'Ten grand?' I said. 'Is he insane? Does he know how many people read what I say? I could call him Jesus and he'd sell maybe fifty extra copies.'

Even that was putting it a bit high. The truth, as far as I had ever been able to tell, was that nobody, nobody at all, nobody except me, ever read a word I wrote. But I wasn't about to share that with her. I felt close to her, but not that close.

'The sales aren't the point,' she said. 'He's got the sales already.'

'And that's not enough for him.'

'Not any more. He wants people to take him seriously.'

'Is he looking to bribe everyone who's reviewing it, or just me?'

'Just you.'

'Why me?'

'Because you're the hard man, and everybody knows it. If *you* say you like it . . .'

'If I say I like *Vagg*, my reputation as the hard man will vanish overnight.'

'And?' she said starkly. 'I mean, so what?'

That stumped me. Her fingers plucked idly at the scars on my hand. I watched them but couldn't feel them. The tissue there is like bark.

'You know what I mean,' she said. 'Don't pretend you don't.'

'I'm not sure I do.'

'I mean, people respect you. They know you're a brilliant critic. But what *good* does that do you?'

'If having a reputation's so pointless, why's Vagg ready to pay ten thousand bucks to get one?'

'Because he's got everything else already.'

I tried not to believe she had a point.

'You must have thought about it.' Her persuasive little fingertips nipped at my dead skin. 'You've been writing for how many years? Shouldn't you have something to show for it?'

'Something like what?'

'I don't know. A house. A wife. Kids.'

'I believe I have a house. What do you call this structure I just fucked you in?'

'I'd call it a shack. A hut. And do you even own it?'

'Why? So I can sell it when I'm dead?'

'You live like the Unabomber.'

'Ten thousand dollars won't change that.'

'Forget that. I'm saying beyond that, in general. I'm saying, why is Barrett Lodge the chief reviewer and not you?'

'Because this is the way the world works. I wish I could remember being so young that I didn't know that.'

'Money is good,' she said. 'It's *good*. You must have thought about these things.'

'Do you often bribe book reviewers?'

'No. This is a first.'

'And it was Vagg's idea?'

'This is *his* version of how the world works. You want a result, you pay for it.'

'And what's your cut?' I said.

She stopped plucking at my hand. 'Who says I'm getting one?'

'I sense it.'

She hesitated. That wasn't like her. Yeah, she was getting a cut all right. Her whole body was tense with the information. I hoped her mouth wasn't about to deny it. That would put a regrettable dent in our relationship.

'Five grand,' she finally said, and her eyes lit up again.

'Out of my ten?'

'No, on top of your ten.'

'Fifteen all up? Jesus. He *is* mad.'

'So what are you thinking? You're thinking about it, aren't you?'

'I didn't say that.'

She rolled off me and slid off the bed. She went over to the big bookcase against the wall. Keeping her back to me, she tilted her head and checked out my library. She hadn't got up for good, but she was letting me know how I would like it when she did. Also she was letting me take a long leisurely look at her body. I did so. What else was I going to look at? Her flesh was ample but not loose. High on the back of her right thigh was a pair of grape-coloured bruises. Somehow I hadn't seen them until now. That was remiss of me. You could call them lovebites, but you'd be stretching a point. They looked more like gunshot wounds. They were fresh. There were black tracks around the fringes that had to be teeth marks. I wondered about the freak who'd put them there. It certainly hadn't been me. Did he own her, or had he just been passing through? I wanted to tell her he was a fool and a scumbag either way. But I thought we'd have other chances to discuss him. I thought there would be other days.

'Be honest,' she said, without turning round. 'How long would it take you to make ten thousand dollars? Normally?'

'A while.'

'How much of a while?'

'A fucking while.'

Finally she came back. She lay down on top of me and sighed. The sigh entered my body and ran all the way up and down it like an electric charge.

'Didn't you expect more, Ray?'

'More what?' It was the first time she'd used my name.

'Out of your life. You must have expected more.'

'Jesus. I'm not dead yet.'

'What was the plan, though? You must have had one. Was it that novel of yours? Was that the big gamble? You put all your eggs in that basket?'

'Something like that.'

'You thought it'd make you rich?'

'I don't know. Maybe.'

'And now what?'

'And now I'm not.'

'So what now? You plan to live like this forever?'

'We're getting a bit close to the bone here.'

'Should I shut up?'

'My life's simple and I like it like that.'

'You don't ever get the urge to complicate it?'

'Sometimes. I always end up regretting it.'

She pouted. 'Always?'

'Maybe I should apply for your job,' I said. 'Publicising people who are famous already. It doesn't sound all that hard.'

'It isn't.'

'That can't have been your dream. Dishing out bribes on behalf of lowlifes like Vagg. You're way too good for that.'

She propped herself up on both elbows, as if about to favour me with something significant – a secret, a confession. Then she thought better of it, or seemed to.

'Say it,' I urged her. I got the feeling I was meant to. Do women pick up these tricks along the way, or are they born knowing them?

'It's nothing.'

'Bullshit.' I gave her rump a playful slap. I'd been waiting for a good excuse to do that, or even a bad one. 'Spit it out.'

'Okay. You want to hear my retirement plan? One day I'm going to go through the slush pile, and I'm going to pull out the shittiest manuscript I can find.'

'Isn't that how they found Vagg?'

'Shut up and listen.' She dug the blade of her chin into my chest and looked up at me. 'People like Vagg – you're right, they're famous already. There's no skill in it, selling guys like him. It's just setting up meetings. That's all it is. But what if I found someone in the pile who was just a puppet? A complete nobody. What if I started the selling *then*, when nobody knows him from Adam? What if I slipped him past the editors and –'

'Hang on. How exactly do you "slip" something past an editor? I've been trying it all my life. It doesn't work.'

'This is what I'm saying. Shut up and listen. Your book had no heat on it. I'm saying you need heat on it from the start. *Before* it gets to them.'

'You want to market some patsy all the way to the top?'

'I want to try.'

'Of course, he'd have to be no good *at all*.'

'Exactly. Because that way it'd all be me.'

'An Ern Malley for the age of spin.'

'You think it'd work?' Her eyes flashed wickedly.

'I know it would. They're doing it already. The industry *thrives* on overhyped shit. But what's the payoff?'

'Fifty per cent of everything he makes, forever.'

'In exchange for what? Not blowing the whistle on him?'

'Exactly.'

'Where's the fun in that, though?' We were just talking. None of it had weight. But I wanted to make the scene last. 'You need to think bigger. Hype him all the way to the

Nobel, then blow the lid off the whole thing. Step out from the wings and end the pageant, like Prospero. Rain down shame on the whole industry. *That's* a payoff.'

'I prefer the payoff where I get paid,' she said, 'and it's my plan.'

'Of course, you'll need a critic to whip the top for you. An inside man.'

'Oh will I?'

'Absolutely. A known hard man who's willing to call your Oswald a genius.'

'Someone like Barrett Lodge?' she impudently said.

'Think about it. It'd be you and me against the literary world. Until now it's been just me. That was *much* less fun.'

'Well you're not getting your hands on my fifty per cent,' she said.

'Jade, I feel like I made you up.' I cradled her diabolical skull in my fingers. 'At long last, a girl with a mind as nasty as mine. You think like me but you look like you.'

'If you made me up,' she said, 'would I do this?'

She dipped her face but preserved eye contact. Her mouth moved down my body. When it came to my lowest rib, she bit me harder than I have ever been bitten in my life. Her teeth went in and stayed in. The pain was stunning. Instinctively I raised a hand to hit her. I didn't go through with it, but I came close. That startled me more than the pain. She saw me do it, but was laughing too hard to care. It fleetingly crossed my mind that she was nuts. Then I went back to thinking she was the sanest person I'd ever met. A ring of blood-beads seeped up from under my skin, then sat on its surface like crimson dew. No, I didn't make her up. Thirteen days later, the fading proof of her is still there on my belly. When I press on the welt I get a jolt of pain that sends a blast of white light across my vision. I have had plenty of time to wonder, since her death, if the man who put those bites on her thigh gave her the taste for doing it herself. Or maybe he got the habit from her. For some reason I like that idea less.

'Did you do that to change the subject?' I asked her.

'You're the one who keeps changing the subject.'

'So we've stopped talking about your thing.'

'That's not real. Forget about it.'

'I don't think you should. I wouldn't want the Vagg thing to be our swan song.'

'So you're going to do it?'

'I was until you bit me.'

She smiled. She dipped her head again and licked the blood off me. Her feathery hair fanned out over my chest. She looked like drowned Ophelia, spread wide on the water.

I said, 'Nobody else knows about it?'

'Just you, me, and him.' She brought her face back up.

'Has he given you the money yet?'

'Of course not. But he's ready to, if you say yes. In cash.'

'Has he gone back to robbing banks?'

'These days he doesn't need to.'

'Up front?'

'If you say yes.'

'And if I say no?'

'I guess our lives will just keep going the way they're going.'

Her tone made it clear who would be the loser out of that. Also she made it sound as if my life and hers were still separate things. Even then I'd started thinking they shouldn't be. I'd known her for about two hours, and already she had the power to scare me.

'It won't be easy,' I said. 'The people who read me have an ear. There aren't many of them, but they have an ear. They'll know something's up.'

'Maybe they'll suspect it, but they'll never actually *know*. Not if you do it cleverly enough.'

'What if we ask him for more?'

That she wasn't ready for. 'How much more?'

'What if we ask him to double it?'

'You just said he was nuts to pay fifteen.'

'He is. But if he's nuts enough to pay fifteen, maybe he's nuts enough to pay thirty.'

'I could try. But if he says no, you'll still do it?'

'Relax. I'll do it either way. I'm just saying, let's squeeze him first. Let's shake the old spiv down and see what happens.'

'So you're not a saint after all?'

I've heard all the bad jokes about my name. There are no good ones. But on her lips, many an old thing seemed new again.

'Not by a long chalk,' I said.

She put her mouth on my chest again, and licked at that ring of blood. We were getting back to the part where speech no longer mattered.

'And remember,' I said, before we left the world of words altogether. 'If you ever do that other thing, I want you to count me in.'

◆

There was a hitch. Maybe it was a small hitch or maybe it was a very large one. Either way, I didn't think she had to know about it. The hitch was this. I had reviewed Vagg's book already. Two nights earlier, two nights pre-Jade, I had fired off my thousand words to Skeats. And they weren't pretty. I'd forgotten most of the details, but I retained a vivid sense of the gist. It had been a massacre, an orgy of candour. Why not? Back then, I'd had no reason to lie. Vagg's book was shit and I had said so. I had called his fame a literate person's nightmare, or something like that. I had spoken of the decline and fall of Western culture, hinting that Vagg was largely to blame for it. Perhaps I had ventured a gibe or two about his criminal past. When a man's book gives me that much of a headache, I feel professionally bound to give him a larger headache back. And now the headache looked like being mine again. If Vagg paid fifteen grand in advance and got that review in return, he'd come looking for a refund at the very least. If he laid down thirty he might bring along his pit bull.

That lie cast its cold shadow over us, then, as we lay there twined on the bed. While she nibbled at my body, the truth kept nibbling at my mind. Thinking about it made it difficult, although not impossible, to savour what we were up to. I doubted the problem was fatal. To fix it, all I had to do was move faster than Skeats. History did not indicate that this would be hard. My stuff had never taken less than two weeks to limp from submission into print. Sometimes it took two months. Skeats was a slow-burn man. He liked to maim my prose at his leisure, like a torturer pulling teeth – yanking a comma here, crippling a joke there. It took him time to think of all the ways he could make each sentence worse.

So there was, I felt, no call to panic. Probably he hadn't opened the document yet. I was pretty sure, come to think of it, that he hadn't even acknowledged receipt. All the signs said I was safe.

Still, the fuse to disaster had been lit, and I itched to hit the laptop and hose it down. So when I asked her to stay the night I didn't mean it, and she could tell I didn't mean it, and she was meant to. I regretted it even then, but I thought I could fix it later on, like everything else. I repeat: I thought there would be other days. For the moment, what I craved was an hour or two alone to put things right. After that we could reunite and enjoy a long unvexed future together, beneath a sky unclouded by secrets. So I let her go. I didn't drop to my knees and sink all ten fingernails into her rump and bury my face in the front of her and beg her in a flesh-muffled voice to stay. I let her go. I *wanted* her to go. I watched her tail-lights swing out of my driveway and I was glad. Was I mad then or am I mad now?

Immediately I emailed Skeats. I told him I'd reread Vagg's book and acquired some second thoughts. I told him to spike my first review without reading it. I told him to expect a replacement soon, very soon. I uncapped the bottle beside the laptop and didn't bother with a glass. And I got to work. I began by calling Vagg a stylist. Once I'd said that without dying of shame, anything seemed possible. I upped the ante: I called him an innovator. Again I waited for the outraged God of Letters to strike me down. Again it didn't happen. (Had Skeats replied to my email yet? No, he had not.) On a roll, I called Vagg a good old-fashioned storyteller. If he wasn't one, let somebody else prove it. And who was going to try? Vagg himself? The people who sold his books? The people who bought them? After a while the grog splashed into action, and I *really* went to town. Surfing a huge foaming wave of booze and bullshit, I gave the old hack his money shot. I called him a *master craftsman*. I called his stuff *history as literature*. Or maybe I called it *literature as history*. Or maybe I called it both. Again, who was going to object? People like me? I'm the only person like me left, and even I don't give a shit any more.

It must have been about two in the morning when I dispatched the finished product to Skeats. Even at the time I could hardly remember what it said. All I knew was that it was a masterpiece of venality. When you don't mean a word you say, writing becomes the easiest thing in the world. Maybe I should have done it that way all along. No wonder Barrett Lodge was so prolific. I pictured a lucrative new future: perjuring my way to fame and fortune. I drank to it copiously. I wondered if I'd taken my nightly dose of pills. I thought I had, but couldn't remember for sure. That meant I'd better dose myself again just in case. A double dose can put you on the canvas for a long time, but no dose at all will bring on the apocalypse. Anyway, maybe I wanted to be on the canvas for a while. I already had a sense of what I'd feel like when I woke up, and I was in no hurry to feel like it. A *triple* dose then? Why not? Why not? So I abused a final pill, then resolved to hit the sack for my own safety. Had Golden Boy replied to that email yet – to any of my emails? No. Did that mean he hadn't seen them? Not necessarily. It was three in the morning, but mediocrity never sleeps. I shut the laptop down. On the floor beside the bed I found her black panties. I was drunk enough to assume she'd left them behind by accident. I still thought she was the kind of girl who made mistakes. I took them to bed and considered disgracing myself with them. It would be a fine note for the evening to end on. But it wasn't going to happen. I was sinking away from consciousness too fast. At least I had them in my hand, though. I had clutched that much of her before she melted away.

One night I'll take so many pills that I will stay down on the canvas for good, and people – a few people – will have to wonder if I did it on purpose or by accident. What they won't understand is that the distinction no longer applies, once pain's claws are in you deep enough. You just want it gone. If you happen to blow yourself out of the water too, so what? I've had nights when the risk seemed more than acceptable. So far I've always woken up the next day. But never waking up again has something to be said for it, when waking up feels the way it does to me.

I came around on what I thought was the next morning. The clock beside the bed said five-fifteen. By the time it said five-thirty I'd worked out that the sun was going down, not coming up. I had slept through the lion's share of her last day on the planet. I'd been dreaming there was an axe buried so deep in the core of my skull that nobody could get it out. Some fat bearded lumberjack kept trying. For leverage he'd planted the sole of a hefty boot on my face. I kept telling him to go away and let me die.

I staggered out into the yard and howled at the grass for a while. When that was done I went back inside and tried lying on the couch. I gave up on that fast. There was nothing I could put my head on that didn't feel like a sack of razors.

So I got myself roughly upright and didn't move and just sat there like someone's dumped outfit for a while. I was still slumped there when the details of the Vagg mess came back to me. I groaned. There was nothing I wanted to think about less. I looked across at my open laptop. If Skeats had emailed me while I slept, I needed to know about it. If he hadn't, I needed to know that even more. I looked at the acre of floor between me and the keyboard. I resolved to make the crossing soon, if necessary on my hands and knees. In the end I got there on foot. I woke the laptop up. Its buzzings and machine noises jackhammered my tender skull. When it had settled itself down I pulled up my emails. They looked all blurred, as if submerged in seawater. I knew from long experience that there was no point trying to focus my eyes. It wouldn't work, and it would hurt a lot. I saw through the haze that there was something from Skeats, sent at ten-thirteen this morning. It was entitled *RE: Revised Vagg*. So he had replied, and in reasonable time too. I thought: I will take two seconds to confirm that the problem is solved, then I will celebrate by getting back to dying.

But when I opened his message, all I saw was a white blur. Was I really that blind? I squinted. Still nothing. I scrolled down: there was my original message, with the revised Vagg file properly attached. I scrolled back up. Skeats's half of the window was empty. The raging imbecile had outdone himself. He'd sent me a blank reply.

For a long while I just stared at it, the way the owner of a stolen car will stare at his empty garage. Finally I rallied and sent him a new message. It said: *So you got my Vagg rewrite? You'll scrap the first one and run the second one?*

Back on the couch, I tried to convince myself that not

even Skeats could evade or misunderstand that. I have spent a third of my life repeating myself for the benefit of fools. While waiting on his reply I took a jolt from last night's bottle. I felt more than entitled to one. Hadn't I earned my cut already, for Christ's sake? Hadn't I done enough? I had sold my soul, which should have been the hardest part. I had reviewed Vagg's dismal book twice. I had told the most fantastic lies about it. I had let go of the idea that anything I said mattered. And here I was doing it all again, or still, or even more. I was on bribe-and-a-half time now, the way I saw it. I had a good mind to charge Vagg a vig.

My email chime went off.

I told myself it couldn't possibly be Skeats yet.

I went over and checked anyway.

It wasn't him. It was a piece of junk mail.

I went back to the couch. Maybe a bit of time passed here. Maybe I drank a bit more. I kept thinking about that blank email. Could anyone, even Skeats, send a wordless email by accident? Then again, why would he do it on purpose? To buy time? Time for what? Either he'd slipped up or he was fucking with me. It was hard to say which thing was more likely. He was a master of both forms.

My mail chime sounded again. I went weakly to the machine. This time it was him. He had replied to my latest email. His reply consisted of one word. The word was *Yep*.

Why did that fail to reassure me? Because I knew who I was dealing with. Christ, my head ached too much for this. I scrolled back to my own message, reread it, and hated myself for writing it. I had asked him two questions in one email – a cardinal error. If Skeats was anybody else, you could safely assume he was saying yes to both of them. But he wasn't, so you couldn't. Maybe he had read no further than the first question, and was answering only that. Maybe he was answering just the second one, because the first one had already slipped his mind. Skeats was an incredibly busy and important man. His one-word replies were meant to remind you of that. They were meant to save time. Instead they wasted it. Mainly they wasted yours. But you could make them waste his as well, if you felt like pressing the point.

This time I had to. I had to pin the slapdash fucker down. I was starting to feel distinctly messed with. I looked around for my mobile phone. Finding it through the saline haze took time. Finding his number on it took more. I called it. He didn't answer. That was a worry. His phone was never far away from him. I got his voicemail. I told him to ring me back.

Five minutes later he still hadn't. I tried him again and got the same result. I felt a pang of fear or prescience. I was starting to comprehend how much I wanted Vagg's money. I wanted it a lot. I sent Skeats a text. *Call me.* I waited, but not for long. I called him again. Again he didn't answer. That clinched it. Either he was dead or he was avoiding me. I was beyond uneasy now. I ditched the mobile and went over to the landline, wondering why I hadn't tried it in the first place. The landline was clean, as far as I knew. It wasn't lumbered with the stink of my ID. I waited three long minutes so he wouldn't guess it was me. Then I dialled his number. He picked up straight away.

'Raymond!' he said heartily, when I told him who it was. If this was his impression of a man who was happy to hear my voice, it needed work.

'You got my email?' I said.

'Mate,' he said, 'can I call you back?'

'No.'

'Frankly, this isn't a great time.'

When a man like Skeats uses the word *frankly*, brace yourself for a deluge of lies. 'This won't take long,' I said. 'I want you to confirm that you got my Vagg rewrite.'

'Ye-aah.' He hesitated so long in the middle of that word that he almost stopped saying it. You could hear him wishing he'd started saying something else instead, like 'no'. We were five seconds into the call and already we were chest-deep in bullshit. Something was going on, all right.

'You sound unsure,' I said.

'No, I got it. The second one, you mean?'

'Yes, I do mean that. That's why I said rewrite. Is there a problem?'

'Not really. It's just that it came a bit late.'

'A bit late for what?'

'A bit late to do any tinkering.'

'Tinkering? I'm not asking you to tinker. I want you to scrap the first piece and use the second one.'

'Ah. Well that *is* a problem.'

'In what sense?'

'The deadline's been and gone, mate.'

Deadline. Is there a nastier word in the language? The cold steel of it touched the base of my balls like the blade of a scalpel.

'What deadline?'

'Tomorrow's deadline.'

'Tomorrow?' I gave myself a moment. How drunk *was* I? 'Hang on. I'm talking about something I sent you three days ago. You can't tell me that's running tomorrow.'

'Why not? It is.'

'Pull it. I've changed my mind.'

'It's a bit late for that, Ray. You've missed the boat.'

'Three days? You *never* turn things around that fast.'

'Not normally, true. But a couple of people fucked me on their deadlines, including Barrett. Luckily I had your Vagg thing to throw into the breach.'

'When the fuck,' I asked him, 'were you planning to tell me this?'

'Check your email,' Skeats said. 'I sent you something this morning.'

'That was blank, and I think you know it.'

'Blank? No shit?'

'I sense I'm being fucked with,' I said.

'And I sense you've been nudging the piss.'

'When was the deadline? Tell me exactly when it was.' Why was I still bothering to talk? Why prolong the nightmare? The deal was dead. Vagg's cash had been torn from me like a living limb. There was a bleeding stump where my future had been.

'What's the difference?' Skeats said. 'It's been and gone.'

'I sent you the second review last night. Was the deadline before that or after that?'

'I don't follow you.'

'Try harder. It's a simple question.'

'A *moot* fucking question is what it is, Ray. Christ, it's just a book review. What's your issue? You worried that Vagg might lob round and break your kneecaps?'

'Maybe he'll break yours.'

'Or make you suck on his shotgun. I liked that line.'

'Christ. I said *that*?' Now something was *really* askew: Skeats was praising my prose.

'You don't remember?'

'And you didn't cut it?'

'Why would I?'

'Because you *always* cut things like that.'

'Ray, you did write the bloody thing. It's not like I've put any words in your mouth.'

'What's with the unseemly rush to print? What's going on? Why did you send me a blank email? Why have you been avoiding my calls?'

'Ray, you're being paranoid. Listen to yourself.'

'Am I? Why did you send me Vagg's book in the first place? Why didn't you send it to Lodge? Did you *want* somebody to piss on it?'

'Why would I want that?'

'Good question. I wish I knew. Vagg's exactly the kind of guy you like to starfuck at the festivals. What happened this time? Why the radical change of policy? What did he do, fuck your wife?'

'You want to talk about changes of policy, Ray?' His tone control was starting to slip, finally. 'Let's talk about you. What went on there? One day you think his book's a titanic piece of shit, two days later you think it's a masterpiece. What happened in between?'

'So you *did* read the second thing.'

'I glanced at it.'

'Why'd you bother, if the deadline had been and gone?'

'I did you a favour, mate, believe me. That second thing wasn't you *at all*. What came over you? It was just a bunch of empty praise.'

'I thought you were into that.'

'Coming from you, mate, it makes me smell a rat.'

'Sniff harder. Maybe the stench is coming from you.'

'Were you drunk when you wrote that shit, Ray? Are you drunk now?'

'Mildly. What's your excuse?'

'Ray, this conversation is coming to a close. You want to know what you think of Vagg's book? Read tomorrow's paper. They're printing it already. And next time you want to change your mind, change it faster. Preferably before you file your fucking piece.'

'Let's talk about this rationally,' I said.

'Rationally? Look at your watch, Ray. The presses are rolling.'

'Stop them.'

Skeats just laughed.

I remember swaying on my feet then, and wanting to be horizontal. And I remember resolving to fight it. If I let myself drop I would lose the rest of the night, and that would be a kind of death. In the morning Liam Vagg was going to wake up with a second arsehole, torn by me. And his cash would be off the table and she would hate me, and that would be that. Ten thousand dollars was a lot of money. I was finally starting to get that, now that the deal had gone to hell. How often in your life do you get a shot at a cold ten grand? Speaking for myself: never. Never before, and probably never again. This had been my chance. Had I blown it? Maybe not quite. Until Vagg saw tomorrow's paper there was still hope. But I had to stay upright. I had to stay in the game. Defeat always wants you to make things easy for it. If you don't lie down, you already have half a plan.

I was in no shape to come up with the other half yet, but I could hardly afford to wait till I was. All I knew was that I needed to hear her voice. When I heard it, maybe I'd know what to do. Maybe I would tell her the truth, or part of it. If I did, maybe she would rise wickedly to the occasion. She'd told me Vagg was delivering the cash up front. What if he'd already done that? Would that make the situation more fucked up than it already was, or less? Maybe less. Maybe we could keep the cash and make it hard for him to get it back. If we made it hard enough, maybe he'd stop trying. Was he so rich that he'd give up fifteen grand without a fight – to say nothing of thirty? Was *anyone* that rich? I didn't know. I don't have the kind of life where you know things like that.

In my wallet there was a torn slip of paper with her number on it. She'd given it to me the other night before leaving. I dialled the number. What time was it now? Mid-evening. Nine or maybe ten.

A man's voice said, 'Yeah?'

'*Vagg?*'

'No,' the guy said. 'Who's this?'

'Put Jade on.'

'No Jade here, my friend.'

'Put her on.'

He hung up.

I dialled the number again. Maybe I'd got it wrong the first time.

'Yeah?' It was the same guy. He had a hostile snarl going already, to save us some time.

'Let me speak to Jade Howe,' I said.

'Brother,' the guy said, 'wake up to yourself. Some bitch has given you the wrong number.'

He hung up again. I stood there listening to the dead line. For some reason I believed the guy on the phone. He could have been anyone, but for some reason I believed him instead of her. She'd given me the wrong number, and not by mistake. Why was I so quick to think her a liar? Maybe I'd been rubbing shoulders with Skeats too long. This was getting to be a bad, bad night. I had a sense of things coming apart, of being caught in something I didn't understand. That made me want to talk to her even more, but how was I meant to do that now? All I knew was her name, unless that was a lie too. I was running out of ideas. A bad one came to me. Maybe she'd given me the right number but had got the last digit wrong. I tried a few variants. Different people kept picking up. None of them was her. I think I got the first guy again.

After that a worse idea hit me. Maybe she'd left her number with Skeats. I rang him to find out. He didn't answer.

And then I was standing in the glow of my laptop, punch-drunk but still doggedly in the fight. The internet: last resort of the damned. Her number had to be on it somewhere. Everything was on it, if you knew where to look. Probably you'd find film of her sucking some guy's dick on there, if you were willing to put in the work. Why not? There's film of every other girl doing it. Next to that, a phone number wasn't much to ask for. I don't know how much time passed while I looked for it. Cyber-time moves weirdly, like plane time, like casino time. I don't know where or how I found it, either. All I know is that I did. Did it resemble, in any way at all, the number she had given me? I wish I remembered. But there are many things I wish I remembered. All I can say is that I found it. I must have, because some time later, in the frigid wash of the screen's light, I found myself standing with a phone to my ear and her on the other end of it.

'Wondering how I got your number?' I asked her.

'I gave it to you.'

'No you didn't.'

She thought about that. 'Are you drunk?'

'Profoundly.'

'What's the matter, Ray? Has something gone wrong?'

'Not at my end. How about at yours? Has Vagg paid up yet?'

It was a simple question, but she seemed to pause before answering it. 'Yeah.'

'Did he double it?' I hadn't liked that pause.

'No, but it was worth a try.'

'So you have it now? Fifteen in cash?'

'I've got it. Are you okay? What's the matter? Have you done the review?'

'It's done. It's in.'

'That was fast. When's it coming out?'

'That I can't say.'

'Did you call him a master craftsman?' Her voice sparkled. She sounded almost innocent, but maybe everyone's innocent when measured against me. She thought it was all over. She was thinking about her five grand.

'Why don't you come here now?' I said. 'Bring the cash. We'll celebrate.'

'What's the rush? I'll bring it tomorrow. We can pour it out on that big old bed of yours and fuck on it.'

Yes, she was enviably free of care. She felt like playing around. I didn't. My tone was turning putrid.

'That sounds so good I want to do it now,' I said. 'Tell me where you live. I'll come there.'

'No,' she said. 'Don't do that.'

'You sound strangely adamant about that.'

'It's late, Ray. Plus you are *way* too drunk to drive.'

'I'll be the judge of that.'

'Plus someone's coming over, if you must know.'

'Who?'

'No one you need to worry about.'

'Christ. I wasn't worried till you said that.'

'Go to bed, you dirty old man. You sound like you need to.'

'Who is he?' I said.

'Who says it's a he?'

'Is it?'

'I'll come up tomorrow night, Ray. I promise. Maybe I'll bite you again. I got the feeling you liked that.'

I listened to her trampy little playful voice and knew she'd never use it on me again. She still thought we had a future, but I had seen the damage below decks, the ruinous hole ripped by Skeats. If I was going to get one more night with her, tonight would have to be it. And maybe we could still get something out of this, if I told her the truth. I still wanted to do that. I still craved her wicked input. But I wasn't enough of a fool to try it over the phone. We needed to be in the same room: me, her, the money.

'Don't you trust me?' she said.

'Why'd you give me the wrong number?'

'Maybe you dialled wrong. Maybe I gave you my old number by mistake.'

'You don't strike me as a girl who makes mistakes.'

'Ray, you're starting to weird me out.' She sounded baffled. The magic was leaking out of our relationship, but I had to press on.

'You wouldn't be going cold on me, would you?' I asked her. 'Now that I've delivered the goods?'

'No, but if you don't shut up I might start thinking you have a dickish side.'

'Say something to reassure me,' I said.

'I just did.'

'It didn't work. Try something else.'

'Ray, it's late.'

'Not too late to entertain this other prick.'

She let that one go.

'Something's up,' I said. 'There's something you're not telling me. I can hear it in your voice.'

Again she hesitated. That left me alone with my fears for a while. Whatever she was about to say, it couldn't be nastier than the things I was thinking.

'Okay,' she said. 'I did tell you one little lie.'

I waited.

'I haven't got the money yet.'

'*What?*'

'He hasn't paid up yet. Listen. When you asked me if he had, I didn't know why you were asking. I thought – I didn't know if you'd done the review yet. I thought maybe you'd lost your nerve. So I lied. That was bad. But Ray? That's all. I'm telling you the truth now.'

She was wrong if she thought that would soothe the fire in my mind. Instead she'd supplied it with a lifetime's worth of fuel. I knew now what she sounded like when she lied.

She sounded, when she was lying, exactly the way she sounded when she wasn't lying. The needle of her voice hadn't fluttered. That meant anything she said could be untrue. Suddenly there was no ground under my feet. Maybe she was lying about having lied. Maybe she *did* have the cash. Maybe she was planning to take off with it right now.

'That's who's coming over tonight,' she said. 'Him, with the money.'

'What time?'

'I don't know. He's doing an interview or something, and he's coming over when he's done.'

'Is he coming before midnight?'

'Why? You worried he's going to show me his tattoos?'

It was meant to be a joke, but I didn't laugh. You need to see their faces when they say things like that. Over the phone any horror seems possible. Maybe Vagg was with her right now, with his hack's face jammed right up between her thighs. Maybe she had a fistful of his ponytail, riding it like a pommel while he put a few more of those bruises on her.

'Is he coming before midnight or not?'

'I don't know. Probably. Why?'

'Because I told you a lie too,' I said. 'You told me one, I told you one. The review's in tomorrow's paper.'

I listened to her think about that.

'How's that even possible?' she said.

'I don't know, but it's happening. The paper goes online at midnight.'

'Okay. But so what? Why's that a problem?'

'Because if it gets published before he pays, he might screw us and keep the cash.'

'Why would he do that?'

76

'Why wouldn't he?'

'Don't worry. I trust him.'

'Why would you trust a man like that?'

'I just do.'

'What if he doesn't like the review?'

'Why wouldn't he?'

'Because I told you two lies. The review's not as great as I made out.'

'What are you saying?' Her voice tightened around that question like a noose. Finally she was as interested in the conversation as I was.

'I'm saying I had to keep it plausible. I had to throw in a line or two of stick to make it sound like me.'

'A line or two? Shit, we can live with that. You had me worried there.'

'Still, I want to be there when he turns up.'

'Ray, relax. If it sounds like the real you, that's *good* for us. He knows that. He's not a *total* numbskull. He only writes like one.'

'Tell me where you live.'

'Ray, you've done your bit. Leave tonight to me.'

'Where do you live?'

'I'll tell you one day when you're not hammered.'

'I can't wait that long. Tell me now.'

'Don't come here, Ray. *Don't*, okay? Go to bed. When you wake up, it'll all be over.'

That was the last thing she said to me. And it was the last thing she should have said, if she really wanted me to stay away.

The next part gets hazy. Events were cascading. The world was collapsing around me. I had to grab a falling shard of it and ride it through the night, and catch all the other shards before they came down. I remember standing in the light of the laptop and looking for her address. If I'd found her number on it, her address had to be there too. And I guess it was, because the next thing I knew I was out on the road. The road was the last place I should have been. I don't need to be told that. I'm the one who had to be there while it was happening. It isn't relaxing, driving in that state. The car gets all heavy. It drifts. It feels like a parade float. You have to keep working, all the time. I remember the darkness seeming darker than usual. There was a shadow on the road in front of me, thrown by the headlights of the car behind. It looked like the shadow of my car. It *was* the shadow of my car. I checked my headlights. They were not on. Somehow I'd got that far without them. I lit them up, and the guy behind me beat a startled tattoo on his horn. I gave him a few blasts back but he had a point. No headlights: that scared even me, even then. The trouble with being that far gone is that you don't know how far gone you are until you do something like that. And by then you're out on the road, doing it.

Don't come here. I remember thinking about the way she'd said that. I was ready to hear the worst in it. I remember wondering how much I really knew about her. I thought about the way she'd looked into my eyes while tonguing the flesh of my thumb. Was it possible to fake *that*? Either I was hurtling towards the answer or I was hurtling towards having no answer forever. Drug-fogged as I was, I had the sense to be terrified by that.

I remember being in some all-night roadside coffee place. Was I lost? The place had orange plastic tables. A girl of about Jade's age sat at one of them. I remember swaying over her and saying things, asking her to look at my face and tell me if a girl like her would sleep with a man like me for fun, without some added angle or inducement. I begged her for an honest answer. Was it plausible? Or would money have to be involved?

I remember being back on the road. My jaw buzzed as if a shovel had hit it. I tasted blood. My right hand hurt too. Either I'd hit myself in the face or I'd got in a fight. My hand hurt more than my face. I remember wishing it had been the other way around. Conceivably, the girl in that clean, well-lighted place had turned out to have a boyfriend. If she had, it was more than conceivable that he'd hit me. It had been shitty of me to hit him back, but I had to hope that I had. It was the loftiest option on offer. At worst I'd traded blows with the girl, and won. I remember telling myself to turn around and go home before anything funkier could happen.

And then the recording ends, and one big reel turns emptily on its spindle, and the full reel slaps the rollers with its tongue of dangling tape. The next thing I remember is this: I am driving into the city in the light of dawn. The sun's coming up ahead of me. Why am I still on my way there? How lost did I *get*? A shameful chunk of the night has gone astray. A fifty-minute drive has taken me seven hours. What happened to all that lost time? Did I go somewhere else on the way? If I remembered then, I've forgotten since.

I remember walking up her driveway with the sun still rising. Her red car was there. And a rolled-up newspaper on the cement, with my Vagg review curled inside like an evil fetus. And her front door standing wide open. I remember walking up her carpeted hallway. I remember seeing the corner post of her bed, and then her bare foot. I remember thinking she was asleep. I remember bracing myself to see somebody next to her, maybe even Vagg. At the time, that was the worst thing I could imagine. And then the blood, that supernova of drying slime on the bed and the walls and her. The smell of it in my mouth. And then the irreversible error of looking at her face. Her eyes both open, the look in them like a scream you couldn't hear. There was nothing fake about that look. She had died looking at a man from hell.

I was shaking and almost out the door when I remembered the cash. I made myself go back and look for it. Let's assume I was in shock. I waded back in against the tide, back up the hall, back into her room. I looked everywhere, within reason. I went as close to her torn body as I dared. The money was gone, if it had ever been there.

I remember the drive home. I remember saying aloud: what did you touch in there? Did you touch the doorknob? Did you leave prints? I looked at my hands and there was no blood on them. I remember getting home and heading straight for the shower. I remember flinching when the water hit my ribs. It wasn't just the pain. It was what the pain meant. I looked down. There were two bites on my chest now, not one. The second bite was savagely fresh. Blood still drooled from its deeper notches. I had no memory of how it had got there: only fear.

I remember thinking: Your life is about to change.

3

Flashback over. We are back in the present tense. My curtains are shut. The couch she sat on for an hour has never been sat on since, except by me. My ribcage still has those bites on it. You'd think they'd be gone by now, but I heal slowly these days. Also they were not trivial wounds. One of them still looks a day fresher than the other, and makes me flinch harder when I touch it. And the teeth marks look similar, flagrantly similar. No, not similar: the same. I am no dentist, but I have eyes. Ted Lewin, for all his rigour, has never asked me to remove my shirt. If he ever does, I'll have yet another thing to explain, and even I won't really know if I'm lying about it. Somebody bit me in the middle of that final night. If it wasn't her, we are dealing with a large coincidence. If it was, we are dealing with a tragedy. It would mean I was with her one last time and have lost the whole memory. And if I can forget that, I can forget anything.

There are things on my floor that have been there since she was alive. The glass she drank from is right where she left it on the table. It's not that I want to preserve the scene. It's that I can't muster the will or energy to clean it up. I can no longer see the point of doing things like that. I only knew her for two days, but her death tore something vital from me. The hook of her went deep into my gut, and it came out festooned with my organs. I hate the world because she's not in it. If it wasn't for the people down at my gate, I would no longer shave or shower. I would let myself look the way I feel. But that might give them the right idea, and we can't have that. I have stopped hoping that they will all just leave one day out of boredom. They will stay until something drastic occurs, something terminal. They're dug in now. They're in this too deep. We all are.

When Lewin called me in for my first interview, I thought we were doing something routine. I assumed I was in minor trouble, and believed I could ride it out. I thought he'd lose interest in me pretty fast. After all, I didn't kill her. Why would I? It was Vagg. It must have been. I thought Lewin would work that out by himself, given time. So I sat through the early turbulence and waited for him to do his job. I waited for the Detective Inspector to detect and inspect. I waited for Vagg's name to bob up in the news, like a corpse riding its gases to the top of a lake. Two weeks later, I'm still waiting. The only corpse floating in the newspapers is mine.

Of course I can always throw Vagg to Lewin myself, if I have to. But I don't see how it can be done without sketching in the context: her and me, the rigged review, the ten grand. I'll need to be in a very tight corner before I give up all that. My literary reputation is all I have left. It's a small thing, but my own. But it will go on the bonfire with the rest of me, if the stuff about Vagg ever gets out. I was ready to risk my literary honour when I could get her in return – her and Vagg's fat ransom. But she's off the table forever now, and I never did get that fucking cash. I'm back to having nothing but a name, and I'd like to keep what's left of it. If I give up Vagg so I can get on with the rest of my life, I'll have no rest of my life to get on with.

So every day I throw one more chip on the original gamble. I bet that I'll get out of this unarrested, with my professional name unsmeared. I wait for Lewin to find his own way to Vagg. But he keeps not doing that. And the longer he takes, the guiltier I look; and the guiltier I look, the less reason he has to look anywhere else. Each time I re-enter his room, I am forced to bury myself deeper in lies. The lies started small, and some of them had a bit of dignity; but there was only one way they could go from there. Why was my address in her notebook? Because she wrote me a letter once. What kind of letter? A fan letter, saluting my criticism. (Two lies in, and already we had veered grievously off the fairway of plausibility.) What became of this letter? You improvise, and you get stuck with your improvisations for good. Did she ever come to your house? You have to say yes, in case somebody saw her car. When? Again you can't lie, as much as you want to. So you tell the truth, even though it puts you with her, alone, in blazing proximity to her death. What brought her to your place? Why did she drive all that way? Here the truth must be shunned, spurned, strenuously not told. But what is the alternative to the truth? Only everything else. You can say anything you want, when your only aim is to erase what actually happened. That sounds a bit like freedom. But when you are not free to tell the truth, you are not free at all. You are a man who may breathe anything he likes except oxygen, a man with an all-you-can-eat pass to a smorgasbord of rotten meat. Out in the land of the lie, the only alternative to the bad option is the worse one. There are lies so atrocious that they will finish you on the spot. There are lies you will have to repeat and defend forever, even though you know, right from the start, that they do not rank with your finest work. There are lies whose leaking hulls will have to be plugged and patched, every time you retell them, with increasingly slapdash sub-lies. But you get no time to think ahead, when Ted Lewin is watching you. You get no time to think about quality. You have to pick your lies fast. And the machines will be watching you too, with their flawless memories, the fact-checkers you can't argue with: the networks and the servers, the unsleeping narcs and snitches who hide out in the circuitry of your phone. Lewin troubles me, but he doesn't scare me. Not much does. But the computers do. They have every power of God – plus they exist. And they are everywhere. In the whole of human history, the liar has never had it so bad. *If you knew her for innocent reasons, why do the records not show it? Why did you send each other no emails? How come she never called or texted you? Why is your hard drive so mute about the matter? Why did your lone call to her happen in the dead of night?* You get fuck-all wriggle room, in the age of the machine. You are strapped into an eternal polygraph. Even when you die, you won't be free of it. You see why people finally give up and call for the biro, in rooms like Lewin's. And you see why they look so happy when they do – why their bodies sag with relief as if freed from the jaws of a vice. Truth has an awesome gravity. Resisting its pull is savage work. Even I must submit to its tug now and then, and feed

Lewin a tactical nugget of non-fiction. If I hadn't done that pretty regularly, I'd have been finished long ago. But my fund of non-incriminating facts wasn't all that bounteous to start with, and I am running out of scraps to throw him. Each week I get closer to bedrock – closer to the point where there's nothing left that I know that he doesn't, except for the things about Vagg. Soon the moment will come when I have nothing left to say except everything: the whole truth. Will I know that moment when I see it? If Lewin arrests me, if he puts me in a cell I can't leave, will that be the moment to bite down on the cyanide? Probably, but I won't know for sure until it happens.

And what if Vagg *didn't* do it? That doesn't bear thinking about. He did it. He must have. And each night he sits there in that big old house of his on the harbour, watching me burn. I'm starting to think it's time he got some of the heat. If Lewin won't turn it on him, maybe I'll have to do it myself. Sometimes I think about paying him a visit. Not straight away, but soon. And what will I do there? Kill him? Squeeze him for cash? I don't know yet. I have a hard time, these days, telling a good idea from a bad one. I have a hard time forming intentions. I have a bad tendency to let things drift, and they always seem to drift the wrong way. Last night I looked up Vagg's address. There's a website that tells you the way to the homes of the stars, and Vagg made the cut. I planned a route. While I was at it, I checked how easy it is to buy a gun. It's not as easy as you'd think. I don't know how seriously I take these notions. All I know is that some-thing has to change. Not straight away, but soon.

Tomorrow I'm due back in Lewin's little room.

◆

It didn't go well. Or maybe it did, in that he let me leave at the end of it. Maybe that's the best I can hope for now: not getting locked up, one day at a time. I am never at my best in Lewin's room, either morally or verbally. But the tapes are always rolling to preserve my words. My output is in demand, for once. The things I say in there are more keenly awaited, more eagerly perused and reread, than any sentence I have ever vainly aimed at posterity. Do digital tapes roll? Are they even tapes? My metaphors are behind the times. I no longer know how the world around me works. When did I get so old? One day I was twenty, and the next I was halfway to death.

'There's one thing I haven't told you,' I informed him this morning, straight off the bat. I wanted to seem transparent from the outset today. I wanted to start on the front foot and stay there. 'Your witness is right. I did go in the house that morning. When I got there, the door was wide open. I went in. I saw her body.'

'And?' said Lewin. *And?* The man always wants more. There's nothing about his room I don't hate now: the cold artificial light, the clean edgeless surfaces, the toneless conditioned air. Bad things happen to you in rooms like this. You get told you have cancer. You arrange to bury your dead. Other people arrange to bury you.

'And she was dead. She was naked. There was a lot of blood. I didn't stick around to see anything else. I was in and out in thirty seconds.'

'Why didn't you say this before?'

'Because I knew how it'd look.'

'And how do you think it looks now?'

'Worse, but that was the gamble.'

86

Yet again I'd let him down. His tactic at such moments is just to sit there, and let silence italicise your blunder. Arthritis has warped his fingers into tortured shapes. They look like bits of driftwood. He smells of cigarettes. I looked at his grey chest hair, curling from the throat of his short-sleeved saffron shirt. I looked at his one bad eye and his one good one. Lewin is a decent man, and he deserves a more respectable foe than me. He deserves an old-school meat-and-potatoes villain. Instead he's got me: a lone-wolf writer, steeped in iffiness and private murk. It isn't just self-interest that makes me withhold the Vagg stuff from him. I also have a tender urge not to expose him to the depravities of the literary world. I don't want to drag him into that swamp, with its grifters and grafters, its hucksters and hustlers, its Falstaffian liars and frauds, the people who buy your soul and never even pay you for it. In that milieu I qualify as one of the good guys.

'Did you touch the body?' he asked me.

'"*The* body"? Her body? No.'

'Why didn't you call the police?'

'Maybe I feared I'd wind up in a room like this, trying to answer questions like that. With someone looking at me the way you are right now.'

'If you'd made the call, I wouldn't be asking the question.'

'I'm sure you'd think of another one.'

'Were you with her that night, Ray?'

'There you go. No, I was not with her that night. As I believe I have told you.'

'Let's say we've got proof you were.'

'I'd say that's impossible.'

'Let's say your DNA was on her.'

The room hummed. A wave of ice broke over my thighs and rode its way to the summit of my spine. 'I'd say it must be old DNA,' I heard myself saying. 'I was with her earlier that week. As you know.'

'No.' His voice went gruff. 'This – the stuff I'm talking about was new. It puts you with her the night she died.'

A pair of reading glasses hung round his neck on a black cord. He put them on his nose now, just to have something to do. The DNA talk made him uneasy. So how did he think it made *me* feel? If I could leave my genes on her and not remember it, my life was very close to not worth living. But suddenly I recalled something, or thought I did. I saw her stretched out on her bed, alive. Her flesh was smooth and plump and intact. All her blood was still inside her. She was smiling at me and saying something I couldn't quite hear. It felt like a real memory, but what do false memories feel like? I waited for more. It didn't arrive. Meanwhile the sound of me saying nothing stretched and deepened.

I said, 'Okay. I think I was probably there.'

'Probably?'

'I forget things, Ted. You know that.' Eye contact was mandatory here. 'I'm missing a big chunk of that night. But if the DNA says I was with her, I was with her. I'll take the DNA's word for it.'

'You've told me you don't forget the big things.'

'I lied about that. I assume you can see why.'

Was it Vagg time yet? Was it ripcord time? We were close. We were very close.

'My head lets me down. It's not normal. I'm well aware of that.'

He watched me over his frames, silently.

'We're at the nub of this now,' I said.

'Yeah.' He breathed heavily through his nose. 'I think we are.'

'I forget things. That alarms me as much as it alarms you, I can assure you. But it doesn't make me a murderer.'

He let that one drift and rot in the silence, then get slowly swallowed by the frigid hum of the machines. After a while I said, 'That's when I must have left my fingerprints, too. The night she died. I told you I was there a few nights earlier. I told you my prints got left there then. That was untrue. That visit did not happen. If I was ever there at all – and clearly I was, I must have been – it was on the night she died. So: I lied about that too. Again I assume you can see why.'

But I was pushing it on the assumptions now, as well as on everything else. I was gravely testing the bounds of Lewin's tolerance for nuance. We were well outside the pale of normal innocence now, way out into the badlands that lie just this side of guilt. What I really needed here, instead of a cop, was a reader of literature, if there were any of them left. I needed a fan of Charles Bukowski, a lover of Henry Miller. I needed someone with a fine feel for the gradations of degeneracy: someone who knew just how much of a scumbag a man can be without being a murderer. Lewin, in this crude binary room, had almost entirely ceased to be my man. The way he looked at me, now I was telling the truth, made me wish I was still lying. He looked disappointed: which meant, by a normal man's standards, that he was appalled. On top of that he looked puzzled, thrown by the sheer weirdness of my output: that strange brew of bad lies, bad truths, and bad memory. He looked like a Grandmaster playing a psychotic. His confusion was unprecedented.

And maybe it was the one thing still keeping me out of cuffs.

'You just told me – a minute ago you said you drove to the house the next morning,' he said. 'The front door was open. You walked in and found the body. So – that was a lie too?'

'No.' I steeled myself. Things were about to get weirder. 'That happened. I think I was there twice. I think I went away and came back.'

He waited.

'Stay with me on this, Ted. This is the truth. Maybe you'll see why I kept it to myself. I remember being in the car that night. I remember wanting to see her, and I remember heading there, but I don't remember getting there or being there. You're telling me I made it. You're saying I left some DNA. That doesn't shock me. I've always suspected it. I'm appalled that I don't remember it, but we're not here to talk about my feelings. The point is I was there – for a while. But I left. I took off when it was still dark. Don't ask me why. I wish I remembered, but I don't. Here's what I do remember. When the sun came up I was driving *back* there. You know the rest. It was light when I got there: true. The door was wide open: true. She was already dead: true. All true.'

I thought about lifting my shirt to show him where she bit me. Why not, since he knew everything else? But I still have this stubborn old-school urge to keep a few things to myself.

'Why would you turn around and go back?' Lewin said.

'Good question. Maybe she gave me a call on the road. Did she? You seem to know more about that night than I do.'

His face revealed nothing. 'Why,' he said, 'would you have left in the first place?'

'I've thought about that too. Want me to speculate?'

'Go on.'

'I think she was expecting someone else.' Maybe I threw that out too hastily, too crudely. But I have started to think that subtlety is about as useful as prayer.

'A boyfriend?'

'If I had to guess, I'd say it was something to do with her job.'

'In the middle of the night?'

'She was big on the career stuff. Why don't you ask her boss what books she was working on?'

'She ever mention any boyfriends?'

'No. We never got to that. Remember, we only ever had one conversation.'

'One that you remember.'

'My head's fucked, Ted. Don't rub it in.'

'So what did you talk about, that time you *do* remember?'

'Her job, mainly. Hyping books. Working with writers. She was – she talked about this book she was working on. This new thing by Liam Vagg. She was publicising it. That's the sort of thing she talked about.'

This was beyond bold and close to reckless. If Lewin had checked the newspaper he would know about my review, and the stink it gave off in all directions. But apparently he didn't read my stuff, like everyone else. Nor, more alarmingly, did Vagg's name seem to interest him in any broader sense, or any narrower sense, or any sense at all. Whatever he was fishing for, Vagg wasn't it.

'I notice you still haven't slapped the cuffs on me,' I said, as long as I was sailing close to the wind.

'Do you want me to?'

'Not at all. But I'm wondering why you haven't. I would have, by now. My story stinks. It's true, but it stinks. And yet for some reason you're not laughing in my face. In fact, I have this odd feeling that you believe me.'

He slipped the glasses from his nose and studied the wall behind my shoulder. His tongue went into his cheek, the way it does when he's troubled.

'What is it, Ted? What do you know here that I don't?'

He tapped the glasses against his chest. He was contemplating an indiscretion. Here it came:

'There was other DNA on her,' he said. 'Some other bloke was with her too.'

He looked hard at my face as he said it. I watched his fingers pinch and twist his dangling glasses. Each restless knuckle bore its own hedge of silver hair. His thick driftwood nails were foxed at the edges like old books. What did he expect my face to do? Howl? Look happy? Not care? Finally I said, 'Was she raped?'

'Now why would you say that?'

'Was she or wasn't she?'

Lewin just looked at me in a stern and sickened way, as if the answer was none of my business. How wrong he was about that. But it didn't matter. I could read his silences now. I could see that the answer was no. She'd permitted it. She'd wanted it. It was the answer any sane or decent man would have preferred, but jealousy can do nasty things to the mind. Or maybe I'm just a nasty guy. Either way, I appeared to be in love with a dead girl. That was pretty clear now. If I hadn't known it before, I knew it then.

'So you know I didn't do it,' I said. 'Everything I've told you fits. I left, and this other bastard turned up and killed her.'

'All we know,' Lewin said grimly, 'is that there were two of you. Who was with her last we don't know. Maybe it was you.'

'Come on, Ted. It fits.'

'You'd better hope so. Maybe when we find this other bloke he'll have a better story than yours.'

He meant that mine could hardly be worse. He meant the other guy's anonymous load was the last thing keeping me at large. And he didn't seem to think it would stay anonymous for long.

'This is why you asked me about her boyfriends?'

'Why? You suddenly got someone in mind?'

'No. I told you. The only men she mentioned were writers, people she worked with. Including some pretty rough types, like Vagg. Other than that, no.'

By now I'd sold Vagg's name as hard as I could without attaching a chunk of myself to it. But Lewin's mismatched eyes just looked at me and wanted more. Always they wanted more. What was his problem? Was he a fan of Vagg's work? It wasn't impossible. Around now I got my head started on the task of remembering Vagg's address. Maybe the time for my harbourside house call had finally come.

'Here's something,' I said. 'Somebody bit her. I saw the marks on her.'

'Where?' I had his interest.

'On the back of her thigh. You must have seen them too.'

'How many did you see?'

'Two. Why? How many were on her when she died? More?' Again this was far more my business than his. And again he wasn't going to tell me. 'Why do I get the feeling the answer's yes?' I said.

'She didn't say who did it?' Lewin said.

'No. Feel free to take a mould of my teeth, by the way.'

'We may do that at some stage.'

'Do it. Call a dentist now. I want you to find this fucker, Ted. Trust me, his story's going to stink even worse than mine. It's going to make mine smell good.'

He gave me a weary sort of smile. I am the man who says too much when he is not saying too little. Lewin liked the other guy more already. He didn't know who he was. He just liked him because he wasn't me. Our relationship is like a love affair in decay. He doesn't care how much I throw him. All he wants is the little corner of me that I refuse to give away. I looked at my dwindling future on his face and thought: Fuck it. I'm going to Vagg's.

4

When your head aches, the city is a shimmering hell of things for light to bounce off – traffic and water, glass and steel. By the time I hit the bridge the sun was sinking already, spraying its low angry fire off anything that shone. Even architecture hated me these days. Even landscape. Vagg's house was a dogleg right up the shore, but I didn't go that way yet. I drove inland first, till I saw a big barn of a hardware store looming off the main road. It took me ten minutes and two wrong turns to get there. Inside I went to the aisle that sold knives. I selected a thin evil blade that curved like a sliver of the moon. I got a scabbard too. I was already handing these things to the checkout girl when it struck me that it was insane to be seen buying them. A knife? I'd forgotten who I was. But I was sinisterly in luck: the girl didn't know me either. Another shunner of newspapers. Another non-restless non-seeker of knowledge. If this was a good omen, who was it good for? Me or Vagg? Maybe it meant I should stop now, while the going was still good. Or maybe it meant this was going to be my night.

Back in the car, jamming the knife into the scabbard and the scabbard into my sock, I wondered what else I was failing to see. Clearly I was not at my best. It was late. I was a long way from home. I was low on supplies, and dangerously adrift from my stockpiles. Was the Vagg visit a bad idea all round? I decided the answer was no. The subtle approach hadn't worked for me, recently or ever. I was living in the wrong world for it. It was time I ditched my commitment to nuance and gave crass literalism a try. Look at how far it had got Vagg.

En route to his mansion I kept trying to think about violence instead of sex. It kept not working. I wanted to picture me and Vagg and the knife. Instead I kept seeing Vagg's DNA – in her, on her, drenching her in foul arcs, his teeth in her flesh, her wanting that. Consensual sex with Vagg. Outside of a prison cell, had that ever really happened – anywhere, with anyone, let alone with her? But I had to hope it had. I had to hope that Vagg had sprayed that other load in her and then killed her. If the answer was not as simple as that, I was out of ideas. I was almost ready to let it be me, if it hadn't been him.

I swung the car towards the water. The streets got cooler and narrower. Big old English trees smothered them in shadow. White men had planted them two hundred years ago so they could pretend they were not a long way from home. And now Vagg wrote shit in their shade while pretending the same thing. The royalties had bought him a lot of nice bobbing boats to look at, but he still had to look at them through philistine eyes. That probably gave him a lot in common with his neighbours, who probably bought all his books, and possibly even read them. I'd rather be me and have nothing to look at but a dirt drive and a couple of fat old gums.

I ditched my car at the mouth of his street and went looking for his place on foot. It wasn't hard to find. It had a wide wooden gate set into a high stone wall. The wall was about two feet taller than I was. A row of wrought-iron spikes was set into its summit. The spikes were a typical Vagg touch. They were sort of impressive, as long as you didn't think about them too hard. If you did, you saw that they made getting over the wall easier, not harder. They gave you something to hang on to on your way up. I hadn't come all this way to turn such an invitation down. Clambering to the top without much incident, I threw myself in over the spikes. They weren't sharp. I'd already hit his lawn before I remembered the pit bull on the jacket of his book. I looked around and didn't see it, and tried to believe that meant it wasn't at home. Was I in the mood to stab a pit bull? Not really, but I didn't feel like climbing back over the wall either.

Vagg's lawn was as wide as a fairway and as tightly clipped. It sloped up for a while before dropping off hard to the water, through a jumble of rocks and wet nodding ferns. On the crest of the slope stood the kind of house that military units stay at during wars. It was a hoodlum's Brideshead, a spiv's Manderley. I wouldn't have wanted to live in it, but looking at it made me think about the many ways in which my life had gone wrong. There I went again: thinking. It was time I rethought that useless habit too. I walked up the slope fast, to get the thinking over with and bring the other part on instead. I went to the only door I could see that wasn't a French window and knocked.

I half-expected a coloured maid to answer it. Instead I got the man himself: Liam Vagg, in a satiny white sweatsuit. He looked me up and down and said, 'Saint, you cunt. I've been wondering when you'd show up.'

He showed me into his study. He had one, naturally. It was on the ground floor. There was a French window in it that gave onto a garden full of pink roses. There was a glass bookcase full of leather-bound books that no person among the living, and certainly not Vagg, had ever opened. There was a polished wooden desk that was big enough to sign a peace treaty on. A vintage typewriter sat on its far side, with a spotless sheet of paper furled around its platen. Behind the typewriter was a brown leather chair with arms as plump as boxing gloves. So this was where the tripe happened. The scene looked clinical and staged, as void of life as Vagg's prose. There was not an open book in the room, not a scrap of torn paper, not one chewed pen.

He poured me a finger of Blue Label without asking. He poured himself one too, then settled into his squeaking brown throne. I sat across from him, on the supplicant's side. I looked at my glass and wanted a refill already. For a dirtbag, he doled out his booze in laughably genteel jolts. But he was still trying hard not to be an animal at this point. We both were.

We looked at each other for a while. He was dressed down, by his latter-day standards, although the space-age sweatsuit didn't look like the sort of sweatsuit you were meant to sweat in. Inside its satiny shell his lean greyhound's body looked menacingly fit. His skin was so sun-damaged it looked cured, like salami. A blurred and ancient tattoo was just visible in the folds of his throat. His irises were disturbingly pale, like a goat's. He used no deodorant: his PR people hadn't tackled that issue yet. His study was a large room, but the rat's-piss reek of his body made it feel like a small one. His hair was thin and silver and long at the back. He wore it in a ponytail – like a roadie, like a sex offender. Tight threads of it ran back across the top of his skull, soused with the sort of oil or pomade that was already going out of style when Dick Hickock used it. He looked as if he'd surfaced from a dirty pond and forgotten to remove the weed from his scalp. His chin had a limp delta of nicotine-stained whiskers stuck to it. I could feel him sizing up my scars, as if he were a connoisseur of broken faces.

'How's the other guy look?' he said at last.

'The other guy was a concrete slab.'

'I heard that. Is that why you're so fucked up?'

'It's part of it.'

He kept flicking his tongue out and in over his lower lip, nastily, as if to stress that the lizard part of his brain was still fully functional. I hardly needed confirmation of that. He swirled his posh grog in its posh tumbler and said, 'I'm sorry you didn't think more of my book, Saint.'

'You read my review, then?'

'I got the gist of it, yeah.'

'Hoped it'd be a bit more positive, did you?'

'I hope that about all reviews.'

'Even the ones you don't pay for?' I said.

'Ah,' Vagg said. 'We're going to be honest with each other.'

He did that loutish thing with his tongue again. His stench needled the air between us. Even my ruined nose recoiled from it. Beyond his shoulder there was a long shelf of books. All of them were by him. Each one was brick-thick with a one-word title. To the right of the shelf a large leather map of the world hung on the wall, fashioned from the hide of some huge-flanked animal, or from the skin of the last critic who told the truth about him.

'How much honesty do you want, Vagg?'

'Let's go full throttle.' *Full frottle.*

'All right,' I said. 'I know you killed her. Let's start with that.'

'You think so?' He appraised me with his billy-goat eyes. That thuggish flick of the tongue again. 'Everyone else seems to think it was you.'

'And I'm ahead of them, because I know it wasn't. I know you paid her fifteen grand to fix my review. I know she was expecting you that night, with the cash. I know the next morning she was dead, and the money wasn't there.'

Vagg was smiling a mirthless smile, for reasons I did not yet understand.

'That honest enough for you?' I said.

'I don't know where to start.'

'Pick a place.'

'I didn't kill her. How's that for a start?'

'Unconvincing.'

'Stabbing women isn't my style.'

'What is? Putting a sawn-off in their mouths and demanding money?'

'If I'd wanted to kill someone about it,' Vagg said, 'I'd have killed you.'

'I wish you'd tried.'

'Believe me,' he said, 'you don't.'

His goat-grey eyes looked at me without expression. His facial skin was mottled, a weird quilt of different pigments. Four deep creases ran square across his forehead, like fence-wires on a horizon. I kept trying not to think about the knife in my sock. I had a weird feeling he would read my mind if I did. Do felons have a sixth sense for the concealed blade?

'And what did the coppers say, when you put this theory of yours to them?' *Feory*.

'I haven't. Yet.'

'I didn't think so,' he said. 'I've been watching your progress, Saint. I've been watching you sink into the shit. And I've been wondering why you haven't pulled me in there too. Not that it'd do you any good, but I've been wondering why you haven't tried. Is it because you'd rather drown in it than tell the world you take backhanders to write good reviews?'

'There *was* no good review,' I reminded him.

'Yeah,' he said. 'What happened there? She told me you were on the hook. And you must've been, mustn't you? At one stage, you must've been. You must've done something you're not proud of, or you'd have shopped me to the coppers on day one. Yeah. She had you on the hook, all right. If you're clean, if you've got nothing to hide, what are you doing here?'

'Do we have to put a label on it? Can't two men of letters just get together and shoot the breeze across a vast desk? Surrounded by an incredible amount of leather? We're a dying breed, Vagg.'

'Man of letters. That's what you call yourself, is it?'

'Somebody has to.'

'Man of letters who takes bribes to write good reviews. And then reneges. Having fucked the girl who tried to bribe him, who then turns up dead. Yeah, I reckon I can see why you want to keep a few things under your hat. That little story gets out, it'd *really* fuck up what's left of your image, wouldn't it?'

'I'd say it'd fuck up both our images.'

'I doubt that, Saint.' He gave me a wider version of his smirk. His teeth were startlingly perfect and cashed up, and grotesquely out of place in a shrunken skull like his. 'That sort of thing *is* my image. Bribing a book reviewer – Christ, I've got away with worse than that. But by all means roll the dice on that, if that's what you want to do. Tell the cops. See how much good it does you. I might have to tell them a few things you don't seem to know.'

'Such as?'

He was in no rush to enlighten me. He pulled a cigarette from a flat silver case. These days he had too much class to keep his smokes in the boxes he bought them in. He was above using matches too. Near his right hand there was a nifty old clock with a lighter built into the top of it. In no more time than it would have taken him to light ten matches he got a spark from it.

'This is going to hurt a bit, Saint.' His grey head issued grey smoke. He sat back. Leather accepted him with a rich creak. 'You seem to think the deal was for fifteen grand. It wasn't. The number we agreed on – the number *I* agreed on, after a fair bit of persuasion from her – was twenty-five.'

I said nothing. I looked back into his billy-goat eyes.

'If she said it was only fifteen,' he said, 'she was telling you a little fib.'

Out in the dying afternoon, somebody was rhythmically raking leaves. A lawnmower was running in someone else's yard, or in a distant part of Vagg's. His eerie mouth was on the edge of smiling again.

'I'm touched you think I'll take your word for that,' I said.

'Take it or leave it, mate. I don't particularly give a fuck.'

'Who,' I said, 'would pay twenty-five grand for a good review?'

'I would,' Vagg said. 'Because I *can*. Look out the window, mate. Look out the window.'

'I know what water looks like, Vagg. I saw some on the way in. Then I saw you, in your natty tracksuit.' The low yellow sun speared in through the glass and impaled my aching eyes. Keith Moon played drum fills in my skull. 'You've come a long way, Vagg, but you're still you.'

Vagg said, 'I'm trying to tell you the truth, you ungracious shit.' His lizard tongue moistened his cracked grey-whiskered lip. 'Mind you,' he said, 'I see now that twenty-five was a long way over the odds, for a pat on the back from a cunt like you. But what can I say, Saint?' He leered, relishing what he was going to say next. 'She had ways of bringing a man around. Am I right?'

He sat back and let me enjoy that one for a while. I managed a smile, but only because I was thinking about the knife. It was a miracle I hadn't whipped it out yet, but the evening was still young. Which one of us would die, if I pulled the shank and lunged at him right now? Vagg was an old man, but he radiated homicidal know-how. Then again, he was a celebrity these days, and celebrities have things to lose. He had riches to protect, and maps made out of hide: he was a brand. Whereas what I had was obscurity, pain, lack of money, lack of readers, lack of her. If the blade wound up in me instead of him, I wouldn't wholly care. That made me dangerous, to at least one of us.

'Did prison do this to your personality,' I asked him, 'or were you like this when you went in?'

He sighed. 'Shall we wrap this up, Saint?'

'No. Let's not do that. I'm just starting to enjoy myself. I'm starting to feel a connection here. Aren't you? I mean, I thought *I* was a charmless fucker . . .'

'Yeah,' Vagg said. 'Let's drag this out a bit. A bit, but not a lot. Let's get all your questions answered, so I never have to see you again.'

He swirled his drink. Was that all he planned to do with it? My own glass was empty, although I had no special memory of making that happen. I got up and helped myself to a refill. I made it a big one so I wouldn't have to get up again soon, or very soon. Vagg watched me do it. He said nothing, and I didn't like the way he said it. Until ten minutes ago, the worst man I'd ever sat down with in the flesh had been Jeremy Skeats. Clearly I'd led a sheltered life. I needed to get out more. Either that or I needed to get out less. But I had come here to find things out, and I was finding things out. I could hardly expect to like them. That had never been on the cards in a place like this.

'Whether it was fifteen or twenty-five,' I said, when I was back in the second-best chair, 'it was gone the next morning. I couldn't help noticing that.'

Vagg smiled his refurbished smile, and shook his head,

and looked at me the way you look at a man who just doesn't get it. 'Gone? Wake up, Saint. It was never *there.* This shit about – what was it? She was expecting me to lob over with the cash *that night*? In what – a leather briefcase? Come on. You can't honestly believe I'd give her money *up front*. She was persuasive, but she wasn't that persuasive. The deal,' he said, 'was I'd pay her if and when you two did your bit.'

'Again, it moves me that you think I'll believe a man like you.'

'But you do. Yeah, I can see that you do. Because you know what she was like, don't you. You know how she operated.'

'And what she was like, Vagg?'

'She was a disgrace,' Vagg said. 'Everything she told you was a lie.'

I'd thought I could get through this without pills. I was wrong. I reached into my pocket now. Vagg had the good sense to watch this move with full vigilance. I brought out a blister pack and cracked capsules from its fat foil welts.

'It pains me to have to say that about a dead girl, Saint.' He watched with vague contempt as I popped my pills. 'It really does. But what choice have I got? Cash up front my arse. She was keeping you on your toes, mate. She must have had a sixth sense that you wouldn't come through.'

'Does it worry you, Vagg, that not even ten grand could induce me to say you were any good? Believe me, I don't draw the line at much. But I drew it at that.' Actually I hadn't, but I wasn't about to tell Vagg that. 'What did you want me to call you again? The people's Plutarch? The convict Carlyle? No. Words have to mean something.'

Vagg clamped a fresh cigarette in his lips and spoke through it. 'You poor bastard,' he said. 'You still don't get it.' He applied himself to the antique lighter again, letting me dangle for a while before he went on. 'You keep talking like this was my idea. This was *all her*, my friend. All I told her was I was sick of getting bad reviews. That was it. That was the sum total of my input. It was her that come up with the notion of buying you off. Me, I wasn't that sold on the idea at first. Let's say I had to be talked around to it.' He smiled in a way that made me never want to see anyone smile again, particularly him. 'Wake up to yourself, champ. This wasn't about me, you, my book, my reputation, yours. This was about her getting her hands on a very fuckin' large sum of money. Larger than either you or me thought, apparently.' Smoke wreathed his silvered skull. His nostrils pushed out tusks of smog. 'My idea? How could it've been? Until she threw your name out, I'd never even *heard* of you, had I? Think about it for a minute. Until a couple of weeks ago, it's not like you were a household name.'

'In a household like this, probably not.'

'Nobody I know had ever heard of you.'

'I don't doubt it.' I had started to feel removed from the action now, a spectator of my own demise. The scene felt muffled and skewed, like a bad dream. The world had got things backwards. I was the artist and Vagg was the savage. So why was I the one over here, and why was he the one over there? Why was he the one with Metternich's desk, and Noël Coward's cigarette lighter, and some flunkey out in his infinite garden raking the leaves? Why was I the one in the week-old clothes, slouching towards arrest, sagging under the weight of the dead girl, while he shook her off like a dog shaking off water?

'So it beats me,' he was saying, 'why you have this high opinion of yourself. Have you asked yourself why she happened to pick on you – you of all people? Maybe you should. Maybe it's because she knew you could be bought. And she guessed right on that, didn't she? Or she almost did, unless you want to claim you were never on the hook at all. But we both know that you were. Yeah. You still look haunted by it. Don't be. There's no shame in it, or not much. She hooked me too. She had her charms. But *Christ*. The way she treated people . . . You know what I thought to myself, when the devious little bitch turned up dead? I thought: no surprises there. Some bloke's got jack of it and he's knocked her off. Don't get me wrong, I hope they catch the cunt that did it. But like I say, it wasn't me.' The grey eyes narrowed in the scaly reptile face. 'Was it you?'

'You've cracked it, Vagg. It was me. I came here strictly for the repartee. I wanted to soak up a bit of culture.'

He contemplated my glass, which was empty again. Standing, he uncorked the Blue Label and tilted it at me in a valedictory sort of way. I put my glass out. Accepting his booze felt like a kind of surrender, as if it meant accepting everything else too – his gibes and his slurs, his desecration of my past. That was a lot to give up for the joke measure of Scotch he poured me. I'd have thrown it back in his face, but it would have evaporated on the way.

'That's your last one,' he said. 'I don't want you getting too blind to leave, and I reckon it's about time you did. I've told you everything I know. Whoever she was waiting for that night, it wasn't me. I didn't go there, and I sure as shit didn't kill her. I had no reason to. Frankly, I've come out of this pretty sweet. She's dead, but I'm pretty sure she'd stopped fucking me anyway. Plus I got to keep all my coin. All I copped was one bad review from a deadbeat critic that nobody reads.'

He resank into the creaking mitt of his chair. He trained his dishwater-grey eyes on me. 'Why *didn't* you come through for her, by the way? As long as we're satisfying each other's curiosity.' From the drawer at his right hand he took a wrapped cigar. He unsheathed it languidly, as if I'd had my fun and now it was his turn. That was ominous, considering how much fun I hadn't had so far. 'You could've had yourself a nice little payday there. Not as much as I was actually paying. We've established that. But big enough, by your standards. So why'd you pull the pin? And don't say you couldn't bring yourself to tell a lie. We're big boys, Saint. We don't believe in fairy tales. What happened? She stop fucking you a day too early?'

And still I wasn't killing him. That said a lot for my character, I thought. If I had it in me to hack someone to death, I'd be doing it right now. Instead I stayed monk-still in my chair, butchering nobody. If only Ted Lewin had been there to see it.

'Somebody was with her the night she died,' I said. Here came my last play. 'You're telling me it wasn't you.'

'That's what I'm telling you.'

'You're out of luck if it was. They've got his DNA.'

A sadistic smile took root on his face. If he was acting, he was a leathery master of technique, a sun-dried Lee Van Cleef. 'Oh dear, Saint. Oh dear. I think I get it now. I think I see why your back's up. Some other big-dicked bastard was with her that night instead of you. Or as *well* as you, is that it? And maybe he killed her, too – assuming you didn't. That *is* nasty, I'll give you that. But I'll tell you one last time. Whoever it was, it wasn't me.'

'Maybe I'll throw them your name anyway.'

'Do that, mate. Do it. They'll swab me, they'll clear me, and you'll be back where you are now, except the truth'll be out about our little deal. And your reputation'll be rooted, and that's about the only thing you've got left, isn't it?'

'The rest is bestial.' I looked around his study. It was bestial, all right. There were bits of cured dead animal everywhere: on the desk, the chairs, the books, on that map on the wall, on him.

Vagg sighed. 'You're a hard guy to like, Saint. You walk into my house, you accuse me of murder. You tell me my work is shit. You talk to me like I'm a fool. But brother, I feel for you. Maybe I'd have gone the way you've gone, if nobody gave a fuck about what I wrote.'

I looked at the shelf that bowed under the weight of his oeuvre, all those books of his with their one-word titles. Somewhere in my dusty throbbing head a quotation stirred. When no other part of me works, the literary part still does. 'I'd rather write for myself and have no public,' I said, 'than write for the public and have no self.' It sounded good, but I didn't believe it. From where I sat, having no self looked a lot better than having one.

'I feel like I've disappointed you, Saint.'

'That's hardly the word.'

'No,' Vagg said, 'let's explore this.' He sent a lungload of weed reek across the desk. 'You're acting like you *wanted* it to be me. I don't get that. If I offed her because of that

109

review, it would have been your fault as well as mine. You'd have been implicated up to your throat. And I'm telling you you're off the hook.' He pointed his cigar at me, trailing foul smoke. 'So why do I feel like you wanted a different answer? Okay, you want the coppers to lay off you and focus on some other cunt. I can see that. I get that. That's only natural. I've been there meself, back in the day. But I'm sensing there's more to it than that. I'm sensing you're *unusually* desperate. And I'm watching you go to town on my Blue Label. And I'm thinking, Jesus Christ, I thought *I* could drink.'

'You can't, but go on.'

'And I'm thinking . . . you want to know what I'm thinking, since we're being frank with each other?'

'Go ahead. Say it out loud. Embarrass yourself.'

'I'm thinking to myself, maybe this isn't about the coppers at all. Maybe you need to prove to *yourself* you didn't do it.'

'Pulp fiction,' I said. 'A hack's fantasy.'

'Is it? The papers say you've got a few problems with your head. Are they right? Think hard, Saint. Think fuckin' hard. *Did* you do it? How can you be sure you didn't? I think you liked her a bit too much, pal. There's your motive, in case you think you didn't have one.'

'In polite society, Vagg, we don't kill women because we like them.'

'*Was* it you, Saint? Only you know that – *if* you know it. But I'll tell you something, mate. A little trick of the trade. If it *wasn't* you – if it *really* wasn't you – you'd better find the cunt who did it yourself. Because the coppers, they won't be looking for him all that hard. Not now. Not any more. They're *way* past looking for other blokes at this point. You're the only guy they want it to be. So you'd better find yourself a few other trees to bark up, and you'd better bark up them fast, before your luck runs out. Maybe it was the guy who fucked her. Or maybe it wasn't: maybe that bloke took off and then some other bloke turned up. With her, nothing would surprise me. I'll tell you what, though. You'd better *hope* it was the guy that fucked her. Yeah, you'd better hope that. Because if it wasn't – if they find him and type him and clear him – then you are *gone*, mate.'

He came with me to the front door. Either he was showing me out or he was making sure I was really going. He didn't have to worry about that. I was more than ready to be elsewhere. The walls of his hall were lined with framed photographs: Vagg posing with various other pillars of the culture. I saw Skeats in one snap – not featured, but doggedly self-inserted in the background, slightly out of focus, out there on the rim of Vagg's aura.

On the doorstep I managed a speech, of a kind. 'You want to know why I didn't come through? Why I didn't throw the review? Because you're no good. Even you must know that. You're not even close. You don't even know what good is. And that has to be said, before everyone else stops knowing it too.'

It was true, except for the parts that weren't. But Vagg didn't have to know how hard I'd tried to call him a master craftsman. I could still cling to that secret. Anyway, that was a mere detail. I was talking about higher truths.

'Fuck off, mate,' Vagg said, 'and never come back here again.'

I'd gone there thinking I had nothing left to lose. I would never make the mistake of thinking that again. You always have things to lose, as long as you're alive. She was still losing things and she was dead. Back on the bridge, in a stagnant river of tail-lights, I tried to think of one thing she'd told me that was unimpeachably a fact. Had *any* of it been real? I had a sick feeling I'd never know. One night was all I had of her, and Vagg had vandalised it beyond repair.

Down on the road they used to call a freeway, until they started making you pay for it, the traffic was even worse. I had a long way to go before I could stop being alone with my thoughts. It need scarcely be said that I wanted a drink. I also wanted to put my fist through something, possibly the side window. Her past was a torture chamber. I had been a fool to open it up. Now that I had, there was nowhere to go but deeper in. I could hardly close the case now, feeling the way I felt. Her past was the only place I would ever find her. It was all she was ever going to be. This is an excellent reason not to die. All those things you thought you were going to put right one day will stay wrong forever. You're not a work in progress any more. Suddenly you're under glass, and that's it: that's all you ever were. The wind changed when she was making a face, and she would never get to make another one. She would never be around again to sweeten the record, to ease my mind with a fresh round of sex and lies. Say what you like about lies. At least they prove a girl's alive, and making an effort.

I was halfway home now, but my mind still hadn't left Vagg's. What had she been thinking, when she put her body under his? I knew about female sexuality, thanks. I knew that girls liked fucking too. And I knew that she liked it more than most girls did, and probably most men. But *Vagg*? Nobody liked sex that much. And nobody could like money that much, either. Fifteen grand was a lot, but surely not enough. Or had she planned to take my ten as well? All these answers she would never give me . . .

I had decided, back at Vagg's, to call it a night before any more harm could come to me. I had resolved to drive home, ingest things, shower the Vagg off me, and recline into oblivion. But the further I got up the road, the more cowardly that plan seemed. It was just a recipe for more hell. Passing out on the couch no longer really cut it, as a response to the gathering storm. Unconsciousness had started to yield diminishing returns. I kept thinking about Vagg's parting shot – his final lowlife pensée. He'd told me I was close to finished. He'd told me I'd better bark up another tree, and bark up it fast. Out on the motorway, as the last sweet wave of his liquor lapped in, I suddenly saw that this was very good advice. Drunkenness has its critics, but I love those moments when it delivers the third eye, to say nothing of the third ball. There in my dark rolling coffin, at the still point of the turning world, I saw things with a wicked new clarity, in ultra-sharp HD. I saw the fly's-eye cells in people's tail-lights. I saw the texture of the road: the black varicose veins in the concrete, the glossy white paint of the lines. And I knew that I was utterly finished, unless I did all the detective work myself.

Suddenly I no longer wanted to call it a night. A night was the last thing I wanted to call it. I wanted to call it half a night: half a night so bad that it had to be redeemed, straight away. It didn't really matter how. Whatever I did, it couldn't make me feel worse than I already felt. Bark up another tree, then. But what tree? I knew the answer before I asked the question. Her empty house, back there in the city, back in the heart of darkness. Her body was lost to me but her house wasn't, even if it turned out to be locked. Some locks can be busted down. The pilgrimage had to be made. And I was awake and at large and already halfway there, even if I was driving in the wrong direction.

That part could soon be seen to. I veered into the fast lane. Behind me an idiot truck blared its horn. That made me speed up, at exactly the moment I should have been slowing down. To my right, beyond the rushing Armco, the median was a deep unlit void. A dark breach in the barrier was coming at me fast, hysterically fast. A sane man would have waited for the next one. No: a sane man wouldn't have been looking for one at all. I, on the other hand, hit the brakes, and slid dementedly into the abyss. The truck bellowed behind me. There was a long blind freefalling moment when I didn't know what, if anything, I was about to hit. I had time to reflect that this would be a pretty stupid way to die. How many people have that as their last thought? And then I was deep in the carwash of the median, scything through native shrubs, juddering on a minefield of fist-sized rocks, hearing things snap off my sled, and generally finding out that I had been wrong to think the evening could get no worse.

5

Her neighbourhood was all ghostly concrete and cheap new brick. The same townhouse, endlessly cloned, ran endlessly up both sides of the street. I'd found my way there with an eerie lack of friction, on autopilot, taking no wrong turns. I knew each piece of landscape before I got to it: the wan lanky streetlights that strode up the slope of the road, the bone-pale kerbing that snaked along in their underglow. If I'd been tempted to doubt the DNA, it was vindicated now. I had come here in the dark before. That first night my dick had done the driving. This time my memory was at the wheel – an even shadier operator. Still, it had got me to the right place, even if it couldn't make me remember things. Maybe there was hope for it yet.

I knew her house from the foul shiver that washed over my body when I drew level with it. Her little car was still sitting there in its port, waiting for her like a faithful dog. I drove past, a long way past, and left my car on the street. I came back on foot, not eagerly. My body was clear on the point: it didn't want to be anywhere near that house. The closer I got, the sicker I felt. Meanwhile the cold air was rendering me sober, which didn't help. I hated what I was about to do. I scanned the sepia street for some solid excuse to bail out and go home. A marked police car would have done nicely. A sedan that looked like an unmarked one would have worked too. But I kept seeing nothing. There was no cop standing guard at the mouth of her driveway, or in her carport, or up at her front door. I was in luck, if you wanted to call it that.

The house was an infiltrator's nightmare. The moonlight bathing it was ominously lucid – good enough to see by, and good enough to get seen by too. Her carport and her front door were outrageously legible from the street. The windows of her neighbours, at the back and on the right-hand side, peered in lewdly over her fence. Lights were on in both places. Along the remaining flank of her house ran a narrow lane for pedestrians. The lane was my best bet, although it was partly lit by a deplorably unvandalised streetlight. I went up the lane and moved beyond the pool of the lamp's glow. There was still nobody around. I gripped the top of her fence, vaulted it, and came down in a fiendishly sonorous gravel garden. The noise I made hitting it got me out of it fast, and sent me deep under the skirt of moon shadow that ran along the house's near side.

I sat there for a while with my back against the bricks, waiting for midnight to get closer. There could be no harm in doing that. I looked at her forsaken yard, full of drooping unmowed grass. In life she'd been so wickedly on top of things: her job, her schemes, me. Since dying she'd really let herself go. Her garden had gone rogue. Why hadn't somebody close to her done something about it? Maybe there *was* nobody close to her. Maybe I was it.

When I could no longer take not moving, I got up and did a furtive lap of the house. The high grass whispered against my shins. I tried all the windows, half-hoping one of them would just slide open when I pushed it. None did. That exhausted my window-cracking expertise. There were two doors, a front one and a back one, both deadlocked, both gift-wrapped in big sagging crosses of police tape.

I sat against the side wall again, trying not to let my momentum flag. I had to ride the logic of the night. I'd ridden it this far, to the outside of her wall. All I needed to do now was get on the other side. It was good to have a problem so base, so material. I was sick of the enigmas of metaphysics. If a woman doesn't want you inside her life, there's nothing you can do about it. The same goes for her body. Her house is a different matter, especially when she's dead. If you want to get in there badly enough, you will. And I wanted to a lot. Only a few bits of wood and glass were keeping me out. At the worst I could just find a rock and put it through a window.

But there was no call to bring on Kristallnacht just yet. I hadn't fully applied myself to the doors. I started with the back one, because the front one was more exposed. The back one felt pretty exposed too, once I was out there standing at it. When I pulled at its truss of police tape, it drifted limply away from the frame. Somebody had slit it neatly down the right-hand side. I would have paused to wonder who, if I wasn't standing *in flagrante* at a moonlit crime scene. Since I was, I dropped the tape, stopped thinking about it, turned the knob, and bumped the door hard with my shoulder. I got a promising result. There was give in the lock. The tongue rode through a useful slice of air before hitting the hasp. The jamb shook against my shoulder in an interesting way. I dug a thumbnail into its timber and pried off a damp clump of splinters. The wood was rotten. I'd never kicked down a door in my life, but this wasn't a bad one to start with.

A car was passing on the road. When the sound of its engine peaked I stepped back and gave the door a wild clout with the sole of my right boot. It hurt me more than it hurt the door. The slap of it echoed in the metallic night. The darkness raised an eyebrow. My knee hummed like a tuning fork. I threw in a second kick fast, before the neighbours could start wondering about the first one. This time I regretted the impact less. I heard wood yield with an inner crunch, like a bad tooth meeting a chop bone.

More cars passed. Each time one did, I put in more leather. I was too deep into the bacchanal to stop now. Fuck the neighbours. These were the same feckless fools who'd stayed inside and heard nothing while somebody stabbed her thirty times. Would the sound of splintering timber rouse them from their couches now? And what if it did? All I was doing was kicking down a door. What was so incriminating about that? Who else but an innocent man would be desperate enough to be out here now, in the middle of the night, doing this?

When the frame was one good shot shy of going down, I stepped back and went at it shoulder-first. Wood blew like the spray of a wave and launched me into the dark interior. Something metallic boomed like a gong. The door, flying in ahead, had spanked a hollow sink or washtub. I silenced the steel with my palm, then pushed the door back against its blasted frame. The house tasted of trapped stale air. I was standing in a small tiled laundry. I vaguely recalled having stood in it before. My memory is good for that much: for confirming, too late, things I've already worked out the hard way. I found a light switch by feel and snapped it. Nothing happened. I went to the threshold of the next room and found another switch and got the same result. Her electricity had been shut off. Maybe this was standard practice in the houses of the dead. Anyway, it settled the question of whether I'd be doing things in the dark.

The next room was the kitchen. It too made my memory twitch a bit. I stood in there and waited for a while, getting used to the dark. It wasn't total. The window was uncurtained, and enough light washed in to give you the essentials: the white of the ceiling, the frames of the doors. One of them opened onto a hallway. I stepped into it. Doors came off it to the left and right. I was already looking, however, at the shut and weakly glowing white door at the hall's far end. That door I knew. It was the door of the room she'd died in. I'd have to go through it eventually. Why put it off? It wasn't as if she was still in there. It just smelled as if she was. The odour came down the hall and sort of wreathed me as I approached. It had a familiarity I didn't want to explore. It was sharp and eggy and had something to do with heat. Before touching the door's handle I paused. I wore no gloves. I had no torch. This was madness. I went in.

The room was weirdly lit up. That streetlight out in the lane stood indecently close to the window, leering straight in. A venetian blind carved its sickly light into fillets and threw them diagonally across the carpet. I had a feeling I'd seen these rungs of light before, back when there was still a bed there for them to fall across. The bed was gone now, along with her fouled mattress. But nobody had scrubbed her blood off the walls. That big frank central smear was still there, with its dry flaky tentacles of run-off. It was the baked-on blood that stank. It beat the smell of a dead body, but not by much. The blood looked monochrome in the muffled light: black on grey. That was graphic enough for me. I had no urge to re-see it in colour. But even in black and white it helped me get a few things clear. Somebody had done this to her, in this room, during a hellish animal fragment of a night like this. Whoever he was, he'd hated her with an energy I just don't have. I'm too old for it, for one thing. And anyway I've never hated anyone that much – not even Skeats, not even Vagg, let alone her. It was good to get some moral clarity on this point. I'd heard enough drivel about the thin or non-existent line between me and the man who did this. I'd heard enough pseudo-philosophy about the blur or overlap between love and hate. No. The man who put these smears on the wall had something wrong with him that went well beyond the things that were wrong with me. The line between us wasn't thin. It wasn't even a line. It was a canyon. It was a phylum. There were species between us. I had many a circle of hell to plunge through if I ever wanted to meet him.

I got to work. I drifted around the room, lusting for data. I wasn't sure what I wanted to find, but I knew I would have to find it now. I was never coming back. That much I knew. If the sodden wick of my memory was ever going to get relumed, this was its final chance. And maybe I got a little spark from it now, as I moved through the wedges of carved-up streetlight. I thought I remembered her naked and alive, stretched out on the bed that was no longer there, with this same ladder of light flung over her like a zebra skin. She was saying something. I closed my eyes and tried to hear it. It's like trying to get an old song back. Soon I was just standing there wasting time.

I went back to whatever I thought I was doing. There was a rib-high dresser against one wall. My hungry silhouette arrived in the big wooden mirror above it: this shadowy fool in the house of a dead girl, tossing the place for fresh sources of pain. I opened her top drawer and sank my palm into a tangle of cold underwear. I pulled out a pair and held them to my face. I wanted a living scent, but all I got was the smell of detergent. I tried another pair, but again the cloth was cold and gave me nothing. I pocketed both pairs anyway. I hated myself for doing it, but I'd hate myself more later if I didn't. I dipped into the drawer again, deeper this time, and my fingers hit something cool and smooth and tapered and plastic on the sea floor. I pulled it out. It had decorum, as dildos went. Its girth was modest, its surface unveined. I liked the fact that she'd needed one. I applauded the implication that she'd spent the odd night alone. In the dark mirror I watched myself sniff the thing and then taste it. These acts did not fill me with pride. Then I watched myself pocket it. There was no way I wasn't doing that. But my sense of moral clarity was slipping, and my pockets were filling up with fool's gold. It was time I quit the muff drawer and found something that might do me some good. I'd come here to reverse my decline, not steepen it. So I took one last under-garment for the road, and I pressed it to my thirsty face.

It turned out to be a good move. My lips felt something trapped or hidden in the weave: something small and square and solid, like a tooth. I pinched the cloth till I had the object cornered. It was lodged in the soft cocoon of the crotch, where the fabric was doubled up. Running a nail around the seam, I found a tiny breach in the stitching. I slipped a pinkie through and touched what was inside. It was a flash drive.

How had Lewin missed it? He must have tossed the drawer too piously, with too much queasy respect for the underwear of the dead. I pictured him gloved and sombre, bent on getting the grim rite behind him. He had lacked the genius to linger over the sifting, to probe each pair with the proper lust, to gorge himself on the evidence.

I slipped the garment into my coat pocket, leaving the drive in the haven of the crotch. It was almost certainly time to split now. I hadn't really known what I was there for, but I had ample reason to think I'd found it. A crotch-stashed flash drive: I could hardly hope for better than that. Considering where she'd hidden it, I expected big things from its contents. Yes, I had pushed my luck far enough for one night. For once I could go home a winner. For once I would have a laurel to rest on. I was still thinking that when I heard a key turn in her front door.

My balls tightened like fists. The door opened and then was quietly closed. Then, on the carpeted floor just inside it, there was a terrible lone creak. Then nothing. Nothing at all. I waited. I'd forgotten how to breathe. My heart kicked at my ribs like a drunk in a paddy wagon. It wanted out. So did I, but I was a long way from both doors, and someone was in the way of at least one of them, and anyway I couldn't move. My soles had sent down roots through the carpet. Whatever happened next, it wasn't going to get done by me. I was out of ideas, and my body was out of juice. All I could do was look down the empty hall and hope nobody appeared at the other end of it.

For a long time nobody did. Then things happened fast. A shape bled darkly into view. It was short and solid and seemed to be wearing a hat. The hat was on a strange tilt. It seemed to be pointing my way. Then the shape raged into life and hurtled up the hall at me. The carpet boomed. The shape hit me low and scooped me off the floor and drove me hard into the back wall, where her blood was. Something behind me split with a rich crunch. It sounded like Gyprock but felt like my spine. I heaved out air with a sound I had never heard myself make. My feet scrabbled but got no floor. The guy's arms were locked hard around my elbows and chest. He was small but viciously strong. His hat had come off. He wasn't Vagg. For one thing he was too short. If Vagg was Dick, this was Perry. I heard gurgling. It was coming from me. Perry went back a few steps then slammed me into the wall again. He was utterly insane. There was an anarchic voltage in his body that made this vividly clear. I felt a kind of fear I had never felt before and do not recommend: the fear or knowledge that I was about to die. This guy wasn't going to stop. There was madness in his limbs. And he had killed her too. There couldn't be two guys around like this. He had smeared the walls with her. And now he was going to smear them with me, and there wasn't much I could do about it. He had way too much violence in him. On top of the fear I felt shame, this strange primal shame, as if I was letting him do it somehow, as if I was failing to try my best. Was this why my ancestors had done all that evolving? Was this why I'd read all those books? So I would die in the dark in this airless room, just because I was the lesser animal? I pumped my feet but only one of them grazed the carpet. I had no leverage. I couldn't breathe. His hair was in my mouth. I couldn't see his face. The room was too dark. He had killed her, and I would die without knowing who he was. To take a piece of him with me I opened my jaw around the bitter peach of his scalp and bit into it as hard as I could. I tasted hair and sweat and a hot backwash of salty blood. He reefed his head away, and a rank wad of flesh and hair tore off in my mouth. I spat the flap out and kept spitting. Perry was reeling backwards, squeezing me hard, bearing me grotesquely up off the floor, making room for one more charge at the wall. But he ran out of carpet and hit the dresser behind him. Something huge and heavy came down on our heads, mainly on his. It felt like the ceiling but it was made of glass. It was her mirror. Chunks of it were in my hair. He threw his head back to shake off shards. That put a foot of clear air between our faces. I cocked my skull and lashed it through the gap. There was a flash of white light and a phenomenal crack of bone on bone. It hurt me unbelievably, but it hurt him more. It must have, because it made him let me go. Through the starburst I saw him sag silently to his knees. On his way down he flung out a sick paw and seemed to rip away a fistful of my coat. I stood over him for a dazed second before my humming skull worked out what he'd done. He'd snagged the hanging panties from my front pocket. The crotch drive, her trove. He had my richest pearl in his fist without knowing it.

I could have gone then. I was closer to the front door than he was, and I was on my feet and he wasn't. But I was damned if I was leaving without that flash drive. Also I had a deep animal need to hurt the cocksucker while he was down. When a man tries to kill you, you acquire a distinct urge to kill him back. He'd flipped a switch in me. He'd attacked the wrong man on the wrong day. Never fuck with a writer. We're dangerous, now that the world has no more use for us. We spend half our lives on our knees, begging for next month's job or last month's pay. The hatred builds. It's not every day you get to kick some kneeling philistine back.

I threw my right boot at him with lust, and it hit what I hoped was his face. I heard him moistly grunt and slump. Maybe I *was* as crazy as him. I danced back and threw the boot in again, aiming for his ribs. This time it got jammed in him like a chisel in wood. He'd caught it in his hands. And then somehow, with stunning abruptness, I was off my feet and thumping down hard on the glass-strewn carpet beside him, and he was coming at me sideways through the shards. I clawed back at him. He still had hold of the panties but he didn't know they mattered. I seized and yanked them. His grip tightened reflexively but a beat too late. The cloth stretched, went taut, then twanged free in my grasp. I rolled away from him and balled the prize up tight and crammed it deep into my hip pocket. That gave him time to stand and blast my ribs with a ruinous boot or knee. The pain was pure and astounding. It saturated the nerves like bliss. I rolled away from him and gagged for air. He kicked me again. That one caught me on the hip. I breathed in blood. I'd had enough now. I was ready for a truce. I was ready to go home. I rolled away again, or tried to, but the floor turned into a wall. I looked up at it. It was the wall with her all over it, all those Rorschach blots of her flung blood. Looking at them made me remember what was stashed in my sock.

When he stepped back to aim his next shot I rolled side-ways and pulled the knife and when his boot came surging back at me I drove the blade tip-first into the flying arc of his flying shin. I felt the steel skid off bone and lodge in meat. He made a bovine noise and staggered backwards. I lurched after him on my knees to keep hold of the handle, glass crunching under me, blood lubing my knuckles like crude oil, the sodden fabric around his shin wrenching the knife sideways. Then he kicked berserkly forward, like a spooked stallion, right into the angle of the blade, and I felt the steel slice clean through a steak's worth of calf-meat before the force of his swing torqued the knife out of his flesh and out of my slippery fist and sent it flipping away with a clatter against some distant part of the wall.

I scrambled after it on my hands and knees, frisking the floor in a wide blind arc, blundering into the thick of the broken glass. The carpet was alive with savage teeth. Chunks got stuck in my hands and bit me to the bone when I put weight on them. My skull smacked into her dresser. For some reason Perry wasn't raining leather on me from behind. I looked around. He wasn't there. Then I heard him in the kitchen. I heard a drawer open. I heard bits of metal slide and clatter. Stabbing him had been a bad idea all round. It hadn't worked, and now he wanted some cutlery of his own, and somehow he'd known where to find it. And he was being pretty choosy in there, from the sound of it. He was taking his time. He seemed to have some particular blade in mind.

I decided not to hang around and find out what. I could live with the ambiguity. I went to the window and plunged my bleeding hands through the venetian. I held the latch and yanked at the glass. It didn't move. It was locked. I felt around for the bolt. The blind swished and clattered like a wind-lashed palm tree. Maybe he was still in the kitchen or maybe he was on his way back with the silverware. I was too busy fist-fucking the jangling blind to hear. I found the bolt. She'd left the key in its lock and I loved her for it. My spine felt exposed and tender, like a snail stripped of its shell. I didn't look around. If he was behind me now, it wouldn't do me much good to know it. I flipped the key and yanked the bolt and wrenched the window all the way open. Cold air washed over me but the big steel cobweb of the venetian still hung between me and the night. There wasn't time to roll it up or rip it down. I just hurled myself over the thigh-high sill and tore out into the sky through a mangled blend of bent slats and busted flyscreen. I hit her sorry lawn and rolled and staggered and ran.

I didn't look back till I was over the side fence. When I did, he was back there in the frame of the open window, just standing, just watching, not coming, a dark still shape against the darker room, a nightmare out of Thomas Hobbes: solitary, nasty, brutish and short.

For about two seconds I looked back at him and thought I'd scored some kind of victory. Then I looked at myself and got the point. The pale wash of the streetlight was all over me. I was lit up like a man on a stage. If he hadn't guessed who I was already, he knew now. This was why he had stayed back there in the dark. Unlike me, he could afford to wait. He knows where I live. Everybody does. He can come for me whenever he likes.

All that got clearer to me in the car, as I put miles of churning blacktop between me and him, as my flopping heart slid back down my throat like a clubbed seal. He didn't let me go. I let him go. I had one shot at him and I blew it. This is getting to be my life: perceiving things clearly but too late, never seeing my shot until the shot is gone. By a freak of chance I had found the man I was looking for. And what good did it do me? All I can say is he's on the short side. He wears a hat at night. He knows his way around her place in the dark. He knows where she keeps her knives. For the next few weeks he will walk with a limp. And he has a key to her front door. I have decided not to believe that she knew him, and liked him, and gave him the key because she wanted a guy like that in her life. If she did, it's more than she ever gave me.

Back at home I assembled the ingredients for the next bit: laptop, memory stick, bottle. The adrenaline had ebbed out of me in the car. The agony in my ribs had hardened like concrete. Something was seriously wrong inside me. Raising the bottle to my lips hurt. So did swallowing. When I coughed, a mist of blood appeared on the laptop's glowing screen. I didn't wipe it off. Its presence seemed fitting. Moving like an even older man than I was, I uncapped the memory stick's metal tongue. It would be a small miracle if the contents were not nasty. Just touching the thing made my heart panic and kick in its stall, like a bullock getting its first glimpse of the slaughterer's blade. I slid the tongue into the laptop's jack. An icon appeared on the screen. When I clicked it, a dialogue box opened. It asked me to enter a password.

Why hadn't I seen that coming? Of course she had sequestered the truth behind one last veil. The cursor blinked, counting off time I didn't have. I breathed out and drank in. I tried passwords. I tried her name. Full name, first name only, last name only. I tried Vagg's name. I tried the name of his book. I tried her employer's name. I tried the name of her street. I tried the make and model of her car. I was running out of stuff I knew about her. I was running out of words. Soon the world would have no words left in it that I hadn't tried. Bottoming out, riding despair to its absurd terminus, I tried my own name – as if I'd been more than a stranger to her, as if I'd made a password-sized dent in her world.

It didn't work.

I took the bottle to bed then, and waited for its nectar to slosh in and drown the fires that burned all over my body. One or two of my ribs were broken. They had to be. I was no authority on broken ribs, but I knew what unbroken ribs felt like and they didn't feel like this. Biting the guy's skull had loosened some of my upper teeth. There was a vicious lump on my forehead. Not all of it was made of swollen flesh. Part of it turned out to be a plectrum-sized chunk of glass, buried in there like a tuber. When I pulled it out, I felt hot fresh blood wash down over my face. I lay there and let it flow.

Well, I had made it back alive. You could say that much for my big night out. Apart from that I didn't have much to show. A dildo and three pairs of panties weren't going to stop my slide into hell. And without a password the thumb drive was as useful to me as the dildo was to her. And that was my whole score. I hadn't even looked for money in there, which I certainly should have. I was going broke fast now. If Lewin didn't lock me up soon, I would finally get to find out what it was like to have no money at all. And if anyone owed me a contribution, it was surely her. I was getting poor much slower, before she came along.

A dildo, some panties, and one more locked chamber of her past that I wished I'd never found. These fragments were all the reward I'd scored for kicking down her door.

No, there was one more thing. I'd met the enemy, and he wasn't me.

6

Something is in the middle of happening. Maybe it's my largest mistake yet. There is a TV crew in the house. I don't really remember how they got here. There is a ludicrously attractive blonde girl on my couch, asking me things. I am saying things back. There is a pool of white light around us. Either I'm triumphantly remaking my public image in its glow or I'm drowning in it. When the show goes to air we'll know which. There are black cables taped to my floorboards. There's a big guy on the girl's far side, hunkered behind a camera, training the dark funnel of its lens on me. The girl is blonde but tanned: her skin is darker than her hair, as in a negative. Her skirt is so short that looking at it is the same thing as looking up it. I know her name, in theory. Everybody does. It's on the tip of my tongue. I'm nodding at something she has just said, trying to look like a man who remembers roughly how he came to be in his chair.

Things are coming back to me. I'm piecing them together. I'm getting a lot of money for this thing. Why else would I be doing it? They threw me a bonus to do it in my house. Not taking drugs before they came was not an option. Getting kicked half to death in Jade's house has left me ancient, hunched, semi-mobile. But I seem to have taken way too many. I appear to be dangerously high. I must have mistimed the dose somehow. The TV people must have turned up late. Yes, they made me wait. I remember hating them for it. Conceivably, more than conceivably, I killed the time by drinking too. I should be more worried about all this than I am. I'm worried that I'm not, but I'm not worried much. This must be what dying finally feels like – just gently letting go of past and future, just casting yourself on the soft tide . . .

The girl's name is Missy Wilde. That's coming back to me too. She's said to be sharp, but the people who say it are people like Skeats. She is a feminist of the new school. That means she shows you a lot of flesh but you're not allowed to look at it. I'm looking at it anyway, since I'm the nation's biggest scumbag whether I do or not. Why be the nation's biggest fool too? I wish I had the integrity to look away. In principle she is not my type. In principle I abhor everything she says and writes and does. She doesn't just do TV. She is a queen of new media. She blogs. She tweets. She goes on panels and talks about the politics of body image – while looking like that. She writes columns about how bad her boyfriends are at making her come.

And now she's on my couch, asking me how this giant contusion got on my forehead. She's saying the viewers will want to know. Her lipstick is sort of mauve. I tell her a pissed-off member of the public jumped me a few nights back. This strikes me as inspired, and has the further merit of being half-true. She's wearing stockings with black suspenders. No doubt there is irony involved. And now she's asking if Jade Howe ever came to my house, back when Jade Howe was still alive. The suspenders yank up the rims of her stockings in tight arcs, like the cables of a bridge. Have I used that metaphor already, somewhere? My imagination has stalled. I'm pausing, trying hard to remember what lies, if any, I have told Lewin about Jade coming to the house – and whether I've told different or bigger lies to the people at my gate. My mind feels like a wiped windscreen, when you wait for the crescent of wet grime to vanish so you can see. There is a small currant of a mole in the fluting of Missy's tanned throat. The gears inside my skull are turning but not catching. The cogs have gone all smooth. My memory isn't working well enough for lies. All I'm fit for is the bald truth. So I tell her yes, Jade came to the house. Apparently I'll be going down in a fireball of candour.

I'm wondering how it came to this. I don't have to wonder very hard. It came to this because of Skeats. When he fired me, I had to start thinking about money. And I hate thinking about money, which must be why I don't have any. Hemingway said you go broke in two ways: gradually, then suddenly. For a long time Skeats made me go broke the first way. That was okay, because I could get away with pretending it wasn't happening. And then he sacked me, and the thought of money slipped off its leash and got right up in my face.

And here is the upshot: me neck-deep in this pool of fake white light, with Missy Wilde asking me straight up, in my own home, if I killed Jade Howe. This is what the world wants. It won't pay me to write. But to hear me utter the word 'no' for the eightieth time, it will pay me more than I ever got for a year of reviews. To look at it another way, the payoff that Vagg never delivered has finally come my way, from an even more contemptible source. For an hour of this tripe I'll get more than Vagg would have paid me for my soul. Plus an extra five thou for letting them in the house. What did they expect to see in here? The gore-caked murder weapon in the washing up? A signed confession on the coffee table?

There's a floating scar on my vision shaped like the light rig. I have this odd feeling I'm in a bubble, looking out. My drunkenness has depth. It has *body*. I can hear Missy out there at its rim, but there's a distance between us, like a satellite lag. Now she's asking if I'm an alcoholic. She asks the tough questions, all right. She declines to be thought of as lightweight. She wants to know if I have blackouts. I take a furtive glance at my right hand, just to make sure there's no drink in it. There isn't. In a way this strikes me as a shame, but on the plus side it lets me deny her charge with a bit of heat, a bit of eloquence. And why shouldn't I? I'm an innocent man, after all. We know this now. What have I got to fear? There is something about Missy that makes me want to trust my tongue.

She's done her homework, give her credit for that. No clipboard, no notes. She's doing rigour, as if I don't get enough of that from Ted Lewin. Now she wants to know if my relations with Jade were carnal. I confirm that they were. She asks if I was in love with her. I reply with my standard lie, although by now I almost forget what the lie is for. Still that feeling of floating in a bubble. In a sense we both are. We're adrift in the twilight zone between taping and airing, so what we say is not really going beyond this room, not yet, and won't for a while, and might get cut out anyway, and therefore hardly feels like it's being said at all. Maybe that feeling is dangerous. Or maybe it's useful, since caution has done me fuck-all good in the past. One of us seems to have raised the topic of DNA – my DNA. I can't rule out the possibility that I raised it myself. Either way, I now hear myself making free reference to the other sample – the mystery load, the blast of the second shooter. This is bold. I allege that the guy who left that load was the guy who killed her. This is even bolder. Lewin will hate me for it, when the show goes to air. But I've never got much mileage out of him not hating me. From Missy, on the other hand, I get a welcome recalibration of vibe. Suddenly she's looking at me as if I might not, after all, be a murderer. This is progress.

I'm feeling rumours of agony, now, from the big red beetroot that's planted under my ribs. There is a distant glow in my backbone, like a cane fire on a horizon. The chemicals are retreating from me like a tide. I want these people to pack up and leave so I can top myself up. But we're still rolling. Missy has ditched the homicide theme and is working the human interest angle. She wants to talk, in a friendly sort of way, about my well-documented failure to be a normal respectable non-suspect nine-to-five guy. Is it true that I have no job now? Also, what made me think that being a book critic was a job to start with? Why do I live alone? Why do I have no wife, no children, no real estate? Do I get lonely? Why have I opted out of the mainstream dream? What, in general, is wrong with me?

Some things only women ask, because men know they might get hit in the face if they try. Not that these aren't damn good questions. I think about them myself at night, when I can't sleep. Thinking about them is *why* I can't sleep. But the answers are a bit knotty for prime time. I draw breath to tell her that. And then I think what the hell, and I give her a blast of what she's asking for. It isn't just because she's paying, although there is that. It isn't just because I'm intoxicated, although there is that too. It's more this: I'm in the dock, and somebody is inviting me to say my piece. So why not say it, since every other fool and knave has said his? Clearly, the world will never want my autobiography. I will never get my shot at a *De Profundis*, unless this sleazy televised transaction is it. Yes: I have the floor, and for once people will be listening. This is my shot at the big speech.

So I give it, or a version of it. I tell her I gambled all I had on the life of the mind. If the accountants and middle managers and investment brokers of the world want to call that a wasted life, I am not obliged to agree with them. I tell her I have set my life upon a cast, and I will stand the hazard of the die. I tell her I wanted to purify the dialect of the tribe, but the tribe didn't turn out to be interested. I tell her I live alone because I like everyone else even less than I like myself. Let people who can stand other people live with them. By now I am on a roll that impresses even me. I sound like Richard Burton as Hamlet. O vengeance! I am spraying revelation like an unmanned hose. I tell her about my rejected novel, my filthiest secret. I tell her how long it took me to write it. I tell her that literature double-crossed me, by promising me a future and then ceasing to exist. Now I sound like Othello. My occupation is gone. I am a hunger artist, a rag-and-bone man. I don't ask for pity, but I'll be damned if I'll be an object of contempt.

Lewin won't be the only one in for a shock, when this thing goes to air. I'll be in for one too. I'm forgetting what I say even as I say it. The tide of painkillers has gone out and the tide of agony is coming in. And pain cripples the mind worse than drugs do. I seem to have finished my speech, because Missy is giving a counter-speech of her own, about the power of new media. She is roused. I seem to have pissed her off. She's defending the internet as if she invented it. It strikes me that we may no longer even be rolling. She seems to be sitting on the couch side-saddle, with her feet tucked up under her skirt, and her shoes kicked off on the floor. Are the lights still on us? Am I even still in my chair? Maybe I knew then, but I don't know now. My tenses are starting to blur. At a certain point I found or find myself standing at the sink. I seem to have decided fuck it, I have to get out of that chair. This must mean we're done, or having a break. At the sink, I find myself in a quandary. If I pour myself a drink I'll have to pour one for everyone else, and that will make them stay longer than I want them to. Then again, if I don't pour myself one I won't get to drink it. It's a tricky call. To help myself make it I have a drink. When I turn around, there is nobody in the room except Missy. Everyone else is gone. Their stuff is gone too, the cameras, the lights, the cables. The room is back to normal, except Missy is still in it, curled on the couch with her shoes off, smoking a cigarette, hunched over her phone, thumbing in text. I step or wade over to the front window. The small things seem to be happening in slow motion, the big things in weird leaps. I pull back the curtain and look out at the drive. What I want to see out there is the camera guys, loading gear into the big white van they came in. What I see instead is an empty drive. The camera guys are gone. So is the van.

'I'm telling my followers,' Missy said from the couch, 'that you knocked it out of the park.' She blew out smoke, chuckling at something she saw on the phone. I dropped the curtain. The scene had thumped down to earth now: it had shaken off the creamy haze of the present tense. My buzz was definitively gone. I had lost the last shimmers of it at the window, looking out at that patch of vanless dirt.

'The DNA thing,' Missy went on, her face slack and inane over the phone's glow, 'is going to be a game changer.' How long had we been alone, just the two of us? She was acting as if we knew each other pretty well. Was it possible I'd asked her to stay? That didn't sound like me. I turned my back on her and filled a coffee mug with bourbon. I didn't mind her knowing what was in there, but I minded her knowing how much. Not that she seemed to be in any danger, just yet, of looking up from her phone. T. S. Eliot knew her type: distracted from distraction by distraction. I took the mug back over to the armchair and sat, still waking up in the afternoon's dregs.

'That stuff you said about your novel?' She let her big green eyes drift up at me for just a second. I felt their cursory transit graze me like a breeze. 'People are going to lap that up.' But already her head had dipped back to the phone. 'You can be quite charming when you want to be.'

Her tone said I could expect to have her full attention soon, but not all that soon. This wasn't bad manners. It was the new manners. Everyone did it, so there was no one left to care. I sat there and drank and watched her be bad news. Whatever was happening here, my body wasn't up

138

for it. It was hardly even up for existing. When I breathed, which I had to once in a while, my ragged right lung got dragged over a field of oyster shells. Like a sick old dog I had an instinct to go somewhere private and die. But first I had one more bad scene that had to be lived through, one more pit stop on my road to damnation. Probably, while she frowned and chuckled at her phone, I was meant to be taking a long unmonitored look at her body. I had no great urge to. It had its merits, but it wasn't Jade's. That meant it was wasted on me: the lean glossy torso, the superb teeth, the heaped hair, the fist-sized breasts half-bared by the tight starched top. She was the wrong kind of vamp, and I wanted her out, I wanted her gone, and this was not the urge she was used to arousing. I felt we were both in for a rough half-hour.

For some reason she was smiling now: at the phone, not at me. 'Some woman's asking if you look as good in the flesh as you do on TV.'

'Let me know,' I said, 'when you're talking to me.' Something was coming back to me. I had slagged Missy off in print once, with extreme prejudice. And plainly she didn't remember, if she'd ever known in the first place. Even my victims didn't remember me. Maybe I *had* wasted my life.

Missy smiled again but still didn't look up. 'Don't knock it till you've tried it,' she said. Meaning tweeting, networking, the whole glorious war on nuance. 'Seriously,' she went on, 'you're mad not to be part of this. Get a profile. Leverage your situation while you can.'

'Leverage it for what?' Those teeth of mine were still loose where I'd bitten the killer's skull. Speaking still didn't feel right.

'For connections. For followers.' She shifted around on her tucked-up stockinged feet to get more comfortable. She'd squirmed halfway out of her skirt now, and it had only been halfway on to start with. At its rim, her toes wiggled in a way that would have struck a healthy man as very good news. But I was not a healthy man. The evidence for that was mounting. The extent to which she wasn't Jade was starting to make me feel ill. I do not speak existentially. Looking at her was starting to turn my stomach.

'I don't want followers,' I told her. 'I want readers. Or I did.'

'Well, start a blog then.' Still looking at the phone. 'Why do you take the march of progress so personally?'

'Because it's happening on my throat.'

And all over my ribcage, from the feel of it. The pain was ludicrous. It made me want to cry or bark with laughter, but I was capable of neither. I was getting flashbacks to the primal scene: Jade on the same couch, at exactly this time of day. Unfortunately they kept ending. I kept coming back to the present: Missy's body there instead, all sharp angles and painted nails, my disease hanging between us like a miasma. Was I ever going to get better? I could think about that when she was gone. But a lot still had to happen between now and then.

'*There*,' she said, putting the phone aside with a joke flourish. '*Now* you can be charming.'

'You know something?' I said. 'Until I was a murder suspect, people who found me charming and good-looking and interesting were pretty thin on the fucking ground.'

'But fame's a turn-on,' Missy said. 'Surely you know that?'

She aimed her big green eyes at me and waited. You could see she wasn't used to waiting long. By now the average heterosexual would have been over there on his knees, drooling on the floorboards, reciting a sonnet while removing her garters with his teeth. But I was still in my armchair, riding out another one of those flashbacks. I was starting to regret all those candid looks I'd taken up her skirt. I'd meant nothing by them. But I had sent her the wrong message. Things were expected of me. I half-pitied her for expecting them, but maybe it was time I pitied myself instead. Girls like Missy Wilde don't flop themselves down on your couch all that often. When one does and you want her gone so you can think about a dead girl instead, you have a problem.

'Anyway,' she said, 'Jade Howe did.'

'She what?'

'Found you charming, apparently.' She tilted her head a bit. With a restless finger she caught a loose hanging cork-screw of her hair and started twisting it, as if to remind me she wasn't bald.

'Let's talk about something else.'

'I see. That topic's closed, is it?'

'Yes it is. Well spotted.'

She waited. I saw the assurance in her wide eyes falter for a moment, like a candle flame bent by a breeze. For the dura-tion of that moment she looked lost. Maybe it was dawning on her that she'd picked the wrong dissolute semi-celebrity to slum with. She'd never had to work this hard. Again I almost felt sorry for her. But she was a big girl. She could look after herself, probably better than I could. She flexed her stockinged feet again, tucked up under her like the paws of a black cat. I watched them wiggle. Through several layers and types of ruination I felt the rumour but not the reality of a hard-on, like a shadow in Plato's cave, or the glow of a crushed ember in a burnt-down house.

'I must say it's brave of you to stick around,' I told her, 'considering what I'm meant to have done.'

'People know where I am.' She flashed me a scurrilous smile. 'Anyway, you won me over with that speech. Like I said, you can be quite charming when you want to be.' She waited a bit. 'Why don't you want to be more often?'

An astute question. I thought she almost sounded like Jade then, but maybe the booze was kicking back in.

'Why don't you come and sit here?' she said.

Another valid question. There was no good answer to it. Bad answers were all I had. I said, 'Let me drink this first.'

The flame in her eyes flickered and bent again while she took that in. But the rest of her didn't flag. Her bawdy toes kept wiggling. Her straightened index finger kept playing with her hair. 'I'd love to read this novel of yours,' she said.

'No,' I said. 'Let's not do that.'

She tensed. This time her playful toes froze. 'Why not?'

'I'm doing you a favour. You wouldn't like it.'

'You think I'm not up to it?'

'Christ. It's not that. *Nobody* likes it. Not everything has to do with you.'

We sat there for a while.

Finally she said, 'What's happening here exactly? Do you want me to leave?'

'Why? So you can go home and blog about how hopeless I am at foreplay?'

She smiled. 'So you've read my stuff?'

'Enough to get the gist of it, yeah.'

She liked that more than she was meant to. 'It's okay, Ray. You're not exactly my target reader. And I'm not exactly yours, let's face it.' She picked up a parched black hardback from the stack of classics beside her: Catullus, Caesar, the guys I was still getting around to. Her milky painted nails were nebulae against the cover's night sky. 'Are *any* of these fuckers still alive?'

'Not by a long shot.'

'This is the dead white male section?' Her toes had thawed, and gone back to wiggling.

'Why not? I'm two-and-a-half out of three myself.'

'Half a male?'

'Half-dead.'

'You sure about the other part? I'm starting to wonder.'

'Oh, I get it. Most days you don't have to ask twice.'

'Most days I don't have to ask once.'

'Does anyone in your generation know how to sit still for five minutes?'

'It depends what's going to happen next.'

'I haven't killed you yet. Give me that much credit.'

'If you want me to stay, you'd better say something nice, fast.'

'Who said I want you to stay?'

'Do you? Most men do.'

'Calm down. Can't we just sit here for a while?'

'What's your problem? Are you scared?'

'Of what?'

'Of women. Of me.'

'No, but I can take people or leave people. That includes even you. Also you've caught me at a bad time. In general, and not just in general. Look.' I lifted my shirt. I let her see

143

the damage – the glorious sunset over my sternum. I let the shirt drop. '*That's* my problem, or one of them. Somebody beat me half to death the other day. And I felt bad *before* that happened.'

'So do you want me to go home,' she said, 'so you can get on with dying?' Mischief had come back into the big green eyes. Something about the novelty of my pitch had appealed to her.

'No. I'm just saying there will be no hard feelings if you do. I'd walk out on me too, if I could. Admit it. I'm a disappointment. I'm a disgrace to fame. You've changed your mind. You want to leave. So leave. I honestly won't mind.'

'Oh but you would. You should. You'd be mad not to. May I make an observation?'

'Please.'

'You seem to be a bit obsessed with death. With being half-dead. Maybe you should think of it as being half-alive. Or actually: just *alive*. Still here. Not dead at all. Capable of doing things that dead people can't do.'

'That's not bad. Maybe I *should* read your stuff.'

'Is that what your novel's about? Being half-dead?'

'Let's not talk about that. If we're choosing life here, let's not talk about that.'

'So . . . Can I read it?'

'Jesus. You don't give up.'

'Well, if we're just going to be sitting here . . .'

'You want to read it *now*?'

'Why not? Where is it?'

It was in the bedroom, but she'd guessed that. Where else could it be? In the fridge? Under the sink? She was smiling again. A woman like her does not stay thwarted for

144

long. I picked up my drink and went for the bedroom door. When I was halfway there I heard her get up and come after me. I was surprised she left it that long. These days my life obeys the rules of pulp fiction. When I walk into bedrooms, women wearing suspenders follow me. But my body remains stuck in a bleaker genre. It is a slave to the laws of realism. It's jammed in them neck-deep. It's so real it doesn't work any more. All it can do is feel pain. It can do dialogue, but she wasn't after much more of that. I drifted into the room ahead of her, already wishing I had a fuller mug.

My novel was deep-sixed under the bed somewhere, like a corpse thrown face-down into a river. I checked under my side first. You still have a side, even when you sleep alone. I put my drink on the bedside chest and knelt down into a thunderbolt of agony. I felt around in the dust and found the stiff. When I resurfaced Missy was standing over at my big bookcase with her back turned, scanning its contents or pretending to. Again I got a potent flashback of Jade, standing in exactly that spot, shorter, naked, her dark head tilted in contemplation, those grape-hued marks on her thigh. That was all I needed: her plump little naked ghost in here with us. The scene did not require further fucking up.

I picked up my drink again and dumped the fat type-script on the bed. Missy flopped down beside it and got cosy. She propped her back against a heap of pillows. Hair of that quality did not belong on my weathered bedding. She put the typescript on her thighs. She brought her knees up. Gravity sucked her skirt towards her waist. It didn't have far to go. The manuscript pinned it in place, sort of. Missy didn't seem fussed either way. I got a flash of her satin panties. They were white and plump. They had sheen.

145

She rearranged herself. I saw a black scorpion tattooed high on her left thigh, pointing its pincers the rest of the way up. She made a big show of keeping her eyes on the typescript so I could gorge myself on the view. I tried, but my appetite was stuck in reverse. The better her body looked, the less it belonged on my bed. I had those genre issues still. One of us was in the wrong book. She came from a world where women had thighs that the light bounced off and black suspenders running up them and mother-of-pearl panties and a scorpion up there to wave you the rest of the way in, on the off chance that you were still weighing your options. And I was Jake Barnes home from the war, and my dick was the dick of a dead man.

She riffled my typescript for long enough to confirm it had words in it. Her interest in it petered out at that point. That still put her ahead of the rest of the world. 'You should try shopping this around again,' she said, tapping a luminous nail on the work's top page. 'The night this interview goes to air, you're going to be the most famous writer in the country.'

'For one night.'

'Exactly. It won't last forever. You'll want to milk it while you can. Why don't I hook you up with Jill Tweedy at Bennett and Bennett? Jill does my stuff. You know,' she provocatively said. 'The stuff about how useless men are at foreplay.'

'Bennett. That's where Jade worked.'

'I thought you didn't want to talk about her.'

She put the typescript aside. That made her skirt drop and pool around her waist. She let it stay there. Idly she let her legs fall open, then pushed them shut again, then let them fall back open. I watched them sway. I looked at the place where the brown flesh went chubby and pale before hitting the bunched-up rim of her panties. There was the faintest sprinkling of glossy hairs there, pale in the late light, like fur on a fruit. She kept the rhythm going. The satin of her panties went taut and then slack, taut and then slack. When it was taut, the cleft behind it looked like two segments of a peeled mandarin, or a mouth suppressed by a white gag. It gapped and closed, gapped and closed, pinching silk. I approved of this as a spectacle and wanted her to keep doing it but I had no ideas beyond that. I had always known the pills were a problem and I had always thought I would deal with the problem when it arrived. Well, it seemed to have arrived. A spot of moisture had appeared on the satin between her legs, like the first drop of rain on a swollen white sail. She watched me watching it. Her face was flushed. The heat in her eyes looked a bit like anger. Soon it looked exactly like anger.

'Well?' she said. 'You plan on standing there forever?'

Without looking at her face I said, 'I'm waiting for you to send me some sort of sign.'

She clapped her legs shut. This was her version of playing hard to get. 'Seriously,' she said. 'Are you a faggot, or what?'

I stepped over the event horizon and joined her in the scene. I had to now. The moment could be deferred no longer. And maybe I would turn into someone else when I touched her. It was worth a try. I sat on the mattress, dumping the mug on the bedside chest as a show of good faith. I put a hand on each of her knees. Her skin felt hotter than it looked. I pushed the knees apart again. She let me do it, but she hadn't stopped looking ornery. Maybe I shouldn't have drained the mug before dumping it. Maybe that had been a mistake. Or maybe she was so generally pissed off that she was going to say the next thing anyway, no matter how fast I came to heel. Anyway, she said it.

'I take it you know about Jade and Jeremy Skeats?'

My hands froze on her hot skin. The world narrowed to one humming moment, and I knew I would remember that phrase, and the sound of her saying it, for as long as I lived.

'What about them?' I said.

'You didn't know?' She was enjoying this. 'They had a thing.'

'What kind of thing?' The room wasn't a room any more. I was out on some wind-whipped heath, naked to the howling sky.

'What kind of thing do you think? The kind of thing where they were fucking each other.' She lay there smiling beyond her open legs, watching me die. 'And here I was thinking you knew everything.'

'How do you know?'

'Everyone does. It's common knowledge.'

'So it's a rumour? You don't know for sure?'

'Jesus, you *were* in love with her. You still are.'

'Make up your mind. Am I a fag, or am I in love with a dead girl?' Why do people keep saying it? Do I carry the evidence on my sleeve, on my face?

'You tell me,' she said, and went back to working her thighs, wafting them like the arms of a bellows, as if the Skeats theme had run its course. She seemed to think we could simply move on now, get back on with things, as if no fissure had just opened in the earth. I did my best to behave as if she was right. I slid my hand past the rim of her stocking and over her tattoo and felt the radiant heat of her core well before I reached it. I peeled the satin there to one side. She slammed her legs shut again, but this time she did it to keep me in, not shut me out. She thrashed back against me so hard that I almost took it as a sign of resistance, until I remembered who she was. Her eyes were closed. It wasn't me she was interested in. It was the concept of me: the man on the edge. But I wasn't on the edge any more. I was off it, and plunging. Rancid images were in my head. I shoved back at her hard, matching her violence stroke for stroke. I thought if I got savage enough I could blast Jade right out of my system. It wasn't working. The movies in my head weren't stopping.

I retracted my hand and said, 'Stay there,' and left the room before she could argue the toss. It was a shitty move. Even I could see it. But the inferno in my skull had to be dealt with. I went to the sink and aimed liquor at an empty glass. Some of it landed in there and some didn't, so now my hand burned with that too. As a rule I don't shake. I was shaking now. Jade and Skeats. It was so rank it had to be true. I pictured his terrible golden head doing terrible things. I drank. I sucked in air, like some thrashed boxer between rounds. I remembered something Jade had told me about Skeats. She'd told me she'd never met him. Somebody was telling me a lot of lies. Unless it was everybody else, it was Jade.

When I returned to the bedroom Missy was still there. She didn't look happy, but she was still on her back. It takes a lot to change a woman's mind, once it's made up. This time I went round to her side of the bed. I moved with purpose. My mind was made up too. I wanted to do anything with it except think. I'd finally been put in an animal mood. Her skirt was still pooled around her waist but her legs had gone back to being closed. I prised them back open and unclipped her right stocking and rolled it down her leg and off her foot. When I went to unclip the left one she lifted herself slightly off the mattress, and I saw something high on the rear curve of her thigh. I spent a moment hoping it was another tattoo, but I didn't hope it with much energy. I knew what I was looking at, because I had seen it before. It was a pair of raging grape-coloured bruises. Each one had a pulsing maroon nucleus, then a dirty yellow fringe, then a ragged black circumference made by a set of teeth, and a gnarled and nasty set of teeth at that.

'Who did that?' I asked her.

'Who did what?'

'Who bit you?'

'Are you serious?' She dropped herself back on the mattress, obscuring the view.

'I'm dead serious. Who did it? What's his name?'

'None of your fucking business.'

'Actually it is. Whoever he was, he put the same marks on Jade.'

'They're lovebites, you idiot. They all look the same.' Her legs were still open, but I sensed we were riding an ebb tide.

'Lovebites don't make you bleed.'

'Depends how much he loves you,' she said viciously. 'You're showing your age, Ray. You sound like a prude.'

'I'd rather be a live prude than a dead whore.' I wanted to slap some sense into her. If I didn't do it with words I'd have to do it with my hands. And I wasn't that kind of guy, not quite yet.

'So what are you saying, Ray? You saying this guy's going to kill me?' Where Jade had irony, Missy just had sarcasm. The difference depressed me, deeply.

'Actually I am, if that bothers you.'

'And you reckon he killed her too?'

'That's what I said.'

'You playing detective, Ray?'

'Someone's got to.'

'Well,' she said. 'The guy who did it to *me* wouldn't hurt a fly.'

She thought that ended the discussion. I let her think it. I put my hand on her stockinged shin. She didn't look wholly appeased. I slid my fingers past her knee. She shut her eyes. I kept sliding. She gave a bit of a shudder. When I got to the first bite I put a finger on its crimson bullseye and pressed down hard. She flinched and yelped. And then she shut her legs again, with what finally looked like conviction.

'Fuck you,' she said.

'No, fuck *you*. Who did it? Was it Skeats?'

'For God's sake.'

'Was it Vagg?'

'*Please*. You think I'm fucking my way through the scrawniest old hacks in the book biz?'

'Tell me his name and we'll move on.'

'Move on? I don't fucking think so.'

'Fine. Just tell me his name.'

'I could say it,' she said, 'and it would mean nothing to you at all.'

'Try me.'

'I'll tell you one thing about him. He's a lot less fucked up than you are.'

'Don't bet on it. Next to this guy I'm pretty normal. Say his name.'

'If he killed her, why didn't he kill me?'

'He didn't kill her either. Not the first time.'

'Ever occur to you she might have slept with a few guys who *didn't* kill her? Maybe even a lot?' She was smiling. She was having fun. This would not do.

'You want me to tell you what he did to her?' I said. 'I saw her dead, remember. You want to know what she looked like?'

Out in the main room my phone started ringing. For once in my life I wanted to answer it.

'If you get that,' she warned me, 'I'm out of here.'

We had reached a new low. Missy was giving me tips on phone etiquette. 'I thought you were out of here anyway,' I said, and walked out and got the phone.

A muffled male voice on the other end said, 'How's your face?'

'Who's asking?'

'You know who's asking,' he said.

A cap of ice closed over my scalp.

'How's your face?' he said again. The line sounded tinny, the way phones used to sound, as if the wire was up in a high wind somewhere, swaying.

'How's yours?' I said.

'Last time I saw yours it didn't look so good.'

My ribs pulsed where he'd kicked them. I wanted to be alone with him. I walked the phone outside, to the deck.

'What were you looking for in that house, Saint?' he rasped. 'What did you think you'd find?'

'You worried I found it?'

'You're the one that should be worried.'

'Why's that?'

'They're going to arrest you. You're going down.'

'Christ, I know *that*.' That ice on my skull was melting. It was occurring to me that my nemesis might be a fucking fool. 'Tell me something I don't know, pal. Say something insane. Prove who you are.'

He said nothing for a while, and I got more of that airy sound. I started thinking he'd gone for good. Then he said, 'Raiding a dead girl's bedroom, Saint. That's sad stuff. Sounds to me like you've got problems. Maybe what the papers say about you is true.'

'It is, except the man they're talking about isn't me. It's you.'

'No, Saint. It's you. Most of it's you.'

I waited.

He said, 'Looked to me like all you found was a pair of panties.'

'You think so? You sound nervous. You should be. I found something else.'

'Maybe I'll come round one night and look for it.'

'Please do. I'll be waiting. I had fun the other night.'

'Really? You didn't seem to.'

'No, I genuinely enjoyed the violence. Didn't you? Or did it boil your vibe a bit, taking on an armed man instead of a naked woman? Bit of a change of pace for you there. Not your usual scene at all.' For the first time all day I felt glad to be alive. I wanted this freak with way more lust than I'd been able to muster for Missy. I had problems all right, thanks to this shithead.

'Who do you think I am?' he said.

'I'll know soon enough.'

'No you won't.'

'Yes I will. They've got your DNA.'

'Maybe they do. So what? I'm not on file, Saint. I'm nobody to them. I don't exist.'

'You will,' I said. 'Soon.'

'She wasn't what you thought she was, Saint.'

'And what did I think she was?'

'She manipulated people.'

'Christ, pal. I've worked that part out. You're not much of an adversary, whoever you are.' He kept leaving silences. I kept filling them so he'd stay on the line. 'Is this really all you've got? You talk in clichés. You're meant to be the man who destroyed my life. Live up to it.' Still that airy sound, that high arid whistle from the line or from him.

'She used people, Saint.'

'Is that why you killed her? Did she use you?'

'How did things go with Missy?' he said.

That cap of ice returned to my skull.

'Why do you ask? She a friend of yours? She is, isn't she?'

'Did the camera guys leave without her? Did she stick around for a drink?'

'You bit her, didn't you?' I asked him.

But the line was dead. I walked inside and put the phone back on its cradle. I went into the bedroom. Missy was gone.

I showered and wrapped my wounded body in a towel. I stood in the glow of the laptop and uncapped the thumb drive and slid it haggardly into the machine. That fool on the phone had fed me a major tip. There was something in her house that scared him. That was why he'd gone back there, with his key. Maybe it was why he'd killed her in the first place. Maybe he didn't even know what he was afraid of. Maybe he thought he'd know it when he saw it.

Well, I knew what it was. It was the drive. It had to be. It was the drive, or whatever she'd put on it. I'd heard the fear in the freak's voice. He was even more scared of her secrets than I was.

When the password field appeared I stabbed in some new ideas. *Skeats. Jeremy. Golden Boy. Show pony. Fraud.* None of them worked. I can't say I minded that. It would have been foul to learn that he'd penetrated her life at password level. It was foul to think he'd penetrated her at all, but I'd gone past hoping it wasn't true.

The wide white field of the encryption box stared back at me. For one more night I was out of ideas. The locked drive was getting to be an emblem of my hijacked life. I wished I'd never found it. Since I had, I couldn't give up on it. I had to hack away until it yielded up its bitter dram of revelation. Each time I didn't crack its code I felt guilty relief. Did I really want to know one more of her secrets, even if knowing it would save my skin?

I shut the laptop's lid and took my drink out to the deck. I leant on the rail and communed with alcohol and the night. I thought about Jade and Skeats. Did it mean anything? It meant an atrocious amount to me, but did it mean anything wider? Might Skeats have killed her? I had borne witness, often enough, to the butchery he could inflict on a piece of prose. I had grieved mutely at a career's worth of his literary crime scenes: all those bloody stumps of newsprint where living language used to be. But did he have murder in him?

I had to doubt it. He was a philistine and liar and clown, but he wasn't a killer. He lacked imagination, for one thing. He lacked the verve for the solo project. Anyway, it wasn't Skeats I'd met in her house, or talked to on the phone. The man in the house was a criminal of a different kind: nuggety, effectual, crackling with vicious energy. His head had tasted of sweat, not mousse. He got things done.

I went inside and got my phone. I came back to the deck with it, dialling Skeats. He didn't answer, which didn't shock me. I put the phone down on the rail and wondered if he'd call back. He had no reason to, beyond the dictates of basic civility. I therefore didn't like my chances. I listened to the night. Its silence was so pure it felt ominous, fragile. Some huge and drastic noise seemed bound to shatter it at any second. Perhaps it would be me, howling uselessly at the trees. When Missy had asked me about loneliness I had dodged the question. TV cannot bear too much reality, and neither can I. But the truth was this. Until Jade walked up my front steps I didn't know what loneliness was. Until then I was alone but I liked it. Now I was alone and hated it, but no woman in the world could fix it, because no woman in the world was her. Until she came I was all scar tissue. I was cauterised, insulated. I was numb. Now that I wasn't, I saw that numbness had a lot to be said for it. The best thing that ever happens to you will also turn out to be the worst. Just give it time. I stood there against the rail and wished I'd never met her. I'd never wished that before, and I didn't wish it lightly. But the news about Skeats had broken me inside. Until tonight, I had thought that I'd had her and lost her, and that had felt bad enough. Now I knew worse. I'd lost her all right, but I'd never really had her. Whoever I'd had, it hadn't been her. The girl I knew wouldn't have touched Skeats with a barge pole.

I looked at the sky. It was starless and cloud-smudged. The air on my skin was freezing but I let it bite. I was closing in, I felt, on a moment of clarity. Of course she wouldn't have gone near a man like Skeats – not unless she'd had some wicked reason to, the way she'd had with Vagg. I seized this thought and tried to tame it. It made my skin tingle. Yes, there was a stench here that reminded me of the Vagg angle. With that old villain her motive had been clear enough. He had cash. But Skeats – what on earth could she have wanted from the stubbled Osric, from the sun-kissed musketeer? I sniffed the question hungrily, like a dog circling a henhouse. I was zeroing in on epiphany. Why Skeats? The man had so little to offer that the question answered itself. She'd wanted his influence. It was all he had, so it was all she could have seen in him. Skeats wasn't a man. He was a position. He was a job title in cutting-edge threads. She hadn't wanted *him*. She'd wanted his column inches, his industrial juice. It was the same thing she'd wanted from me, on my humbler scale. With Skeats the scope for literary graft must have been nearly limitless.

I was thinking usefully now. If she'd fucked him without desire I could take it, just about. And she had. I was sure of it now. I knew it with mathematical certainty. The angle was clear: she'd done it so Skeats would give her books an easy ride. I tried to remember the last time he'd let me loose on anything published by Bennett and Bennett. I couldn't, except for the Vagg book. But that one could be left aside. There had always been something odd about it. Vagg apart, it had been a long, long time since a piece of Bennett product had come my way.

By now I was back inside, refiring the laptop. I logged into the paper's archives. I pulled up all the reviews run by Skeats in the last six months. I filtered the list for books published by Bennett. I combed the filtered list for hostile or even mildly negative reviews. It was a lonely search. Apart from me on Vagg, I was looking at wall-to-wall blow jobs. Skeats had channelled her books to his most abject soft-soap artists, with Barrett Lodge kneeling at the vanguard. Why the trend had ceased with the Vagg book I didn't know, for the moment. It was the one review that didn't fit. Otherwise the pattern was flagrant, once you went looking for it. But who was going to look for it? Who was going to blow the whistle? Jade? Skeats? Bennett and Bennett? What was being harmed apart from literature? What was being destroyed, apart from the sacred covenant between writer and reader?

I rang Skeats again. Again he didn't ring back. To kick things along I sent him a text that said: *I know about you and Jade.* It didn't take long to work. The fuse burnt for about thirty seconds, then the phone exploded into life. I picked it up.

'Raymond.' He was feigning joviality, badly. 'I think you just texted me something by mistake.'

'Nice try, but I've just worked out what the two of you did.'

'The two of who?' A dumb man playing dumb is a sad thing to listen to. But the chronic liar doesn't go down without a fight. 'Ray, I'm genuinely not with you.'

'You and the late Jade Howe. The fixed reviews and the fucking.'

There was a very long silence. I knew what it meant. It meant I could scrap my last lingering hope that it wasn't true.

'Have you told the police?' he said.

'Not yet.'

'Good,' he said. 'Don't. Please.'

'I think we should meet.'

'I agree.'

'Tomorrow,' I said. 'And this time we're sitting inside.'

7

He got there before I did. He was sitting inside, all right. He was as hidden from the street as you could get without sitting in the kitchen. For once he had no craving to be seen. There was a black leather satchel down near his feet. He put it up on the table as I sat. The move looked rehearsed. He wanted me to ask him what was in the bag. When I didn't, he started telling me anyway.

'A peace offering,' he said through a queasy smile, reaching for one of the buckles.

'No,' I told him. 'I'm running this.'

'Sure.' He raised a conciliatory palm. 'Sure.' Returning the bag to the floor. 'Later, maybe. Whatever you say.'

He was afraid of me. Good. He waited for me to speak. For a while I left him in suspense. His eyes drifted to my forehead, to that red third eye of mine that won't stop weeping. A waiter turned up with some water and a big plastic smile. He was primed for banter. When he got close enough to see that we weren't, the fake smile turned into a real wince.

He left the water and beat a wordless retreat. Skeats hunched towards me. His breath was rancid with fear.

'My marriage means a lot to me, Ray,' he couldn't help muttering. 'My kids. My wife.'

The golden curls looked less lofty than usual. Whatever he normally did to them, he had lacked the heart to do it today. They looked defeated: out of luck, out of vim. Also his stubble had stopped looking like stubble. It looked unmeant, as if he'd just been too haunted to shave. The cocky smirk, the vain convex chest: the whole Skeats steez was dead. I'd come here wanting to hit him, but there was nothing left to hit. His perfunctory lower face was one big dent already. He had no chin. The thin bloodless lips curled back in on themselves, as if he had a mouthful of something he'd been waiting a lifetime to spit out – something bitter, like the taste of his own pointlessness. Until today, our whole relationship had consisted of scenes I would never forgive him for. For once things would be the other way round.

'What do you want?' he asked me. 'Just tell me what you want.' His phone bleated wretchedly in his coat pocket. He made no move to answer it. It rang until it stopped, like the phone of a dead man. That clinched it. We were in radically new terrain.

'I want you to tell me everything,' I said.

'Okay,' he said. 'But there's not much to tell.' His fingers tortured a sugar sachet, spraying the table with fine white grains.

'Did you fuck her the night she died?' I asked him.

'Ray. Be serious. You can't think I had anything to do with *that*?'

'Somebody was with her that night. Was it you?'

162

'No. I swear. We were through by then.' He said it with unusual force. When a liar gets a chance to tell the truth, he hammers it hard.

'How long did it go on?' I framed each question carefully, as if dismantling a bomb. I wanted information, but not enough to blast any fresh holes through me.

'About a year, on and off.'

A year? He said it casually. The words had no weight for him. I envied his airiness, but my contempt for him as a man acquired a new sub-basement floor. If he'd had her for a year and could say it like that, he wasn't really alive.

'When did it start?' I asked him. 'When did it stop? Who ended it, and why? Who started it?' I was ready to up the tempo now. I wanted to yank out the rotten tooth and get home fast.

'Who started it? At the time, I thought it was me. Looking back, I think it was her.'

'Let me guess how it went. You met her at some literary event. A party. A festival.'

'A book launch.'

'And she made the running, right? She came to you. Probably you couldn't believe your luck. And you were right not to, because it wasn't luck. She wanted your clout, not you. She had it all mapped out. She wanted you to keep her books away from the hard cases – from the guys like me. And you did. You slipped them to the pushovers like Lodge, so he could dance the old soft-shoe on them.'

'More often than not, yeah.'

'Jeremy. No. Come on. You were doing so well. Focus. Reread the situation. There's no wriggle room here. I looked at the archives last night.'

'Sorry, Ray. Yeah, that was it. That was the arrangement.'

His shoulders drooped like a wrung-out sponge. The trouble with watching him squirm was it made me want to squirm too. Defeated, he was a disgusting spectacle. The man you have on the ropes is never quite the same man who pissed on you when you were down. You have to remind yourself, firmly, of what he'll do to you if you're ever enough of a fool to let him back up.

'Can you blame me?' he abjectly said. He leaned in even closer. His breath was like an exhalation from a crypt. 'You knew her, mate. She was a little bit hard to turn down, am I right? Plus,' he said, 'I'll be honest with you. I'm not all that fuckin' sure I did anything wrong. All I really did was, I funnelled the bulk of her books to Barrett. What's so outrageous about that? The guy *is* our chief reviewer. Most probably I'd have thrown him most of those books anyway. It's not like I told him what to write.'

This was more like it. He felt some slack in the straitjacket. The Houdini of untruth was giving it one last shake, one last reptilian writhe.

'Lodge wasn't in on it?'

'Not formally. He didn't need to be.'

'She was spared the horror of fucking *him*.'

'That would have been superfluous, mate. Accentuating the positive is Barry's natural style. The old soft-shoe, like you said.'

'The critic as cheerleader.'

'I know. I know. He's predictable as buggery. Can I tell you something about Barrett?' He glanced cautiously at his leather bag. 'Between you and me, he's not going to be around for much longer. That's one of the things I want to talk to you about.'

'Let's stick,' I said, 'with what you *don't* want to talk about. Let's keep talking about that. Go back a month. Suddenly things change. She's flogging the Vagg book. It's got Lodge written all over it, but for some reason you send it to me. A radical shift of policy, that. I'm guessing it was her idea.'

'It was.'

'She explain her thinking?'

'No, but I could have a guess at it.'

'Go on.'

He exhaled. That pack of sugar in his hand was springing leaks all over the place. 'Lodge's praise was getting a bit shopworn, obviously. From her point of view, his use-by date was looming. So was mine, if I'm going to be honest about it. The phone calls, the *tête-à-têtes* . . . she was starting to phase them out. I think she was moving on to new challenges. Like you. If she could get a good review out of *you* . . .' Repulsively he raised his eyebrows. 'Doesn't take a genius to work out what she did next, Ray.'

'Clearly not.'

'Well. Whatever she did, it seemed to work.'

'Not for her.' I gave him time to think that one over. I wanted to see if it would kick his conscience out of its coma. But it would take more than a subtle phrase to do that. It would take more time and patience than I would ever have on my hands again.

'You double-crossed her,' I clarified. 'You sent me the book early, before she could get to me. Probably you lied to her about the dates. That's why you sent it in proof, and by express. I'm starting to remember these details now. I should have seen that something was up. All that strange *efficiency*, the weird haste to get me into print. By the time she turned up on my doorstep it was too late. I'd sent you the hatchet job already. And for once in your life, a hatchet job was what you wanted to run. Not for the good of literature, but to stick it to her. When I asked you to hold it back, you still could have. You just didn't want to.'

'Yeah. Sorry about that, Ray.'

'You wanted to rub her face in it. You wanted to show her you were still boss.'

'You could say that.'

'What else could you say?'

'Nothing. You've said it already. I could feel her forcing me out of the loop.'

'And you couldn't have that.'

'Not if I could still help it, no.'

'You couldn't have her going over your head and fucking your reviewers instead of you.'

'That was part of it. And I don't know, maybe I thought there was still hope for us. For her and me. Which was a delusion – I can see that now. Getting Vagg's book to you, I reckon that was the last job she needed me for. Maybe I could see it even then. Maybe I thought: okay, you little bitch. You're finished with me? Well, here's something to remember me by.'

'She didn't get to remember it for long.'

Behind his face there was a flicker of something that came close, but not all that close, to introspection. I'd got him thinking, at long last. After years of yanking at the slot machine, I'd finally scored this dribble of a payoff. 'You don't think . . .' His sunken chin sagged. 'Surely you don't think the *review* had something to do with . . . with what happened?'

'It must have occurred to you. Jesus Christ. The review came out at midnight. A few hours later someone took a hatchet to *her*. The timing's never struck you as strange?'

'What are you saying? You think it was Vagg?'

'I did once. I don't any more. That doesn't mean there's no connection.' Was that true, or did I just want it to have been Skeats's fault?

Skeats said, 'I've been assuming it was the other bloke.'

I looked at the ravaged sachet in his fingers. A song played on a radio somewhere: a girl singer, singing things I couldn't hear. More things that were just beyond me, more things I didn't quite get.

'What other bloke?' I said.

'She had somebody else. Some young prick.'

'What makes you think that?'

'She told me.'

'That's all? Maybe she was lying.'

'Why would she?'

'Because she lied about everything.'

'Only when she had a reason to. She had no reason to lie about that.'

'Maybe she wanted to keep you on your toes.'

'Christ, Ray. I was on my toes already. I was on my toes the whole time.'

'So who was he?'

'I don't know. She wouldn't tell me his name.'

'Could she have been talking about Vagg?'

'*Vagg*? No. I'm talking about somebody young. More like her own age, maybe younger. He was long-term. In the picture well before me. I got the impression he was a bit of a moron. I think I saw him once, one night at her place.'

'Keep going.' I was already thinking about the voice on the phone. Young, possibly. Moronic, certainly.

'Or maybe it wasn't him,' Skeats said. 'I don't know. I saw somebody.'

'Describe him.'

'I can't. It was dark. It was the middle of the night. I was walking up her driveway, this other cunt was walking down it. All I saw was a shape.'

'Shortish? Solid?'

'Maybe. Yeah, if I had to say. Why? You think you know him?'

'Possibly. Keep going.'

'That's all I can tell you. He wasn't Vagg, I can tell you that much. And he wasn't you. Beyond that, I'd be scratching. I didn't see his face.'

'You think he saw yours?'

'I know what you're saying. I've given that some thought, believe me, considering what happened to her. But I don't think he could have. It was black as – it was as black as night. But I'll tell you this much. When I got up there, up to the house, you could smell what they'd been up to. This is the guy, Ray. Trust me.'

'You think she was serious about him?'

'How do you mean?'

'In love with him?'

'Love?' Skeats scoffed. 'Turn it up, Ray. That was hardly her style. Nah, I got the feeling he was like us.'

'Us?' Was this how far I'd plunged? Was I the equal of Skeats now?

'Another one of her useful idiots,' he said. He must have caught the look of revulsion on my face, because he quickly added: 'Don't blame yourself, Ray.'

'I don't.'

'Good. You shouldn't. Blame her. I do. The media goes on like she's some kind of dead saint, but you and I know better.' He said it in a spirit of solidarity, as if we were brothers in harmless graft and mild sexual humiliation. 'Whatever game she was playing with this other guy, I reckon it backfired on her. He got sick of it and he did something about it. And it won't take the cops long to work that out, Ray. This kid, I got the impression there was something wrong with him. He was some kind of fuckup. She told me that much. He won't stay off their radar for long. All you've got to do is be patient, mate. Sit tight. Don't say anything you don't have to. You won't, will you? About me and her? Frankly, there's nothing to be said. I've told you all there is to know. It was a dalliance, that's all it was. A dalliance, plus the scam with the good reviews. Apart from that there's nothing to tell. I didn't kill her. I don't know who did. I couldn't tell the cops anything I haven't just told you. So let's not go fucking up my whole life for no gain. It'd achieve nothing, except my marriage would be over, and you and me would be out of a job.'

'I thought I was out of a job already.'

'Ah. Let's talk about that. Can we talk about that, Ray?' His hand oozed down towards that black bag of his. 'I want to talk about that, if you do. As long as we're . . . long as we're cool on that other subject? Are we, Ray? Are we cool on that?'

'I'll think about it.'

'Maybe this'll help you.'

'What's in the bag, Jeremy? Cash?'

'Cash? Ray. Come on. We're civilised men. We're *literary* men.' He put the satchel on the table. 'But yeah, in a way. You could think of it as cash, if you wanted to.' He hadn't opened the bag yet. He had a preamble to lay out while he had my attention. His breath was starting to stink less, as if he thought he'd weathered the worst. 'First,' he said, 'let's be honest about something. You and me, we've never been that close. Have we? Let's not bullshit about that. I mean – we're beyond bullshit now, am I right? What I'm saying is, you don't let people get close. And who knows – maybe I don't either. But Ray – it doesn't have to be like that. Not any more. Not after today. Let's use this thing, is what I'm saying. Regrettable as it is, let's build on it. Let's view it as a chance to do some business.'

This was grotesque, and I wanted it to end. I said, 'Enough foreplay. What's in the bag?'

He reached inside. He brought out the galleys of a book, bound by a black plastic comb. I had never seen a fatter set of proofs. It must have run to 1200 pages. He dumped it between us. The cover said: *The Tainted Land, by Dallas Fingle.* Below that was a slab of fine print about permissions and embargoes. The book was under wraps for six more weeks.

'You know about this?' Skeats said.

'Should I?'

'It's going to be huge,' he said. 'And I want you to review it.'

'You want to un-fire me?' The transaction had the familiar stench of a Skeats lie.

'You never were fired, and here's your proof. In six weeks

this book is going to explode. It's going to be massive. I need somebody good on it. I want it to be you.'

'*The Tainted Land*? It sounds like it's about two hundred years of white oppression.'

'It is. They reckon it'll be a shoo-in for the Miles.'

'Sounds like the sort of thing you'd normally give to Lodge.'

'Exactly. And now I'm giving it to you.'

'So it's my lucky day?'

'This isn't just about the girl, Ray. It's *partly* about her. Why pretend otherwise? But there's a bigger picture here too. Frankly, Lodge is starting to give me the shits. I'm getting jack of the prick. It isn't just that his stuff's getting worse, although it is. He's starting to blow his deadlines too. He's a drinker, but unlike yourself he can't drink and still do the business. Between you and me – *strictly* between you and me – I've decided to put the bloated old deadshit out to pasture, effective pretty bloody soon. Which means there's a vacancy coming up in the top chair.'

He seemed to think this was pretty big news. He sat there for a while so I could soak it up. Then he said, 'Now, I'm not going to sit here and tell you the job's yours.'

'Why not?'

'Ray. Come on. Like I've said, we're beyond bullshit here. You as chief reviewer? That'd be a hard one for the industry to swallow cold. I get enough pissed-off phone calls about you as it is. If I suddenly gave you the top job, they'd be burning my effigy in the streets. No, we'd need a bit of time for this. We'd need to lube them up for it first. Plus we have to wait till the cops are off your back. Who knows how long that'll take?'

'I can think of one way to move it along.' I wanted to needle him while I still could. Maybe it did me damage, but it did him damage too.

'Touché,' he said through a lipless grimace. 'But you can still move it along without mentioning me. Tell them about the short-arse boyfriend, by all means. I'm not averse to that. Tell them what I saw on the driveway. Just tell them you saw it yourself.'

'I thought you didn't see anything.'

'He was short. He was solid. He was *there*, for Christ's sake.'

'And what about the rest? You want me to morph into Barrett Lodge?'

'Not fully. But again, let's not bullshit each other. The chief reviewer's got to be able to speak for the paper. Not for himself, or not *just* for himself.'

'Or not even.'

'I'm trying to help you out here, Ray, believe it or not. I'm trying to tell you how to get ahead in the real world – *if that interests you*. I'm making you an offer that most blokes in your position would consider a pretty generous one. I'm inviting you into the tent, mate. I'm inviting you in from the cold. Consider this book a trial run. Let's see what you can do with a bit of water-cooler literature.'

'If it's a piece of shit, I'll say it's a piece of shit.'

'I wouldn't expect anything less, Ray. But Jesus. Why do you immediately assume it's a piece of shit?'

'It *looks* like a piece of shit,' I said. 'It's got the title of a piece of shit.'

'Well, I don't get the sense that many people will be saying that in six weeks.'

I laid a wary digit on the typescript and rotated its bulk towards me. 'What kind of name is Dallas Fingle?'

'They reckon he's some kind of boy genius.'

'Who are "they"? I thought *we* were they, and we haven't read it yet.'

'Ray, give me a bit of credit. Remember, I'm plugged into the industry in a way that you're not. I've heard what people are saying about this book. They're saying it's extraordinary. They don't say things like that all the time.'

'Yes they do.'

'Okay, they do. But this time they really mean it. Trust me on that. I'm giving you a bit of context here. I'm not telling you what to write. Obviously I'd never do that. I'm just giving you the background. I'm saying, in six weeks' time, this is the book that everyone's going to be talking about. And I'm saying: What do I look for in a chief reviewer? I look for someone I can rely on to be at the centre of that conversation. Think about this, Ray. You're a smart guy. Think about the game you're in, and play it.'

I eyed the proofs. He eyed me eyeing them. We both knew he wasn't going to give me Lodge's chair. He didn't want someone who would speak for the paper. He wanted someone who'd speak for *him*. He wanted me to stand on the throat of my song. I'd done that once before, for Jade, and it hadn't worked out that well. It had stopped being rewarding pretty fast. If I did it for Skeats, it would be unrewarding all the way.

But when I stood up, Fingle's breeze-block galley was tucked under my arm. A job was still a job. Ten minutes of fun and the old order had reasserted itself. We were back in the real world, in which I needed Skeats more than he needed me. I hated myself for that. I hated the world for it. But when I am not getting paid to write, I am nothing. I'm just a man who spends half the day drinking and the rest of it sleeping. I knew what unemployment tasted like now. It tasted like death.

'That other thing,' said Skeats. 'We've buried the hatchet on that? You won't say anything to the cops?'

'Not unless I have to.'

'And you don't,' he said. 'This other bloke, he's a clown. They'll find him soon enough. Until they do, you stay smart. You've got a future after this thing's over, Ray. Part of that future's with me – if that's what you want. I do, if you do.'

I didn't like his tone, but then again I never do.

8

Be careful what you wish for. I was getting paid to write again, but before I could write I had to read: 1259 pages of this Fingle character. I never piss on a book without reading the whole thing first. I do have a few principles, and that's one of them. At home I hit the couch and assembled a lie-down workstation: notebook, pen, the fullest bottle I could quickly find. I propped the proofs on my one good lung and got instant emphysema. I flipped to the first page of text. It was an Author's Note. The note was ominously long. In it, Fingle explained that his novel, although set in the past, was a work of fiction and not of history. This meant that only a fool would read it in quest of historical 'truth'. The quote marks around the word *truth* were Fingle's. Having cleared that one up, he laid out his general vision of what novels were meant to do. They were meant to meditate on something he called symbolic truth. Suddenly the quote marks were gone. After that he went on, for a bit, about the power of mythology. I got his drift. It wasn't complicated.

Saying false things about the past was how you exposed its real nature. As long as your heart's in the right place, you can be as free with the facts as you like. Fingle was a trail-blazer, all right. Never before had I hated a writer so much so early. His book hadn't technically even started, and I was sick of it already. At this rate my career as the new Lodge was going to last about two minutes.

I turned the page. I saw half-a-dozen hefty swinging epigraphs: from Dostoyevsky, Céline, Genet, Camus. No doubt about it: Fingle knew how to read a dictionary of Euro-quotes. I turned to the next page. Chapter One. A few more epigraphs. And then, under a sky leaden with the zingers of better writers, the action started. In an unnamed harbour, a creaking wooden ship was dropping its anchor. We seemed to be somewhere in the eighteenth century. A longboat full of white marines in red coats peeled off from the ship and rowed for shore. They were drunk. This, you were apparently meant to think, was a pretty unforgivable thing for them to be. But wait: now one of them was standing up in the boat, in order to urinate into the bay. Again Fingle seemed to think this a self-evident outrage, as if the guy should have held out for the nearest mulch toilet. While that baddie defiled the ecosystem, the redcoat beside him was ominously shouldering a rifle. He pointed it towards the beach, cocked it, and shot a strolling Aborigine.

End of page one. 1258 pages to go.

I got the remote and switched on the TV. I was going to be on it in half an hour: me and Missy Wilde, back when we still had chemistry, back before our relationship went to hell. Watching it wouldn't be much fun, but it would beat reading more of Fingle's prose. Waiting for showtime, I skimmed the rest of his polystyrene opus with as much energy as I could muster. It had sweep – I was ready to give him that. The action stretched, like a flimsy old pair of pantyhose, over the fat white expanse of the last two hundred-odd years. The central characters were all descended from the genocidal honky on the longboat, or maybe from the guy who pissed in the water. To work out which, I'd have to read the whole horrible book. Apparently the bad guy's son grew up to be a grazier who made his fortune by raping the virgin land. The son of *that* guy, or maybe his grandson, was a top-hatted goldminer who got his kicks from being racist to immigrant labourers. Later on you had a corrupt media mogul, a warmongering politician, a timber tsar with a thing for the unsustainable razing of old-growth forests. Fingle's prose was as perfunctory as his ideas. He wasn't just bad, or even unbelievably bad. He was *suspiciously* bad. I felt like the victim of some weird post-modern scam. Maybe Skeats had slipped me a dummy text written by a child, to check just how compliant I could be. If I could be induced to praise this slab of styrofoam, I would never have to be worried about again. Yes, I had a paranoid sense that someone was testing me. But surely such things didn't really happen, even to me. I put the proof aside, resolving to revisit the question some other day, in that ideal future when my head won't be too smudged by pain or other things. For now I was left with the feeling that someone, somewhere, was taking the piss.

Then it started, the Missy and me show. I lay there watching myself say things I'd forgotten I'd ever even thought. Some of them weren't bad. Tightened, rejigged, the broadcast had a coherence that my memories lacked.

Missy looked better on my TV than she'd looked on my bed. I found myself wondering why on earth I'd wanted her off it. What had I been thinking? I watched her body on the screen and forgot the personality that went with it. I tried to look up her image's skirt, as if I'd see something up there that I hadn't seen before. Maybe this time there would be no teeth marks, no complications.

At the bottom of the screen there was a scrolling ticker for live social media feedback. The world was reviewing me, in real time. To start with, it was a rolling slurry of bad news. But as Missy peeled her way towards the inner me, the odd chunk of pro-Saint sentiment started bobbing up in the stew. Some spirited cyber-thinker ventured the word 'injustice' – with a question mark, but it was better than nothing. When my image told Missy's about the mystery DNA, the tide really turned. Somebody floated the word 'innocent'. Someone else said something about a cover-up. By the show's end something unprecedented was going on. I had *fans*.

About an hour after the credits rolled I got an email from Jill Tweedy – senior editor at Bennett and Bennett, mentor and publisher of Missy Wilde. She wanted to meet. How would tomorrow be, at her office?

I looked at the excruciating bulk of Fingle's book.

I wrote back and told Tweedy I was free.

In the offices of Bennett and Bennett, the walls have no corners. They have curves instead of angles, and they're covered with salmon-pink carpet. The lobby is like the waiting room of an upmarket brain doctor. There's a big white horseshoe desk personned by multiple receptionists. The firm's name is bolted to the wall in heavy but sleek chrome letters. I'd never been on this side of the ramparts before. It looked a lot better than my side. The chairs for waiting in are padded and plush. I sat in one and thought about money. Never before had I been so close to having none of it. The TV cheque hadn't turned up yet. Christ knew when it was going to. When it did, it would take two or three days to clear. Ruin was so close now that days were starting to matter. The Fingle money was of course irrelevant: it was eight weeks away even if I could bring myself to review the book, and a cheque of that size would make no difference anyway. The haemorrhage would blast it straight into history. Conceivably, Tweedy was my last shot. If I didn't walk out of this place with a cheque, or better still some cash, the shuddering little stunt plane of my finances might finally hit the ground instead of looping back into the sky. Of course Ted Lewin could always fix things at any time by locking me in jail. That would put me back on my feet straight away. But for the moment I was stuck with being an unarrested writer. Sitting in the Bennett lobby, I thought I might finally be in some kind of luck. The place stank of lucre.

It stopped doing that, once you got past reception. It started looking like my place instead. Stepping into Tweedy's office was like going backstage at a sausage factory. I saw things in there that no civilian was meant to see: the offal and filler of the book trade, the waste products of the industry in its terminal phase. Life-sized cardboard photographs of Bennett's star writers were heaped randomly around her walls. I saw Liam Vagg in his best threads, flanked by his pit bull. I saw a game-show host whose trademark was to hold up his thumb while smiling. I saw a celebrity chef lifting a silver lid off a white plate. Between the lid and the plate there was an oblong hole in the cardboard, where a book would be displayed when the effigy hit the stores. I doubted it would be the *Critique of Pure Reason*.

Jill Tweedy had the air of a canteen lady who took no shit. I sat on the other side of her desk and watched her eat a leafy lunch out of a square plastic tub. She was my age and looked it. I was my age and looked like me, so I could hardly point the finger – the finger that was bent and scarred at the best of times, and now full of bone-deep shards from a dead girl's mirror. Tweedy glanced at the fading pink bruise on my forehead but didn't ask about it. Not caring about things like that was part of her hard-bitten style. We were on the same page, Tweedy and I: we were old enough to know that time blows by you like a typhoon. Our days of squandering it on fake pleasantries were behind us. You weren't meant to like her, and I liked her for it.

Even so, it had to be recalled that I was on enemy turf. The desk between us was chaotically duned with Bennett product: bound and unbound proofs, mocked-up dust-jackets, paperbacks garnished with the flaccid praise of Barrett Lodge. Christ knew how many of Tweedy's books I'd taken down over the years. It had to be a lot, although I couldn't remember their names. She would, though. I knew that much about the trade. I saw a bloated hardback on my side of the desk, half-hidden by all the other slabs of wasted forest. I angled my head to read the spine. *The Tainted Land*, it inevitably said. I'd thought I was here to get away from it. Apparently that was not going to be feasible.

I picked it up.

'Careful, now.' Tweedy stopped chewing. She went all tense and headmistressy. 'That one's embargoed. Hot off the presses.'

It was less heavy than the proof copy, but not by much. There was nothing on the jacket's front except the title and the author's name, in stark white text against an ochre background. The font was austere: it spoke, grimly, of Fingle's deep seriousness as a writer and man. You could take the font's word for this. You didn't even have to read the book. You could just buy it, stick it on the shelf, and wait for the prize committees to endorse your good taste. I checked out the back-flap photo. Fingle looked like James Dean, only dumber. No wonder he was no good. He hadn't suffered. Never trust a non-ugly writer.

I opened the text to a random page. Tweedy stiffened some more.

'You know the rules,' she said. 'No peeking.' She tried to sound mock-stern instead of real-stern, but it didn't work. Some people like their humour dry. Tweedy seemed to like hers non-existent. Conceivably she had tried laughing once, in her youth, the way another person might try mescaline. And it hadn't been her thing. Creases of underuse ringed her slot of a mouth, like cracks around a scorched billabong. Again this was okay by me. I was pretty much out of gags myself.

I let the book drop shut. Apparently she had no idea I was reviewing it. That interested me.

'You've heard about him, of course,' she asked me, or told me.

'Of course.'

'Guess who plucked him from obscurity? I found it in the slush pile, believe it or not. Over the transom, totally cold. Which *never* happens. The dream novel. The one that reminds you why we got into the business in the first place.'

So it was her fault. I considered telling her that obscurity existed in order to keep people like Fingle buried, forever. That was the whole point of it. Instead I said, 'What's he like?'

'As a person? Ooh. Interesting. Reclusive. Moody. A bit of a mystery. Tough life. In and out of institutions as a kid.'

Not educational ones, to judge from his prose. I put the book back on the desk and said, 'My commiserations about Jade.'

Little as I liked throwing around her name, I liked throwing around Fingle's even less. Also I thought she had to be mentioned early, for form's sake. I shouldn't have bothered. Tweedy had gone all rigid again, as if I'd raised the name of her least favourite dead person.

'She'll be missed,' she stingily said. She left it to me to sketch in the rest of the sentence: She'll be missed, *but not by me.* Apparently Jade, in life, had done something that rubbed Tweedy up the wrong way. Whatever it was, getting murdered had not been nearly enough to make up for it.

'I got the feeling,' I said, 'that she was a workaholic.' Since Tweedy didn't want to talk about her, I suddenly did.

'She certainly got results,' Tweedy grimly conceded.

'She went the extra mile.'

'She did.'

'She ever talk about her boyfriends?'

'Not to my knowledge.'

That was a strange way of putting it. I wasn't here to add Tweedy to my list of suspects, but this was a chart-busting performance.

'Ex-boyfriends?'

'No.'

'Some young guy?' I said.

'I knew nothing about her personal life. She played all that stuff pretty close to her chest.'

She sealed her lunchbox with a resonant little click, as if dropping the lid on the whole topic. 'We should talk about you,' she said.

I sat back. 'So Missy told you about my novel?'

Tweedy gave me a blank look. 'You're writing a novel?'

'I've written one already. I assumed that's why I was here.'

Apparently I'd assumed wrong. Well, that solved one little mystery. I'd been wondering why Missy had done me that favour, or any favour. Here was my answer. She hadn't. I should have seen that coming. I had thought my head was at its best this morning, more or less. I hadn't even brought a flask. But maybe my best was worse than I'd thought.

'First novels are a tough sell, Ray,' said Tweedy with a pro's savvy. Yes, I should have seen that she'd called me here with implausible urgency, if my novel was what she'd wanted to talk about. For my novel, any amount of urgency was implausible.

'So tell people it's my second.'

'What's it about?' Tweedy said briskly. 'Sell it to me in one sentence.' She meant that the sentence might as well be a short one, since it would be a waste of breath at any length. She wanted to move on. The topic inconvenienced her.

You don't mention an unsolicited book in a publishing house. I had broken the laws of good taste and commerce in one gauche stroke, like a man offering a dead pig to a kosher butcher.

'I don't think I can do that.'

'Well if *you* can't do it, Ray, what makes you think I could do better?' She was back in her element now, setting me straight with her blokey little maxims about the bottom line.

'Maybe you could read it,' I proposed – since I was here, and since I never would be again. No doubt I was wasting my time, but what was another five minutes on top of the life I'd wasted writing the thing in the first place? 'Let's think outside the box. Read it, and see if you think it's any good. And if you think it is, let your sales people worry about selling it. Isn't that their job?'

Tweedy, in an effort to hurry things along, had started shaking her head long before my little speech was done. 'Come on, Ray. You know the score. Fiction's dead in this country. It's just the way things are.'

'Fingle's book,' I pointed out, 'is a first novel.'

'Ah,' she said. '*Well*. Not everybody can write like that.'

'No?'

'*Tainted* is a once-in-a-decade kind of book.'

'And what's *it* about, in just one sentence?'

'I'll tell you what it's about in one *word*. It's about Australia. It *is* Australia.'

If that was true I was swimming out on the next tide. I left a moment's silence to mark the passing of my novel, the official death of my one big shot. But really it had died a long time ago, the way we all do, a day at a time. No wonder

I was a failure. I'd got hung up on this idea that books had to be *good*, when all they had to be was fat and full of big ideas. Yes, writing was like long-haul trucking. If you could load a book with heavy issues and get it from page one to page 1259, that made you an important writer. End of argument. Give the guy a prize. Quality? What had I been thinking? I'd spent my life worshipping a dead god. Maybe it was time I lowered my sights, devoted my remaining years to humbler ideals. Paying the rent. Eating. Maybe it was time I took the hint and knelt down in front of money.

I hefted Fingle's barbell of a book again. This time I opened it and kept it open.

'No peeking,' Tweedy said again.

'It's okay,' I said, 'I've got the proofs at home. I'm reviewing it.' Perhaps it was the wrong move, but there was a look on her face I was dying to wipe off. I got that result, instantly.

'Who for?' she asked with horror. 'Not for Jeremy?'

'Yes, for Jeremy. You didn't know?'

I watched the cogs churn behind her eyes. She'd been bargaining on Barrett Lodge. No doubt she'd already pictured his limp garland on the paperback: *humane, monumental, coruscating . . . a masterpiece.* And instead she'd landed me. What had she done to deserve that? She stole a tiny but telling glance at her phone. It wasn't hard to read her mind. She thought she could ring Skeats later and get me booted off the job. Let her try it. She'd be in for a shock.

For the moment she picked up an apple and looked hard at its grainy surface, so she wouldn't have to look at me. 'Have you read it yet?' she said.

'It would be improper of me to say.'

Tweedy kept looking at the fruit. At a similar moment Jade had given me her full gaze, not too long before giving me everything else. Tweedy, to her credit, was not about to give me either. Instead she said, 'Look. Tell you what. Shoot me a synopsis of that novel of yours. Two pages. Can't promise anything. But if I feel like it's got . . .' She fell silent and snapped her fingers a few times to suggest some elusive thing that could not be verbalised, something like pizzazz, or marketability, or proximity to the blazing virtues of Dallas Fingle. Whatever she was thinking of, she wouldn't find it in anything written by me. 'If I feel like it's got something,' she elaborated, 'we can take it from there.'

It was a tepid effort, as bribes went. I'd had better. But you had to remember she thought Fingle's book was *good*. She didn't see how anyone, even me, could think otherwise. How nice it would have been to inform her, right now, that her boy, her baby, was a raging illiterate. But why ruin her surprise?

'So what am I doing here?' I asked her.

'*Well*,' she said, swerving away from the other stuff with relief. 'I saw you on the telly last night, with Missy. And I *loved* the way you reframed the narrative. I certainly think there's a book in *that*, if you're interested. The crime, the investigation, the whole "person of interest" thing. Have you thought about it? We'd be interested, if you are.'

'A celebrity memoir?'

'More than that, I'd hope. Much more than that. The trial by media. The headlines. The struggle with alcohol. Depression, if you have it. This is the kind of stuff I *can* sell, Ray. Reality stuff. Life writing. You know what the climate's like. Let's operate within the parameters of the real here. And look, maybe you've had other approaches already, I don't know. If you haven't yet, you will. That's your business. What I *can* tell you is what we can offer you. The brand, for starters. That logo on the spine. Lot of history there, Ray. Generally I'll sit here with a writer and I'll reel off some of the names we've published over the years. You of all people I don't need to do that with.'

'Of course not.' Sample names: Vagg, Fingle, the guy in the chef's hat. But her central point was sound. I was, after all, still sitting there, still listening, still lashed to the chair by reality's parameters.

'And the beauty of this is that you're a writer already – in the sense that you've written a lot of short stuff, a lot of newspaper stuff. So the writing element shouldn't be much of a problem. I think we could persuade the board of that.'

My eyes were fixed on the cloche of the celebrity chef. My mind was fixed on the stark facts of my penury.

'In terms of money,' she pertinently said, 'the days of the swinging-dick advance have been and gone. We both know that. Anyone who tells you otherwise is lying to you. That being said, I think we could put *something* together.' Her tone said I was lucky not to be paying her. 'And there's – there's your novel too. *Maybe.* I don't know. We'll see. All this is contingent, of course, on what happens to you in terms of your legal position.'

'I'm innocent, if that's what you're asking.'

'Good. Good.'

'Although you've published the odd felon in the past.'

Tweedy thought about that. 'Maybe, but no one who's killed an innocent girl in cold blood. There are limits, even in this landscape. But look: let's not get morbid. Let's assume this thing'll have a happy ending.'

'I'm working on it.'

'Good,' Tweedy said. 'Think it over. I'm not asking for an answer here and now. Take a day or two. But bear in mind that there *is* an element of urgency, with any project like this. Your viability's at a peak right now, today. It won't stay there forever. We'll want to leverage it while we can.'

'Before people forget who I am?'

'Yes, to be frank. It happens. What people are interested in is current affairs, with the emphasis on current.'

'Who wants to be read by people like *that*?' She was making it damned hard to maintain my dough-focus.

'I keep forgetting you're a critic,' Tweedy said.

'This is what things have come to? Books for people who don't like books?'

'We've got our prestige books too.'

'Like Fingle's?'

'Exactly. But they can't all be books like that.'

'Some of them have to be books like mine.'

'Assuming you want there to *be* a bloody book, yes.'

'To make back the money Fingle loses by being so searing.'

'Jesus Christ, Ray. I was sort of under the impression I was doing you a favour here. Do you have any *idea* what people in this industry think of you?'

'I assume they think I'm utterly beyond the pale.'

'Okay. So you do have some idea. Anyway,' she said with an air of finality. 'I've told you what I can offer you. If you're not interested, you're not interested.'

I looked at the hall-of-famers stacked against the wall

behind her. I looked at the game-show host with his raised thumb. Money, Jade had told me, is *good*. I still thought that was untrue. I thought it now more than ever. But there was no denying the other thing. Lack of money is a nightmare. It makes you stop being you. When you don't have any, money starts thinking your thoughts for you. It makes all your decisions. And finally the worst happens: it writes your words.

'Now, Jill.' I looked her in the eye again. I'd made enough futile gestures for one day, if not for a lifetime. 'I don't recall saying that.'

There are things you finally learn, if you live long enough. When a stranger stops her car and opens the door for you, get in. When a man sticks out his hand at you, shake it. Think about the consequences later, if at all. Take what you get offered, not what you deserve. If you wait for that, you might be waiting forever. The future never comes. It's a myth, like the afterlife. Don't subtract yourself from the world and hope that a different and better world will spring up in its place. It won't. No matter how fucked you are, someone else is always worse off. In a day or two it will probably be you. Try not to drink too much. You still will, but you won't drink as much as you would have if you hadn't tried. Never turn down a shot at sex or money. Don't look too hard for the hidden catch. There will always be one. You'll find out what it is soon enough. Waste no time trying to please other people. Not even they know what they really want. Pursue the truth if you like, but don't imagine that it matters all that much to anyone else. Make a big noise, or the world will forget you're there. Do all these things and hope they add up to a life.

This is what it's like to be a writer.

Maybe it's what it's like to be anyone.

Maybe that was the night I turned up at Liam Vagg's. Or maybe it was some other night. The encounter seemed blurred even while I was having it. I don't believe he asked me in. At any rate I never made it past the front door. I don't remember driving there, and I don't remember driving home. I will never be sure I didn't dream the whole thing. But if I dreamt it, why didn't I dream myself some better lines?

'I told you never to come back,' Vagg said.

'I came here to apologise,' I told him.

He started closing the door. I stopped it with my foot.

'I was wrong to think you killed her,' I said. 'That showed a sorry lack of imagination. I thought you were the nastiest guy she knew. I was wrong, by a long way. She had somebody worse. I've heard his voice on the phone. I've tasted his skull. It won't be long till I find him. I'm closing in. Things are swinging my way, Vagg. Guess what? Your pal Jill Tweedy offered me a book deal. A true-crime quickie. A ruffian's memoir. I'm coming after your title, champ. This hasn't all been a waste. I'm finally getting my payoff after all.'

'I wouldn't bet on it.' Vagg looked bored. 'What's the advance?'

I quadrupled the true sum and named the result. It still wasn't enough to wound him.

'I'll believe it,' he said, 'when she sends you the cheque.' Even at midnight the Brylcreem, the designer sweats.

'Believe it now,' I said, 'and save yourself some time. She's hot for me. She wants my infamy. I'm a marketable scumbag, like you. Mind you, I'm not really a criminal. You're one up on me there. But you know something? Suddenly I don't mind looking like one. Yeah, I sort of *like* the spotlight now, Vagg. I'm starting to see the point of it. Maybe I want to stay in it a while longer. Maybe I don't *want* them to catch the guy who really did it. Not just yet. Why kill the goose now?'

'Try that and you'll end up in prison, mate, very fucking fast. You think Tweedy'll want to touch you then? Don't bet on it. She'll be wanting that advance back, too.'

'All publicity's good publicity, Vagg. I hardly need to tell you that. And my publicity's even worse than yours. I'm coming for your mansion, pal. I'm coming for your readers. I'm younger, I'm more desperate, and I write better.'

'Well, you'd better write fast. You're already starting to smell like yesterday's news.'

'You don't smell so fresh yourself. You know how many copies of your book I saw in Tweedy's office? Try none. They've got a new blue-eyed boy over there. His name's Dallas Fingle. They're about to throw everything they've got left at him, so don't be surprised when they stop throwing it at you.'

'I've heard all about him,' Vagg said. 'He sounds like a cunt.'

'He is. That's another apology I owe you. I didn't know what a bad book was, until I opened his. At least your stuff's honest. I should have said that when I reviewed it.'

He was about ready to shut the door now, whether my foot was in the way or not.

'Wait,' I told him. 'I've got one more thing to say. Ready? I wish I could write the way you do, Vagg. I mean it. I wish I had the common touch. I wish I could treat it as a day job, like baking bread. I say that without malice, or without much. I wish I could write a page of prose without worrying about how good or bad it is. Maybe I'll start now, with the junk memoir.'

'Go for it. Here's my blurb. You're a drunk, you seem to take a lot of pills, I'll be surprised if you survive the drive home, nobody cares about your reputation except you, and you were ready to throw it all away for one night of phoney sex.'

'Actually it was two,' I told him, 'plus some cash that never turned up.'

'Also,' he said, as the big expensive door closed on me, 'I still reckon you killed her.'

9

Something dull and heavy was on my chest. I thought a man was kneeling there. My eyes were shut. I tried forcing them open. It didn't work. My brain had risen from sleep but my body was locked below the surface still, paralysed. It happens to me sometimes. I fear it says bad things about my lifestyle. It's like waking up in your own corpse. I don't recommend it. You can think but you can't move. This time I started to fear it would never end. It had never gone on for so long. There was panic in me but it had no way to get out. The thing on my chest felt like the dead body of a big soft animal. It was crushing my maimed lung. I heard birds singing. They sounded way too loud. Was I outside – in the scrub, on the lawn? Had things come to that? A strangely fresh wind was fingering my hair.

My eyes came open, but the rest of me stayed entombed. I was on the couch, on my back. I looked down the length of my body, racked out in its coffin of air. I was fully dressed, boots included. It was the middle of the day at least. I lost patience and tried thrashing life back into my limbs. This is exactly the wrong thing to do. It's like trying to lift a fridge with your mind. The thing on my chest was Fingle's manuscript, flopped open like a fat dead albatross. It was crushing the breath out of me, and I couldn't get it off. I was dying the way I'd lived, under a suffocating mudslide of talentless prose.

Not before time, my concrete body surged up out of its shackles. It jerked sideways and flung Fingle's schlockbuster to the floor. Then I lay there shaking on my flank for a while, sucking air like a beached fish, taking things in. The door behind my head was standing wide open. That was where the wind was coming from. I didn't remember leaving it open, but that didn't mean much. Those singing birds were not outside. They were with me in the room. There were two of them. They were perched on a curtain rod above the sink, painting the wall below them with liquid shit. They were strangely small, considering their output of noise and waste. Somehow I'd have to get them out. That had to be done soon, but by no means yet.

The clock said it was two in the afternoon. On the coffee table beside my head was a kit of morning essentials: pills, water, a modest amount of liquor, a pen. I must have prepped them the night before, when I was thinking straight. The only thing missing was a bucket, or preferably two. I hauled myself away to the can and made it happen. A lot of bad things had happened to me lately, but vomiting through broken ribs was a hot new contender for the worst. When I was all wrung out I came back and redumped myself on the couch. My bed was softer but it was farther away. Also I was in no shape to lie down. I had to sit up straight and cradle my howling pink newborn brain for a while. The song of the birds ripped into it like an endless downpour of barbed silver arrows.

I shut my eyes and tried to reassemble the shards of the preceding night. Vaguely I recalled having dropped in on Vagg. Apparently I had then made it home, lurched inside, failed to shut the door, and fallen asleep reading Fingle's book. What a waste of time that last part had been. Whatever I'd read, I couldn't remember a word of it. And now the proofs were splayed on the floor like the head of a mop, and my place was lost forever. But wait. One thing I *did* remember. At a certain point in the evening, just before I went under, something in Fingle's book had stirred me. Some tin-eared phrase or scene in there, some stray stroke of hackery, had lit a fuse in my mind. I recalled a period of mental smouldering, as if I could smell a distant burning but couldn't find the source. And then, when I was on the point of sleep, a lightshow of revelation had burst behind my eyes. Something profound had come to me. Was it something about Fingle, or had I landed on some wider answer? Whatever it was, I'd written it down. Yes. Now I remembered that too. I had hauled myself up off the couch, found a pen and a pad, and written it down. It had to have been something pretty vital, if I'd forced myself to do all that. Maybe it was the answer to the whole thing.

For some reason I hadn't left the pad within reach. It was down at the far end of the table, still flipped open. I didn't bother wondering how it had got there. I felt a general optimism that trumped such questions. The future was on my side for once. The answer was right in front of me, in plain sight, even if I had to get off the couch to reach it.

For a while I didn't. I just stayed where I was, looking at the pad but making no move. Time had slowed. I thought I could afford to savour the moment. Finally I got up and went over and looked down at the pad's top page. It was empty. There was nothing on it. I pawed through the pages under it. There was nothing on them either. I flipped back to the first page. Running down its left edge, jammed in the pad's metal spiral, was the ragged remnant of a missing sheet, with a few severed loops of my handwriting still clinging to it. I'd written something down all right, but some fuckstick had ripped it out. I had a strong feeling it hadn't been me.

I was already headed for the kitchen bin. The birds saw me coming and freaked out, exploding off the curtain rod and flapping around my head in black ragged circles, screeching like rusted hinges. I threw my hands at them. They didn't seem to care. I removed the bin's lid. What I wanted to see right under it, crowning the rest of the trash, was a balled-up sheet of fresh white paper. Instead I saw the typescript of my dead novel. What was *that* doing there? I pulled it out and plunged my hands into the deeper garbage. They delved and rummaged. They got wet. They found nothing.

The birds were back on the curtain rod but they hadn't shut up and they hadn't stopped shitting. It was starting to feel like a bad day. I glanced over at my bedroom door. The day got worse. The door was closed, and I never closed it except when I was in there, and I wasn't in there. I wanted to believe it had blown shut in the wind, but the wind was blowing the other way. I found myself moving towards the door. Why was I doing that? Why wasn't I walking away from it, fast? There was something inevitable about the whole scene. Somebody somewhere had written all my moves for me. I had walked towards a door like this before. I had a bad feeling about this one too. Somehow I knew what was behind it. If I was right, I'd better know it now. If I was wrong, whatever else was in there couldn't be worse.

I opened the door – not all the way, but far enough. I wasn't wrong. Missy Wilde was lying on my bed again, exactly where she had lain the other day, wearing a similar outfit, striking an identical pose. Her knees were up. Her legs were parted. Her skirt was pooled around her waist. This time, on the other hand, she was dead. There was something drastically wrong with her face. Her shins were purple and waxy. On one of them a fat fly was moving.

I shut the door on her. I looked at the grainy peeling surface of the wood for a while. In bad fiction, the women stay good-looking even when they're dead. Missy hadn't. She looked the opposite of good. She was a splayed effigy. She was driftwood in the shape of a person. She was rag and bone. I didn't want to look at her again, ever. But I had to. There was no getting around it. For one thing, I'd already started to doubt she was there.

I opened the door again. This time I went into the room. There were a few things I had to check out in there. Her face wasn't one of them. I let myself look as high as her throat, but no higher. The skin there was the colour of a foul sky. She had been strangled, with wicked force. I didn't think it had happened here, on the bed. The sheets looked thrashed, but no more thrashed than usual. There was no blood. There was nothing wrong with the bed except that she was on it. Her pose was flagrantly familiar, and it was meant to be. Someone was messing with my mind. Her feet were bare.

Her toenails were painted cherry-red. The bite marks I'd seen the other day were still there, high on the inside of her left thigh. They had faded to yellow, like stains on an old book. She had healed fast. She was still young, or she had been. Near the top of her other thigh were two additional marks, blood-red and new. Her killer had given her a couple of fresh ones for the road. She didn't smell yet, according to my shattered nose, but maybe that fat and sated fly on her shin knew better.

Light-years behind me, back in the other room, those idiot birds left their perch again. I heard them smack a wall or two before making a screeching inevitable swerve for the open bedroom door. I went to slam it shut but got there too late. So now they had joined the party too, the idiot birds, flailing around the bed in pointless circles. I tried slapping them back out but they wouldn't go. That gave me another reason to leave the room for good. But I had one more piece of business in there. Under the bed was a ripped and sagging cardboard box stuffed with all my drafts and cuttings and cast-offs: the story of my life, the sorry codex of my collected works. Also, somewhere in that casket of shame, lay dead Jade's dead panties, and her retired sex toy. And right at the bottom of that nasty carton I had stashed the flash drive – the only hard evidence I'd ever had, the only proof of my innocence, if that's what it was, that wasn't in my head. If the drive was gone, if he'd found it and taken it, I was finished. I might as well turn myself in today. The box was around on Missy's side, naturally. It was right under her. If I didn't check it now I would have to check it later, when I would dig the ambience even less. So I skirted the bed, pointing my head at the wall, and knelt down to take delivery of my future, if I still had one. And it turned out that I did. The drive was still there. I put it in my pocket, feeling heavy and tired and old. A lot of me had wanted it to be over there and then.

Head averted, I stood back up. As long as I was there, I opened the window behind her head. Hitting her with a fresh breeze – so far it was my only plan. It wouldn't cut it for long. While I was at it, I shoved the flyscreen out into the yard. Maybe those idiot birds would have the wit to fly out, although I'd be a fool to bet on it. With my luck more birds would fly in. I went out the door without looking back and shut it behind me and left them to it.

Back on the couch, I felt something close to panic. No doubt that was the proper thing to feel. I wanted a drink, but not as much as I wanted to be sober. I wanted to have a normal man's head. I wanted to feel clean, cloudless, mentally scrubbed, fully present in time and space. I was working on a theory. It was unpalatable, but all the available theories were going to be that. She'd been killed somewhere else, by somebody who wasn't me, and she'd been brought in here dead. But when? Yesterday, when I was out of the house? No. That didn't fit with what I'd woken up to: the open side door, the closed bedroom, the missing page of my pad. It had to have happened last night, while I was sleeping on the couch, if sleeping is the right word for what I do there. He'd entered through the door that was four feet from my head, and he'd carried her body right on past me. If I'd flung out a slumbering arm at the wrong moment I'd have touched his depraved balls, or her dead white panda face. In the bedroom he had taken his time, laying her out, posing her, exhuming my poor novel from under the bed and dumping it sadistically in the bin. So he was a critic too, or maybe a publisher. On his way out, still taking his time, he'd stood over me and read my open notebook. Whatever he'd seen on the top page had made him rip it out and take it with him. And when he went he left the door open, and the birds had come flying in.

How would this theory go down with Ted Lewin? I wasn't about to run it by him. I could hardly swallow it myself. But somebody had laid her out on that bed, and it hadn't been me. I was meant to think it had been, but the man who wanted me to think it had a cheap imagination. He was the Dallas Fingle of sex crime. Like Fingle, he had the raging pointless stamina of the imbecile. He'd strangled her, dumped her in his car, driven her here, lugged her up to the house, smuggled her in past me, posed her. All that labour for one cheap effect. I wondered which way he'd brought her in. Not through the front gate, past the TV people. He must have parked up on the hill and hauled her in the back way, through the bush. And what about the pose? How did he know she'd struck it for me? Had he watched us through the window? I doubted it. He'd made a lucky guess, that was all. It wasn't an unusual pose, especially for her. She must have struck it for him too, and not just once. On at least two different nights he had moved his head up her, or down her, and sunk his teeth into her body's crux. On at least one of those nights it hadn't bothered her.

He'd put us into the endgame now, whether he'd meant to or not. He was coming out of the shadows. He was taking risks. What would he have done if I'd woken up as he dragged her past me? Killed me? Why hadn't he done that anyway? Maybe there was method in his madness, or maybe he'd gone clean off the fucking rails. Either way, my current life was not going to last much longer. If the façade held for long enough to let me bank Jill Tweedy's advance, it would now be a miracle. At a minimum, there was the question of Missy's corpse. Some decision would have to be made about her soon. Not today, but soon. Her use-by date loomed. To ignore that would be unthinkable, even for me. And getting her off the bed had been hard enough when she was alive. There was bad stuff in my near future, all right, no matter how things played out.

The birds had stopped flailing around in the bedroom. They'd landed on something. For what it was worth, I hoped it wasn't her. I looked at the bottle near my knees. Not drinking from it had got me about as far as it was going to get me, for today. Anyway, I had an obligation, sort of, to drink one to Missy. I owed her that much. I wished I'd been nicer to her, within reason. She'd deserved her chance to grow older and less obstreperous. She was still making her plans. I'm still making mine, and I'm forty-five. What would my life have added up to if he'd snuffed me out on the couch last night, while I slept? Nothing. Nothing at all. A prelude to a washout, foreplay to a non-event. My payoff or redemption, if I'm ever going to get one, has not come yet.

Uncapping the bottle, I resolved to chase my dreams harder. Revenge for Missy was suddenly a big part of them. I craved a rematch with the man who had done that to her. I wanted to be alone with him one more time – one *last* time. That was about all I still wanted out of life. Finding him, taking him down – *that* was something to drink to.

I drank to it.

◆

I didn't get to drink to it for long. About an hour later, just as the short day started to wane, I heard a car come crunching up the drive. I hadn't drunk nearly enough to make this seem acceptable. I heard a handbrake crank on. I heard the slam of a door. The world won't leave you alone, no matter how grimly you shut it out. It will always track you down. Beyond the mottled glass of the front door, a dark and stolid male shape came up my front steps, rising like smoke. I watched the shape blur and fatten until it filled the panes. The shape was wearing a fedora, a Jack Ruby hat. There is only one man in my world who wears a hat like that.

He knocked. I moved to the door. Getting there seemed to take a long time, as if I was wading through thigh-deep water. The figure on the door's far side had not stopped looking like Ted Lewin. This horrified me less than it should have. Maybe it didn't horrify me at all. Let the rest of it get taken care of by Lewin, and by solemn experts in latex gloves and paper shoes: the processing of the scene, the shrouding and removal of the body. That way I'd never have to go back in there again.

I opened the door. Lewin looked at me without expression. Then he was inside, removing the Ruby hat, drifting across to my armchair, sitting down there, rotating the hat's brim in his fingers. He looked all slack somehow; his eyes had gone all rheumy and old. If he was here to arrest me, he was hiding it well. He glanced around the room without rigour. The closed bedroom door didn't interest him. With mild disapproval he contemplated the survival kit on the coffee table: the bottle that was no longer very full, the curled blister packs that no longer contained many pills.

For a second I thought I saw him cock his head at the empty air, as if he smelt something that I still couldn't. But the moment evaporated. His senses had lost their acuity, their threat. I half-wished they hadn't. He breathed out hard and said, 'They're taking me off the case.'

I was back on the couch now, facing him, waiting for him to say more. He didn't. I said, 'I'm sorry.'

'Who for, Ray? Me or yourself?' He looked exhausted, beaten, out of his element. His poignant singlet showed through his short-sleeved shirt. His cricket club tie was badly knotted.

'Both,' I said.

'You should be. You'll find things are about to change.'

But things had changed already, and he didn't know it. For once I was ahead of him. He was a corpse behind the times. Maybe he didn't even know she was missing. If he did, he didn't think it had anything to do with me. Nor was I about to raise the topic myself: not any more. My chance had been and gone. There are only two good times to tell a cop about a dead girl on your bed: straight away or not at all.

'This next bloke won't be as nice as I am.' Lewin looked at me with his mismatched eyes. The bad one was an egg fried over way too much heat. 'He thinks you did it, for starters.'

'And you don't, do you, Ted? You never have.'

He looked at me with something like disgust and said nothing. My heartbeat had steadied. This wasn't, after all, going to be the end. It was just one more scene to be ridden out on the way.

After a while he said, 'They reckon I gave you too much slack. I'm starting to think they're right.'

In the bedroom, the open window let in a blast of wind. The door bumped softly against the jamb. Lewin looked at it briefly, then back at me.

'That TV thing was the last straw,' he said.

'I had to defend myself.'

'It wasn't smart. It made us look bad. It made *me* look bad.'

'Yeah, but it made me look good. And I've got to look after myself, Ted. If I don't, who will?'

'This next bloke won't, I'll tell you that much. He'll go in hard. He'll put the dogs on you. He'll tap your phone. You'll have company wherever you go. In your car. On foot.'

'I don't go out much anyway.' He was talking about abstract threats, nightmares for a future I no longer had.

'He'll be out to break you, whether you did it or not. And he'll be wasting his time, won't he? Because you didn't.'

'No, Ted, I didn't. But how do you know that? You knew it before I did. How?'

'Now why should I tell you *that*,' Lewin tiredly said, 'when you've never told me nothing? This whole time I've had to wring things out of you, drop by drop. You've never given more than you had to. I've never understood it. You're a smart guy. You know I don't give a bugger about your secrets. I just wanted to catch the bastard who killed her. I could have been done with you in a day. It's like you *wanted* to stay in the frame.'

I hated seeing him like this: perturbed, hat in hand, clueless on an away pitch. Outside his miked-up room he was just an old man whose old wife dressed him, badly.

'I'm in love with her,' I said. 'But you already know that. You worked that out before I did too. I didn't love her until she was dead. Maybe *because* she was dead, I don't know. And maybe *because* I hardly knew her. These are dark themes, Ted. Some of them I don't even understand myself. Can you blame me for not wanting them in the papers? Plus, I've started to lose her. I've only got one or two solid memories of her left. If I talk them away, I'll have lost everything. That enough truth for you?'

Not even close. He did the thing where he looks at you and says nothing and waits for the silence to break you. This time I decided not to let it. I waited for it to break him first. And then, in my bedroom, those idiot birds reared up screeching off their perch, and started rattling around the walls like dice in a cup.

Lewin looked at the door.

'Birds,' I told him.

'Eh?' His eyes were on the door still.

'A couple of birds flew in there. I can't get them out.'

He pondered that claim without much interest. He was free to walk over there and open the door, if he really wanted to know a secret. Instead he just looked wearily back at me. His fingers resumed their workout on his hat, running lap after lap of its brim.

'I don't suppose,' he said flatly, as if already aware he was wasting his breath, 'that you broke into her house the other night?'

'What other night?'

'The night you got that big red lump on your head.'

'No.'

'Well. Somebody did. There's glass all over the floor. And blood. They're testing it. If it's yours, I think you might finally have ruined yourself.'

Again he spoke of a future that wasn't coming. I sat there, waiting for him either to speak again or leave. Our whole relationship had flipped. Now I was the one who could just sit there, and let the other man drown in silence. I tasted power, and didn't like its flavour much: not if its victim had to be Lewin.

'I came here to give you one last chance,' he said. 'There's still things you're not telling me. We both know it. Whatever you haven't given me, give it to me now. Off the record, man to man. No cameras, no tapes. It's still not too late. I've got one more day. After that, you'll have this other joker to deal with.'

'And he won't understand me like you do.'

'I can assure you that he won't.'

I was starting to want the old man gone. He was an irrelevance now. He was cramping my style. What was he here for? Friendship? I had nothing left to give him. All my leads had been abject red herrings. Skeats, Vagg . . . It was all just literary politics that meant nothing and led nowhere. And Lewin didn't police the literary world. Nobody did. So what else could I tell him about? The girl on my bed? The voice on my phone? The flash drive? No. The end was going to be hot and nasty and violent, and I wanted it all to myself. I had earned that.

'She had somebody young,' I offered.

Lewin said nothing.

'He's a biter,' I said. 'He bites people.'

'I know that. You know I know that. Give me something I don't know.'

'Look at her job. I think he had something to do with that.'

'Last chance,' Lewin said.

But we'd hit bedrock, at long last. I had nothing left to give, apart from the whole truth. Were his powers of empathy subtle enough to forgive that? Were anybody's?

I said nothing. Lewin shook his head and put his hat back on. And that was that. One last disappointment for the road.

'You're a prick, Ray,' he sadly said.

I'd reduced him to saying that. For some reason it felt like my most shameful failure yet.

10

As soon as he'd gone I wanted him back. You haven't been alone until you've been alone with a dead body. It tests your taste for solitude. You start to crave company, no matter how sick of life you thought you were. Those birds were still back there, squawking around in the bedroom with her, but they didn't count. I wanted the human touch, for once. I even picked up *The Tainted Land* for a while, in the hope of getting some spark of animation or fellowship from Fingle. But I had as much chance of finding life in there as Missy had of bursting into song. Say this much for Missy: at least she'd been alive once. Fingle wrote like a mannequin. Even by accident he couldn't write a breathing sentence. And yet something he'd written had stirred me last night. Somewhere on the featureless salt flat of his dud epic, some shred of pertinence had caught my eye: a dropped stitch in the vast flaccid tapestry of his irrelevance. If I'd found it once, maybe I would find it again. Or maybe it was the freakish absence of any such stitch that had got me thinking. Maybe his utter worth-lessness was the key.

The phone rang. I picked it up. I knew who I wanted it to be.

'You find her?' his voice said.

I had my wish. It was him: my *semblable*, my *frère*.

'How could I miss her?' I said. 'Not much subtlety there, even by your standards.'

'Dealt with her yet?'

'Why don't you drop round and find out? I think it's time we met again.'

'We will,' he said, 'but not yet.'

'I almost know who you are.'

'You have no idea.'

'I know you're young. I know you're not that bright. This is what Jade used to tell people. She told them she had this boyfriend who wasn't that bright.'

'What people, Saint? You don't *know* any people.'

'She told them there was something wrong with you. She was on the money there.'

'I could have killed you last night.'

'You should have. Next time I'll be ready for you. You fucked up. I feel reborn.'

'The state of you on that couch.'

'Yeah, I'm the sick one. Talk about the crooked timber of humanity. You're riven, mate. You're *sawdust*.'

'Maybe you should ask yourself why I let you live.'

'Because I'm not a woman?'

'Maybe I want you around a bit longer.'

'Why don't you come back tonight? I believe you know the way.'

'I'm busy tonight.'

'But you missed something. You left something behind. That thing I found in her room. It's a thumb drive. It's encrypted, but one of these days I'll crack it. Or maybe I'll get sick of trying and give it to the cops, and let them work it out. And that'll be it for you. Whatever she had on you, it's on that drive. You want to bet against it? I know you don't. Because that's the sort of thing she did, isn't it? We both know it. She was smarter than everyone else, especially you. That's why you went back to the house. You knew she'd have some way of fucking you up from the grave. Well, I found it first. I'm zeroing in on you, pal. You're a brainless sack of shit, but for some reason she had a use for you. When I work out what it was, I'll have you. I'm close now. I'm so close. But I think you know that. You saw what I wrote on that pad.'

'That was nothing. You weren't even close. If you were, do you think you'd still be alive?'

'So why'd you take it away?'

It was a mistake to ask. 'Because I knew you'd forget,' he said. 'You're pathetic, Saint. Aren't you ashamed of yourself?'

'You're going to ask me about shame?'

'Don't dodge the question.'

'I'm not here to answer your questions, champ. What do you think we're doing here? Matching wits? Don't flatter yourself. Play to your strengths. Come back tonight and try to kill me. Come for the stick before I crack it. I sleep with the doors unlocked, as you know. You want this thing to end, let's end it.'

'I don't want it to end. Not yet.'

'It's ending, whether you like it or not. Come here tonight. This time I'll be ready for you. No cops, for now. Just you and me. You do your best, I'll do mine.'

'I've told you,' he said. 'Tonight I'm doing something else.'

I should have hung up then. We'd covered the essentials, and I was sick of the sound of his voice. But any sound beat the sound that was waiting for me when he went, the sound of Missy in that other room. Silence is one thing. The silence that will never end is a bit much even for me.

I said, 'You're getting desperate, aren't you? You're start-ing to panic. Why'd you kill Missy? What did she do wrong? She burn you in one of her columns? She go public about the size of your dick? Or did she ask you one of her probing questions? Something like: "How did Jade Howe get the same bite marks on her that you put on me?"'

'If you'd kept your mouth shut, Saint, she'd still be alive.'

'Why? Did I give her the right idea?'

'You shoot your mouth off about things you don't under-stand. You're getting dangerous to know.'

'What's that mean?'

'It means people around you keep dying.'

'Because you keep killing them. Christ. People around me? There *are* no people around me. Not any more.'

'I could name one or two,' he said.

'I wish I could.' Did I know what he had in mind even then? 'There's nobody left.'

'There's your boss,' he said.

I felt something like an electric shock – the mild kind, the not unpleasant kind.

He waited. He said, 'You don't like him much, do you?'

'Now what makes you think that? Are you in the business?'

'No. But I'm telling you the man's in danger, and for some reason you don't seem to care.'

'That's what you're telling me, is it?'

'You know it is.'

'Maybe I don't think you're serious.'

'Sounds like you want me to be.'

'Killing a *man*? That isn't your style. Even a man like Skeats.'

'Jade didn't like him either,' he said. 'She thought he was a fool. She thought he was pathetic.'

'That's nice to hear, but what's your beef with him?'

'What's yours? The fact that Jade fucked him a lot?'

Something was dawning on me that would have dawned on me days ago, if my head wasn't always so full of pain and pills and sloshing booze. 'You *are* in the business,' I said.

He said nothing. I took that as confirmation. He was in the ink trade. You didn't have to be to want Skeats dead, but it helped. Yes, this freak was in the word racket, like the rest of us. Why had I taken so long to see it? Just because he was an amoral and embittered dunce? On reflection, that hardly ruled him out.

'Who are you?' I said. 'A writer? Did I give you a bad review once? Did Skeats publish it? Did Missy Wilde give you one too? You're a failure of some kind, clearly. But what kind? A washed-up poet? An even more failed critic than me?'

'His family's out of town tonight.'

He left a silence I didn't fill.

'Tonight it's just him.'

'Who is this? Lodge, is it you?'

'Let's be clear about what I'm saying.' He said it petulantly, almost in a whine.

'I get it,' I assured him. 'You're really not that subtle.'

'And you don't care.'

What could I say to that except nothing?

'I assumed you'd want to talk me out of it.'

'Would it make a difference?'

'Maybe. I don't like doing these things.'

'So turn yourself in.'

'No. Someone has to stop me.'

'There's plenty of people in the phone book.'

'This is your boss I'm talking about. The man who publishes your stuff. And this is the best you can do. I find this strange.'

'You should get out more.'

'The man who puts your words into print.'

'In butchered form, my friend.'

'So it's only fair that we butcher him?'

'Not we. You. *You*. I don't make other men's decisions for them. I can barely make my own.'

'You're making one right now.'

'Is that right? Everyone's a moralist now. Even you.'

'You're no better than I am, Saint.'

'No, I'm quite a lot better than you are.'

'Bullshit. You want this fucker to die.'

'I've told you what I want.' I was tired. I was in no mood to debate ethics with a man who murdered women and posed them like dolls. 'I want you. Here. Now. Tonight.'

'You know what I'm doing tonight.'

'Don't do it. Is that enough for you?'

'Say it like you feel it.'

'That's all the feeling I've got left. If it's not enough, do what you have to do. Just leave his family out of it.'

'Like I told you,' he said, 'tonight it'll be just him.'

Again that sense that the answer wasn't far away. I knew this man somehow. Was it Skeats himself, checking to see whether I'd piss on him if he caught fire?

If it was, he had his answer.

'Let it come down,' I said.

After that I thought I started to smell her. I got a towel and soaked it with water and plastered it into the crack under the bedroom door. The smell propelled me out of the house then, out the side door and across the width of the deck. But even out there the stench was still with me. Maybe it was in my clothes. Or maybe it was under them. Maybe the dead smell was coming from me.

I leant on the rail and looked out at the trees. I noticed I had no drink in my hand, or even near it. This was telling. I'd brought my phone out instead, and had laid it on the rail. There was more of the afternoon left than I'd feared. I had time to think for once, just when I didn't want to. I wanted night to hurry up and come down and take things out of my hands. I wanted to bail out of consciousness and let darkness take its course without me on board. I am better at behaving badly when I am asleep. Awake, I have a bad tendency to develop second thoughts. But bedtime was still a long way off, even by my clock. Like a spooked animal, the night had sniffed me and declined to come any closer: it could smell my thirsty evil. I felt stationary in time and space. I could shape the future instead of freefalling through it. Conceivably, being sober always felt like this. It would have been nice to have this clarity when it might have done Jade some good, or me, or even Missy. Why did the lucky day have to be Skeats's?

The palm trees crossed swords in the high wind. The air played with my hair the way Jade used to, once. Exactly once. My appetite for Skeats's death was souring. It wasn't that I didn't want him dead. I just didn't want him to be dead because of me. There was a big difference. Even the moral idiot on the phone could see that. Would the world be a better and less stupid place without Skeats in it? Of course, but this was no time for idealism. What mattered was living with myself. Would that get easier or harder, if Skeats turned up dead in the morning? I thought I knew the answer, and didn't like it, which probably meant it was right. You make the big decisions in your gut, and then you work out the reasons in your head. The truth was that I had enough corpses on my conscience already. Throw Skeats on the stack and I would vanish under the weight. I would sink right down into the earth with him. I would have no self left to enjoy his being dead with. There was no getting around it. He had to be warned. Calling him was the least I could do, as well as the most. Not doing it would be a whole new kind of disgrace. What failure on that scale would taste like I did not want to know. So why had I still not called him? Why chew the foul cud any longer than I had to?

The gum leaves hissed high in the breeze, like applause heard from a long way off. Somebody half-smart said you regret the things you don't do more than the things you do. Whoever he was, I doubted he ever put a man to death.

If he did, what were the things he regretted *not* doing? By now I'd looked at the phone for so long that I saw its shape when I blinked. The scene had the texture of something I would remember forever, no matter what happened next. The best I could do was make sure I remembered it for the right reason. Would Skeats have saved my skin if our positions were switched? I doubted it, but that was exactly why I had to save his. Wasn't I better than him, at least by a bit? If I didn't have that to cling to, I didn't have much.

I dialled his number.

And he didn't answer. Of course he didn't. I pictured him glancing at his phone and seeing my name on it and glibly turning away, spurning the call that would save his worthless hide. Part of me, a very large part of me, wanted to let that be his last bad decision on earth. But the larger principle had to be remembered. I wasn't saving him for his sake. I was saving him for mine. That's all there is, in the end: just you.

I went inside to landline the prick. I sat there by the phone and waited a bitter eternity before redialling him, so he wouldn't guess it was me.

He answered. When he heard my voice he inevitably said, 'Ray, can I call you back?'

'No,' I said.

But I was already talking to a severed line.

He didn't call me back.

And even then I couldn't let him die.

11

One last time into the vile city, then. One last drive and I would be out of good deeds. Not drinking before I left, or even while I drove, was part of the martyrdom. My body was an inferno before I hit the plains. My phone was on the passenger seat in case Skeats called back. He hadn't yet and he wasn't going to. Till the end, to the death, he was not going to make things easy for me. It had never been his style.

From the foot of the hills to the city an endless chain of tail-lights stretched ahead through the dusk, glowing ruby-red like my spine. A river of metal and light going nowhere, and everybody in it was going to get there before me. The memory stick was in my pocket. I hadn't been stupid enough to leave it behind. Missy was still on my bed. For some reason I hadn't liked leaving her back there, alone. But what could happen to her now that hadn't happened already?

The drive was endless, but it ended. Near the lit-up offices of the newspaper I found a dark lane to ditch the car in.

Then I went through the paper's revolving glass front door for what would surely be the last time, no matter how the rest of this went. In the lobby I summoned a lift and rode it up to Skeats's floor. When it got there I stepped out into the mid-1960s. That was the last time the place had turned enough profit for a revamp. There were bent grey venetian blinds on the windows. The laminated floors were the colour of month-old avocado. The desks were cubbied off by ranks of chest-high tin filing cabinets set at right angles to one another. The place was vanishing even as I walked through it. Half the floor space had just been sold or let out to some IT firm. Two guys with nail guns were erecting a plaster wall across its width right now. Fresh blue carpet had been laid on the far side of the frame. I caught the sweet rubbery smell of it. The light was brighter over there. I saw virgin white workstations standing in its glare, and ergonomic chairs still sheathed in plastic. I saw cutting-edge computer towers. A stylised logo on the wall said something about networking solutions and synergy. Here was one more reason to let Skeats live. He was being walled off into the past anyway. He was more like me than I wanted to believe.

I was halfway to his corner office when I got a rogue urge to swing by Barrett Lodge's warren en route. I thought I could afford the detour. I thought I'd done the hard part already, just by making the drive. And something about the Lodge factor gnawed at me. He was anomalous somehow. I'd checked out everybody else, so why hadn't I checked out him?

Lodge's filing cabinets were sandbagged almost to the ceiling with old proofs and review copies, with every book he'd ever glazed with the lukewarm drool of his approval.

The old fool was so torpid he'd never even got around to selling them. Or maybe Skeats paid him so much that he didn't need the extra cash. His little den was an Alamo of overpraised books. Until the last moment you never knew if he was in there or not.

This time he was: slumped at his strewn desk like an overfed vagrant, wearing the trench coat he never took off even when he was inside on a rainless day. His big body was formless and necrotic, like his prose. His huge mad thatch of hair was uncombed. He looked like a badly stuffed mastodon. His meaty paranoid face swerved up at me, bent into a rictus of hatred and fear. His mouth sagged open and I wished it hadn't. He had more missing teeth than extant ones. His gums were a moist pornographic abyss, pink fretted with brown. On his post-apocalyptic desk he'd hacked out a rough clearing for the thing he was currently reading. It lay there open in front of him, an implausibly thick set of proofs. I'd have called it the thickest set of proofs I'd ever seen, but I'd seen it before. It was *The Tainted Land*. I knew its girth all too well. Lodge was about halfway through it. Pencilled exclamation marks and underscorings festooned the page. Apparently he liked what he saw. Of course he did.

'Are you reviewing that?' I asked him. Patently the answer was yes, but I needed time to start believing it.

He frowned, as if he found the question strange. And why shouldn't he? Fingle's book was big, local, no good. Of *course* he was reviewing it.

'For Skeats?' I asked.

'Who else?'

'And what do you think of it?'

'They reckon it'll be a shoo-in for the Miles.'

'But what do *you* think of it? What do you *think* of it? Off the record. Man to man.'

I looked into the wet chasm of his maw while he said: 'This is a *fine* novel. Huge, ambitious, epic in scope, Dallas Fingle is a stylist, a throwback to an age when literature still mattered, and a timely reminder that it matters still . . .'

We're all kidding ourselves if we think we have a future, but some of us are kidding ourselves more than others. When I surged into Skeats's office he was on the phone. He saw me and looked away fast, but not fast enough. I had seen the panic in his eyes.

'Sure,' he said into the phone, while I sat down across the desk from him. 'That's not an issue. If he wants me to cover that, I will.'

I waited. He wasn't looking at me but he wasn't looking away from me either. His shoulders had gone taut. He knew something was up. He could sense I had one more reason than usual to want to vault the desk and maim him. He knew that one of his lies had veered off the road and reduced itself to wreckage. He just didn't know which one yet.

'I'll do that, Jill.' He nodded eagerly into the phone. His curls were back at full loft tonight. His shirt was a radiant sheeny white: like his teeth, like Missy Wilde's underwear. 'I'll do that.' He looked at me without looking at me. 'Whatever he prefers. Whatever he prefers.'

I waited while he said a few more things like that. When the call was done he put the phone back in its cradle. 'Jill Tweedy from Bennett and Bennett,' he explained through a zestless smile. 'I'm interviewing Dallas Fingle tomorrow.

Lady Muck wanted to dish out a few riding instructions.'

This was meant to sound airy, conspiratorial – as if I was his great chum and Tweedy wasn't. 'It's going to be a weird scene,' he flailed on. 'They're playing it like a movie junket. Fingle gets to sit in a comfy chair all day, not moving. Us hacks come in to interview him in shifts. Fifteen minutes each, plus five minutes for the photographer. Strictly no more. Apparently he's not big on photos. Reckons they drain him spiritually.'

'Funny you should mention Fingle,' I said.

'Why's that?' He reached for a pencil and started tapping it against his side of the desk. Looking at it gave him a half-plausible excuse not to look at me. This thing was getting off to a bad, bad start.

'I swung by Barrett Lodge's desk on the way in,' I said.

Skeats said nothing.

'Guess what I saw on it?'

'A rat?' Skeats tried to grin, but his face wasn't buying it. He'd stopped tapping the pencil.

'Close. I saw Fingle's book.'

Skeats lost the smile and tried on a frown instead. He couldn't make that work either.

'Lodge seems to think he's reviewing it,' I said.

Skeats looked over at the closed door, as if to confirm that there was wood between us and Lodge. Either that or he was checking escape routes.

'Okay,' he said in a low voice. 'I won't bullshit you.'

'There's a first time for everything.'

'Keep your cool, Ray. I'm not fucking *you* here. I'm fucking *Lodge*. You're still my Plan A. I threw him a copy for backup. I had to. This book's a big deal. I can't afford to take any chances on it. I needed a safety net in case you get a last-minute attack of the . . . of the Gore Vidals. But as far as I'm concerned, you and I still have an agreement.'

'Which is? Remind me of it.'

'As long as you come up with something usable,' he said, 'I'll use it.'

'I don't remember agreeing to that. I remember sitting there while you said it.'

'In that case you can hardly blame me for taking an each-way bet.'

'Define "usable".'

'Christ, Ray. We've been through that.'

'Let's go through it again.'

Skeats made a big mistake now. He heaved an extravagant sigh and went into Polonius mode: as if the fool in the room was me. 'This book,' he said patiently, 'is going to be the biggest Arts story of the year. They're holding a *junket* for it, for Christ's sake. Take it from me, this is not normal. Fifteen minutes I get with him. Timed by some flunky with a stopwatch, if you please. When there's a minute to go, they're going to ring a little bell. You think this is normal? This is a first-time novelist we're talking about. Normally they'll sit down with you for as long as you like. Longer. You can't get rid of the fuckers. Not Fingle. This guy's special. No one even knows what he looks like yet. They're keeping him under wraps, like he's the phantom of the fucking opera.'

'I know what he looks like.'

'No shit?'

'I saw the book in Tweedy's office.'

'What *does* he look like?'

'I won't spoil your surprise.'

Skeats shrugged, as if he'd be seeing him soon enough. 'You get what I'm saying, though? Tomorrow I interview him. Saturday week the interview goes on the front page. And I don't mean the front page of Arts. I mean the front page, as in page one. Two weeks after that we run an extract from the book. And two weeks after *that* it's our lead review. By which time a certain momentum will have built up. Are you with me, Ray? You still want me to define "usable"? Usable is something that'll be consistent with that momentum. Something that won't confuse people. Something that won't make them wonder, are we talking about two different books here, or what? Something that won't make the industry wonder if I've got a madman working for me.'

'As opposed to a toothless stooge.'

'If you force me to run Lodge's, I'll run Lodge's. I might as well be frank about that.'

'Last time we talked, you told me he was on his way out.'

'Barrett's a safe pair of hands, Ray. Don't underestimate what that means to me, being a safe pair of hands.'

Out on the floor, those guys with the nail guns were still going at it. Otherwise there was the sound made by a modern newspaper: the sound of not many people doing nothing much, on equipment that made no noise.

'So who're you sleeping with now?' I said. 'Jill Tweedy?'

'Ray. That is *way* beneath you.'

'What's the payoff then?'

'Grow up, Ray. You know this isn't about money.'

'What's it about?'

'It's about knowing which way the wind is blowing.'

'And which way,' I asked him, 'is the wind blowing?'

'Not your way, mate. Not the way you're going.'

Now he'd upshifted from confidence to aggression. Another bad play, at this delicate stage of proceedings. Another bad life choice. No, this was not going well. My resolve was taking dents all over the place.

'Lodge called him a stylist,' I said. 'Is that the sort of thing you want me to say?'

'I'm not telling you what to say.'

'You're just telling me what *not* to say.'

'No, I'm telling you I have an editorial policy, like every other editor in the history of the business. It'd be nice if you remembered that's what I am, mate, in the end. The editor. *Your* editor. It'd be nice if you at least *pretended* to respect me.'

'I thought I always had.' We were finally getting to the nub of things – now, at this faltering hour, a bit too late in the day to help either of us, especially him. This wasn't about Lodge, or Fingle, or Jade. It wasn't even about me, or just me. It was about rank. It was about Skeats's thirst for deference. If you didn't give him that, he felt like a man who looks in the mirror and sees nothing there.

'Does Lodge have any idea,' I asked him, 'what a stylist *is?*'

'Do *you?* A stylist is somebody that Lodge *says* is a stylist. End of story. They put it on the back of the book and it becomes a fact. This is the way the real world works.'

I half-wanted to tell him he was making a big mistake, talking to me in this tone. But I also wanted him to keep making it. I'd reached the point where it made things easier for me, not harder. I said, 'Have you read the book?'

'Ray, you're becoming a bit of a bore on this.'

'*Have you read this book?*'

'You know I haven't.'

'Well, I have. And there's something wrong with it. It reeks. It's like Fingle's *daring* you to call his bluff. It's like he's doing an Ern Malley.'

'Ray, do you ever wonder if you're in the wrong game?'

'No,' I lied. 'Do you?'

'A critic is meant to articulate what people are thinking. And who else thinks what you think, at this point? Does anyone? The trouble,' he said, 'is that you don't really seem to like books.'

I was still thinking about Ern Malley. It sounded like something I'd said before. Long ago, in a different life. I wanted to nail this impression down, but Skeats kept talking over my thoughts.

'And I happen to rub shoulders,' he was saying, 'with a lot of people who *do* like books. And I'll tell you something. All of them, to a fucking man, are *raving* about *The Tainted Land.*'

'Who are these fools? Name one person who's read it and says it's any good. And don't say Lodge.'

For a moment he hesitated: he seemed to be on the brink of saying something I *really* wouldn't like. Then he changed his mind and said: 'Ray, let's broaden the scope of this chat.'

'Yeah. Let's do that.'

'I feel we're at a crossroads here. A watershed.'

'So do I.'

'We may even be reaching the end of the line.'

'I feel that too.' I was drifting out of the scene now. I pictured myself back out on the road, driving into a future from which Skeats was already fading.

'I mean, I don't know what more I can do here.' He heaved a big terminal sigh. 'I've offered you the chance to play ball. And I don't just mean on this book. I mean in general, in the future, for good. And you don't seem all that interested. Which is fine, fair enough, okay. It's your choice. As long as you understand it's a permanent one.'

'If you've got no further use for me,' I said, 'then I've got no further use for you. Think that through.'

'That a reference to me and Jade?'

'Among other things.'

'I have thought it through, as it happens.' He looked over at the door again. It was still shut. It hadn't turned its own knob and freed its own latch since the last time he'd looked at it. He lowered his voice and said: 'You're a smart guy, Ray. Too smart, in some ways. But you play the percentages. And her and me, there's no percentage in it. You must be able to see that. I didn't kill her and I've got no idea who did. I knew her a bit, I fucked her a bit, we fixed a few reviews. End of story. You want to tell the world that, go ahead. But I don't see you being that stupid. That *cheap*. I can't see you smearing a dead girl for no good reason. A girl who's no longer around to defend herself. I can't see you telling the world she was a . . . Well. *We* know what she was really like. But nobody else does, not yet. And I don't see why you, of all people, would want to ruin their fantasy about her. It wouldn't be your style. After all, you're better than all the rest of us, aren't you? Isn't that your shtick?'

'I wouldn't bet on it.'

'I'll tell you what I *will* bet on,' he said. 'You liked her. You liked her a lot. And I don't think you want the tabloids to turn on her. I know you don't give a shit about me. You probably don't give a shit about my wife and kids either. Fine. But Jade's another story, isn't she? At least to you.' Here it came: one last clean wide revolting grin, one last drastic over-rating of his own wit. 'I'm calling your bluff, Ray. I just don't see you pissing on her memory in public. If you don't keep it sacred, who will?'

'Speaking of your wife,' I said, 'I hear she's out of town.'

'What the fuck,' he said with some surprise, 'has *that* got to do with it?'

I waved a careless hand. Nothing. Pure hatred is like pure love. It makes your decisions for you. What man could look at Skeats's vain and vacant face and not want it gone forever? Not me. That much was now clear. Somebody better than me, maybe. Somebody who knew him less well. But not me.

'Otherwise,' that face was saying, 'I don't think we've got much left to say to each other. I tried offering you more work, and look where that got us. There *is* no more work for an inflexible cunt like you. You refuse to see the big picture. Look around yourself, mate. The whole business is dying. And you want to argue the toss on whether some guy's a *stylist*, for Christ's sake.'

'And you want to save it by giving good reviews to bad books.'

'Pretty soon there won't be any books *at all*, Ray, good or bad. Is that what you want? What do you plan to review then? Don't you get it? If the ship goes down, so do we.'

'Maybe it deserves to go down. The industry fucked *itself*, Skeats. You can't keep selling people shit and telling them it's gold. Sooner or later you run out of customers.'

'I tried, Ray. I did my best with you. I cut you way more slack than anyone else would have. I'm starting to forget why I bothered. You just never got it.' He said that a bit sadly. A bit sadly, but not a lot. He thought the grave he'd just finished digging was mine.

'So we fend for ourselves now.' I was about ready to leave. 'Both of us are on our own.'

'Oh, I'll do all right,' Skeats said.

'Goodbye, Jeremy.' I stood up. 'It's been pointless knowing you. I never really worked out what it is you do, except fuck up people more talented than yourself.'

I was a step shy of the door when Skeats said to my back: 'Who did you think you were, Ray? Kenneth Tynan? Cyril Connolly? You were just a newspaper reviewer. That's all you ever were.'

I looked back at him. 'That's all they were too, you fool.'

'Once upon a time, maybe. Those days are dead. They're never coming back.'

Again I turned to go. I was out of memorable comebacks, and anyway Skeats wouldn't get to remember them for long. He looked half-embalmed already. The lofted hair, the plasticky witless face, the pale lipless smile. I was talking to Yorick's skull. Gel your flaxen locks an inch thick, pal. Gravity's coming for them.

I was touching the doorknob when Skeats said, 'You want to know who liked Fingle's book?'

He had one more knife to fling at my spine. Like a fool I turned around and let him fling it into my heart.

'Jade,' he said.

'Bullshit.'

'It's a fact. Take it from me.'

'No. She was *much* better than that.'

'That's where you're wrong. She was the first person I ever heard talk him up. She used to lie there and rave about the prick, well before anyone else had ever heard of him. She told me he was the real deal. Oh yeah, and she called him a stylist too.'

'Then she was lying.'

'She wasn't. She liked the book. She liked *him*. You think you knew everything about her? You only ever fucked her twice, by your own admission. No, Ray. There's a few things about her you never found out. Let's add this to the list. Matter of fact, she didn't just like him. She discovered him. This book was her baby.'

'Now that I *know* is bullshit. Jill Tweedy discovered him.'

'And who told you that?' Skeats demanded with a leer. 'Don't tell me. Let me guess. Jill Tweedy, right?'

That one caught me flat-footed. It was an arid feeling: standing there at the net and watching Skeats pass me with a cold winner. It made me feel old, clueless, dead on my feet.

'Sometimes it *stuns* me,' he was saying, 'how little you really know about this business. Jade's dead. She's gone. You think a leathery old warrior like Jill Tweedy is going to sit back and let a *corpse* take credit for the biggest book of the year? You think a senior editor's going to admit that Fingle got discovered by a *publicist*, and a dead one at that?'

Still that foul feeling of having nothing to say. After all those years of hacking away at my words, he'd reduced me to silence at last. Not that it mattered any more. Anything I said was headed straight for the abyss, unless I remembered it myself. But that had been the story of my career.

'She was his biggest fan, Ray.' He was talking to my back now. 'If you don't like it, go home and take it up with her ghost.'

I didn't wait that long. I got the inquest started in the car, where there were no other ghosts in the way. My memory of her was in the last stage of collapse. The gutted edifice of her lies was finally coming down. If she had really liked Fingle's book, I had no more shreds of her to cling to, and not much of a self left to do the clinging with. I was unravelling as fast as she was. Soon one of us would be a shapeless heap of rags on the floor. It was a race towards non-existence, and I didn't care who won it. I looked at the hard grey road in front of me, bone-pale in the headlights, and wondered what was keeping it there. Everything else had been snatched from under me. Why not that too? I drove fast, so I would make it home while the earth still held.

She couldn't have liked Fingle's book. If I knew one real thing about her, that was it. I was ready to concede almost anything else. For all I cared she'd fucked the guy. If she'd met him, she probably had. The fucking I could take. I'd grown numb to that. But the idea that she'd liked his stuff – *that* stuff. If that was true I was ready to die. The world was a meaningless place, and I wanted no part of it. If *The Tainted Land* was her kind of book, I hadn't known her at all.

The road ahead, in the ashen wash of my lights, was starting to look like the same scarred stretch of tarmac all the time, endlessly cycling on a cheap loop. The landscape was in re-runs, like my brain. A half-hour shy of home, when I could wait no more, I dropped a couple of red-and-whites. They would take about an hour to bite, and when they did I would be down for the day. Thirty more minutes on the road, thirty on the couch: that was about as much consciousness as I was up for. After that, the fog would come down.

Maybe I hadn't known her. The prospect had to be entertained. I almost wanted it to be true. It would mean I could let her go. It would also mean I was a madman, but who said I wasn't? Nobody except me. Maybe Skeats was right: maybe my standards were so out of whack that I was effectively insane. If I wasn't, a lot of other people were. Maybe Fingle *was* a genius. Maybe I *did* kill Jade, and Missy too. Maybe the voice on the phone was a voice in my head. Maybe the man who would visit Skeats tonight would be me.

All that horseshit had to be considered – for about thirty seconds. And then it had to be shovelled aside for good, because time was running out. Fingle's book was trash. It didn't matter how few people could see it. It remained a fact. It was an epic for fools, and the girl I knew had not been a fool. Yes, she had used me. Yes, she'd told me a few lies. Yes, she had fucked Skeats and Vagg and probably Fingle. But I still thought I'd known her in a way that they had not. If I was wrong, I didn't know myself either. But I wasn't wrong. Not all of it had been lies. She'd given me wit, and nothing is less fakeable than that. She was the opposite of a fool. She knew what bullshit smelt like, and Fingle's book smelt of nothing else. Of *course* she hadn't liked it. That meant she'd been lying to Skeats when she said she had. More than that: it meant she'd *gone out of her way* to lie about it. Now why would she have done that?

By now I was at home. I drove through the front gate without slowing, without taking questions. I had about ten minutes left to think straight in. I needed to lie down. I'd have liked to do it on my bed, but I was ready to assume that Missy was still there. I wasn't about to go and check. The bedroom door was still shut. The undergap was still plugged by a towel. I lay on the couch instead. Jesus: she was still in there all right. Her stench had ramified while I was gone. Was it a metaphor for something? My rotting life? My dead career? I heard a muted sound in there that might have been the buzzing of flies. I wanted to stop hearing it. I got up and dragged the couch as far away from the bedroom as it would go. It knocked something over that smashed. I didn't bother checking what. I stepped on a shard of it and the shard went in deep. I left it in there and let the blood spill. Why not, since there was blood everywhere else? I lay down again, feeling the first billows of the descending haze: the dope mingling with my pain like blood in bathwater. She'd lied to Skeats. She'd told him Fingle had talent. She'd laid claim to discovering him. Why this rush to claim credit for a cretin? The answer was close. I almost had it. It was like a balloon that kept drifting down from the ceiling to my fingertips. I kept trying to seize it, and it kept squeaking back up out of reach. And I was falling away from it now, sinking away from lucidity. I wasn't going to get it, not tonight, not in time to save Skeats. I had dropped those pills a fatal ten minutes too early. He came into my head now – softly, a ghost already. I was falling away from him too. I had done my best. I'd driven there to warn him. But before I could save his life he had tried to take mine, by telling me I would never write again. To a writer that is a death threat. If Skeats knew anything he'd have known that. One man in that room was going home to face oblivion. Why should I have let it be me? I've got integrity, but not that much.

Just before I went under I had one last thought. It went something like: You didn't do enough. It's not too late to do more. If you don't, you'll regret it forever.

But that was it. My flesh was weak. It always has been. I was out.

I woke in the dark and knew he was dead already. I knew it because I knew everything. Four or five hours of sleep and my brain had tightened around the truth like a fist. I knew who'd killed her and I knew why. I knew there was no hurry any more. I knew Skeats wouldn't answer the phone if I rang him, now or ever again. I dialled him to prove it, and stood there in the dark while his phone rang out. The old ritual, one last time: me calling, him not picking up. Finally he had a solid excuse. I tried to picture the scene at the other end, him in his empty house, splayed there in his share of the dark. Strangled? I doubted it. The man who had killed him was small in every way. Even when killing women he liked to skew the odds. He'd have taken a blade there at the least. He had killed Skeats for his own benefit, not for mine. For his own reasons he needed him gone by tomorrow. I pictured a dark room with darker splashes on its walls. I saw defensive wounds on Skeats's palms, like pursed lips. Had he died with his eyes open or shut? Either way, they were closed to the big picture. His killer's face would have meant nothing to him. He had gone out as he'd lived, understanding nothing.

I put the phone down. I had another job to do. I hadn't hit bottom yet. I opened my laptop and stuck the flash drive in its socket. The password box came up. I put the word *Fingle* in it. It didn't work. She was craftier than that. I tried *The Tainted Land*. That failed too but I kept going, like a crazed marathon man in sight of the finish line. Each defeat was one more necessary stride towards the tape. *Ern Malley*, I typed. No result. *Punchinello*. That's what Fingle had been, and still was even now: her puppet, her clown. Still no result. *Stewart*. Nothing. *McAuley*. No. *Frankenstein*. *Prospero*. *Oz*. Then I typed the word *Caliban*.

It worked.

A square window came up, showing the drive's decrypted contents: her insurance policy, her rainy-day Fingle file. The window had two icons in it. One was a folder called *The Tainted Land*. The other was a video file with no name. Rashly, I opened that one first.

With computers there is no time for second thoughts. The video started at once, and suddenly there was no prospect of looking away. The image was subdued and barren-looking: a moving picture, although nothing was moving in it yet. I saw a double bed in a dark room. A venetian blind threw fillets of streetlight across it. I knew the *mise-en-scène*: her bedroom, pre-blood stains, pre-murder, pre-me. The camera, I guessed, sat on the dresser I had raided on the night Fingle tried to kill me. The scene waited darkly for someone to enter it. I wanted to rip the drive from its socket before the action started. But my body wouldn't do it. I had to watch what was about to happen, even though I knew it would never leave my head. It was going to be a snuff film, and the victim was going to be me.

Here they came, first her, then Fingle. She was leading him by the hand. They were both naked. His cock, inevitably, was larger and nastier than mine. It was horribly half-aroused, a windsock on a blustery day. When his back was to the lens she looked past him and broke the fourth wall – just for a moment, but pointedly. She knew about the camera and he didn't. Then she sat on the bed's near edge and lay back and opened her thighs. And the worst novelist in the world knelt before her, and the gates to heaven were eclipsed by the moronic rear of his head. He gorged himself there in vicious silence, like a mole burrowing its way to the earth's core. The James Dean hairdo dipped and bobbed. I watched now because I knew I would never watch again, once the horror show was done. This would be my last look at her living body. Those bites were not on her thigh yet. Before Fingle's head got in the way I'd made a point of looking, and the site was clean. I had a feeling it wouldn't be for long. Yes: watch now. His unlettered primeval face was getting bored. It roved back down towards her knee, or back up to it – the geography was inverted. Then he roved back the other way, seeking paler flesh, like a starving man who'd finished the fruit and still wanted the rind. Soon he reached a soft place that would have been her buttock if she was standing up. His neck went tense and she uttered a ragged yelp: one-eighth pleasure, seventh-eighths pain. I knew how deep his teeth went because I had seen the wound myself, days later, maybe weeks, when it looked like a wine stain fringed by rusty staples. And I had thought, while looking at it: one day, when I know her better, I will ask her about the degenerate who did that. And here she was, telling me. I watched her seize a fistful of his hair – not to pull his head away, but to force it deeper in. Whether or not she liked Fingle, she liked what he was doing. I couldn't fool myself about that. But how could she have believed that it would have no price tag? It always does. She had been so young, and I had never felt so old.

I reached for the drive's plastic hilt. I was ready to shut the show down now. I believed I had caught its drift. But before I could yank the plug she broke the fourth wall again. She raised her gaze from the top of his skull and looked straight down the barrel of the lens, at me. And our eyes met, and I knew they would never meet again, and I didn't have the heart to break the clinch before she did. She had thought she was bulletproof. She had thought Fingle was the clueless one, the one in over his head. She was smarter than he was, but not smart enough to know that smartness doesn't matter. The sword is mightier than the pen. The barbarians always win. But even I had been too young to really get that, until about yesterday.

Finally she looked away from me, forever this time, and in one fast slithery move she pushed him to his feet and slid off the bed and knelt on the carpet and dipped her face to send him to paradise and me the rest of the way to hell. Before either of us could get there I yanked the drive like a rotten tooth. The screen froze and went grey, then black. And then it was just me in the dark again, with the laptop's speakers uttering a barren howl of protest. I'd have uttered one too, if I'd thought there was any point.

When I felt like moving again I restarted the machine and was rebathed in its light. The worst was over now. The rest could be safely predicted. Redocking the drive, I re-entered the password and opened the folder labelled

The Tainted Land. Inside it were two documents. I clicked the first one and scanned a few pages. It was Fingle's transom draft of the novel. It made the published version look like something by Rilke. Here was how the tackler of the big themes thought you wrote sentences and spelled words. If the final text had looked like this I'd have been quicker to suspect him of derangement. Not of multiple murder, though: it stunned me that he'd had the wherewithal to pull that off. It stunned me that a man who wrote like this could pull off anything, including tying his own shoes. But Jade had made the same wrong guess. Fingle wasn't a straw man. He just wrote like one.

The second document was the work as I'd read it in proof. It was Fingle's abysmal manuscript touched up by a literate hand – that of Jade. Literate, but not literary. She hadn't turned it into anything worthwhile. There had never been any chance of that, and anyway it hadn't been her aim. No, she had preserved his essential worthlessness. All she'd done was put a little makeup on the turkey, knowing that a little would be more than enough to fool the likes of Tweedy, and Skeats, and Lodge. Plausibility, and then hype. In literary circles, what else is there?

I hadn't been blind, I'd been deaf. She'd told me about the whole scam. Fingle was her long con, her retirement plan. Fifty per cent for life, in exchange for never blowing his secret. She *had* pulled him from obscurity: not because she thought he had talent, but because she knew he had absolutely none. She was sick of the usual drill: ho-hum books by so-so writers, ingeniously marketed by her. She'd wanted to prove it could be *all* her: a bubble of pure promotion, spun around a product that had no property except bulk.

So she'd raided the slush pile for something even worse than usual. And she'd found Fingle – a selection that confirmed her genius. His book wasn't merely no good; it also thought itself a searing masterpiece. It had size, scope, ambition – all the things a marketer could *really* sink her teeth into. Sell them hard enough, get a big enough ball rolling, and people would forget that the concept of quality had ever existed. Jade wasn't ahead of her time, and she hadn't wanted to be. She was *of* it, fully and audaciously: she was deeply in tune with its resonances. She'd pulled off the perfect postmodern swindle.

It was her masterpiece, and she'd told me all about it. All she'd lied about was the tense. It wasn't something she was saving for the future. She was pulling the scam already, even as we lay there. All along it had been happening right in front of me, with Fingle as her wretched Pinocchio. She had knocked off his edges and slipped him into the machine. And she couldn't resist telling someone, and the someone had been me. Here was my consolation at last. She hadn't told Skeats, or Vagg, or Jill Tweedy. She'd told me. Had she seen the same fire in my eyes that I saw in hers? Did she feel we had a future?

She was magnificent. You had to hand it to her. *The Tainted Land* was an enormous piss-take, a vast fraudulent happening, an act of glorious and wicked subversion. And it had all worked perfectly – until the bodies started to fall, starting with hers. She hadn't guessed that Fingle would be a psychopath. Maybe she should have. A semi-literate who thought he was Tolstoy: that reality-gulf should have given her pause. More than that: it should have scared her. Delusion on that scale is not harmless. Instead of a stooge she'd got a monster, with a few ideas of his own. If only I'd been on hand to tell her about writers and madness. Even good writers have their pride, their fears, their insecurities. We all think we're better than we really are. We're all a bit nuts. Those of us who are a lot nuts should not be toyed with. She'd been playing with fire.

Well, so was Fingle now. I yearned for daybreak, even if it turned out to be my last. There was just one body left to fall. No more thinking, no more ceaseless arguments about merit or subjectivity or taste. Just two deluded scriveners going at it, *mano a mano*, one last time. The way I felt, that didn't sound like the end of the world. The way I felt, the end of the world didn't sound like the end of the world either.

12

In a spirit of closure I swung by Skeats's house en route to the junket. His blood wasn't on my hands but it was in my head. Seeing it for real would be my punishment, my penance.

But when I found him I felt something dangerously close to nothing. I was punch-drunk on dead bodies. His front door was wide open. In a big central room he sat posed half-upright in the angle of the floor and wall. I hung back beyond the reach of his stains. I didn't want him on my boots. He looked the way my prose looked after he'd improved it. His eyes were open. His face wore a look of mild bafflement, as it pretty much always had. It asked the same question in death that it had asked in life: how did a man like me end up in a position like this? His hair was a riot of golden loops still, moussey to the last, a live pooch sitting vigil over its dead master. It had been a mistake, I already saw, to grant him the seriousness of death. From now on he would no longer be around to remind everyone what he was really like. They would talk about his services to literature. Not existing would be a clear plus for him. I looked at him and thought: You finally beat me. You're out of it and I'm still here, looking at the worst thing I have ever done. Maybe I owed him an apology. I could subtract it from the many he had died owing me.

I went to his bedroom and found his press pass, and a white envelope containing three polaroids of Jade. Only a very bad man would have wanted to keep them. I kept them.

In the big old hotel, at the entrance to the function room, I flashed Skeats's ID. The skinny blonde on the door gave a mild shrug and let me go by. From my angle she didn't look that young. From hers I looked so generally middle-aged that she saw no difference between me and the mugshot of Skeats. That hurt, even through the haze of everything else. My craving for apocalypse went up a notch.

The function room was a big glossy sanctum with a parquet floor and panelled walls the colour of burnt toffee. Its function, on any normal day, would have been to keep a man like Fingle out. Today he was the guest of honour. The walls were draped with big silk sails or banners stamped with the cover art of his book. They looked as classy and restrained as ten-foot-high advertising materials can. I half-recalled a line from Ern Malley: something about the hoisted banners of praise. There were about fifty people in the room and all I saw was their backs. Their faces were all aimed at a vividly lit clearing at the room's far end. I drifted towards it as if in a dream. And I *was* in a dream. I was in Jade's dream. In her version she had been here too, and I probably hadn't. In her version she hadn't been dispensable. Beyond the crowd, on the near shore of all the fake white light, two big guys in semi-sufficient T-shirts were tensed over a pair of TV cameras. Out in the core of the light's glow were two swivel chairs. In one of these sat the current doyenne of TV news entertainment. In the other chair was Fingle.

I already knew what he looked like, so I'd thought I was in for no more surprises. But I hadn't guessed what he would wear on his big day out. Who could have? Nobody was that good at guessing. He wore black pointed boots, tight purple jeans, a collarless white shirt and a chocolate waistcoat. Above all he wore a black broad-brimmed hat with a white feather stuck in its band. I recognised him after a second or two, but only because Jimi Hendrix was dead. Fingle was talking, and the doyenne was listening gravely, nodding her head. Who could listen gravely to a man wearing those threads? They reeked of clinical madness. Couldn't she smell it?

I drifted towards the action, unperceived by Fingle or anyone else. So this was what he looked like out of the shadows, the man who had destroyed my life. The shadows had a lot to be said for them, clearly. I thought I deserved a less laughable nemesis. One has a right to demand that one's executioner shall not be a clown. But this was how fragile my happiness had been. It had been shattered by a buffoon. I kept drifting towards him, still unseen. I had a weird sense that I no longer existed. All these lights and cameras and people, and none of them pointing at me. My star was fading. All I saw was backs. One of them belonged to Jill Tweedy. She was standing up at ringside, watching her adopted boy shine. Was the world really this desperate for cultural icons?

When I got to the outer ring of the white light I propped. I didn't want Fingle spotting me just yet. But Jill Tweedy had a sixth sense for the uninvited guest. She turned and saw me, and her face crumpled with vexation before she could stop it. She strode over and whispered, 'Ray.'

'Jill.'

'I was expecting Jeremy.'

'He had a rough night.'

'Or even Barrett.'

'I'm afraid you're stuck with me.'

She didn't bother to hide what she thought of that. I had lowered the junket's tone. I was fucking up Finglefest. It didn't matter that I was one of her authors too, sort of. Right now she was wearing her Fingle hat: she was repping the prestige end of the slate, the prize-wrangling end. And I belonged with the crooks and the dieters and the celebs. I watched her ponder, briefly, the scorching phone call she thought she'd be making to Skeats later on. And then she looked at her watch with resignation. She had a pep rally to run, and I was the next cheerleader whether she liked it or not. Briskly she talked me through the basics of Fingle etiquette. No personal questions, or Fingle would walk. No soul-sucking photography. ('He's got a black eye anyway,' Tweedy said.) Fifteen minutes of face-time all up, with a warning bell at ten minutes and a final bell at fourteen. What would happen if I was still there a minute later she didn't say. I found it a moot question myself.

Fingle still hadn't seen me. The TV people were done with him now. They were killing their lights, collapsing their tripods. He sat there in the sudden gloom and inspected his shirt front. He didn't bother scoping the room. Why would he? He knew Skeats wasn't showing up. He thought he had the next fifteen minutes to himself. His fan club splintered and drifted to the side wall, where a row of trestle tables was decked with the kind of food you get at book launches or when someone has died. With Fingle you had both things at once, although his fan club didn't know it yet. They were a complacent-looking bunch, Fingle's crowd. They didn't look much like people who read books. They were dressed too well, for one thing. Whoever they were, they seemed to think the main event was now over. The moving pictures and sound bites had been snared. All that remained was for the loners like me, the revenants of print, to slink up there like Oliver Twist and receive Fingle's dregs. This part didn't qualify as a spectator event. The cognoscenti could half-watch it from a distance while talking about other things. That suited me fine. I needed a crowd, but I didn't want an audience. I strolled towards him. He had removed his hat to confirm that the feather was still present and upright. It was. This pleased him. I had time to see, while the hat was off, the mangy bald spot I had conferred on him with my teeth, that night in Jade's house. The wound was leathery and textured and brownish-red, like an old six-stitcher. With a smirk of lowbrow satisfaction Fingle put hat and feather back on his head. When he looked up and saw me filling the empty chair beside him, he stopped having a good time.

I said nothing for a while. I let him think about what was happening. His face had gone slack, with a makeshift smile draped across it for show. Behind it his vestigial brain was in overdrive, pedalling for traction like a cartoon dog

stuck between cliffs. I watched him weigh the permutations.
I found them a bit confusing myself. He knew who I was,
but he didn't know if I knew who he was. We had talked on
the phone. Two nights ago he had dragged a corpse past me
while I slept on the couch. Once in a dark house he had tried
to kill me hand to hand, and I had done my best to kill him
back. What he didn't know was if I'd joined the dots yet. On
that question he was still in suspense.

For the moment I let him stay there. A PR girl had swept
into earshot and was buzzing around us like a fly. It was the
blonde who'd looked right through me at the door. Looking
right through me again, she put a fresh glass of water on
the knee-high table between me and Fingle. She put a big
fat copy of his book there too, in case I'd missed its name
on my way past all those ten-foot banners. She wanted to
be noticed, but not by me. She had eyes only for Fingle:
Fingle in his Hendrix hat and Civil War waistcoat. If worn
by anyone else, these threads would have made her laugh
out loud. But Fingle was a celebrity. He had the gravity
of fame, and that changed everything. I wanted to tell her
what he did to literature-loving publicity girls, but maybe
that wouldn't bother her either. I waited, wanting her gone.
I was desolate and sick of an old passion. I yearned to be
alone with him. Her lust for him was trivial next to mine.

But still she loitered, still she fussed. She was starting to
throw me nonplussed looks, as if she thought I was squandering my face-time with the master. It hadn't occurred to
me that the clock was running. I threw him a softball question for show. Tell me about the title, I said. Tell me about
the taint. You seem to know an awful lot about history. Fill
me in on the big picture.

Through a tight smile he did his best, but his best was even worse than usual. His voice was the voice from the phone, but it had lost a lot of its sass. He kept looking queasily down at my notepad. It was open, but I wasn't writing down what he said. I was ready to put on a show, but not that much of a show. Being this close to his body sickened me. All those things it had done. Nor was I feeling that crazy about myself. No matter how civilised you are, you feel somehow shamed and inferior when faced with the man who has ruined you with violence. Or maybe I was just less civilised than I thought. The quadrant of his face that I'd headbutted in her room was still discoloured by a rich saffron bruise. Here at least was one thing to be proud of: my last act of literary criticism, and possibly my finest.

The PR girl was running out of reasons to stick around. Maybe Fingle had thrown her a crumb or two of encouragement earlier in the day, but he was in no mood to throw her another one now. Finally she got the message and went away. So now it was just us, me and Fingle in the wash of the room's noise. A few faces were pointed our way from the buffet table. They could see us but they couldn't hear us. I took my chance while I had it. I leant towards him, put an intrigued book-chatter's frown on my face, and said: 'If I'd known who you were, I'd have hit you harder.'

Panic washed over his face like a wave full of sand.

'Don't get out of that chair,' I told him. 'If you do, it's over. Stay put. Stay calm. Nothing's going to happen. Not here, not now. If I was going to raise a stink I'd have raised it by now. Do you understand? We're going to talk. That's all that's going to happen. Nod your head, Fingle. Smile. Look like you're being interviewed.'

He nodded. That ailing smile twitched on his lips like a dying moth.

I said, 'I know everything. Don't bother hoping I don't.'

He said nothing.

'Nobody else knows, not yet. Maybe they don't have to.'

His crippled smile writhed and squirmed, flicking its dying limbs in the air. There was an alarming heat in his eyes. I wondered if I'd miscalculated. Maybe I had made Jade's mistake, and revved the little engine of his brain a needle-notch too far. For a bad few seconds it seemed possible that he would blow his foul wad here and now, and do his thing in the middle of his own coronation. And I didn't want that. This wasn't the time or place for Armageddon. I wanted the earned climax, the crafted denouement.

'For Christ's sake, relax,' I told him. 'People are watching. Smile. Nod. *Say* something.'

'I don't know what you're talking about,' he said.

'The story of your life,' I said, 'and for once it's not true. Tell me: does part of you wish she was still around?' For the sake of the spectators I had uncapped my pen. Its tip quivered in the churning air between us. 'You must, at times like this. You must wish she was here to pull a string and make you talk. Make you sound like a real person. But you made your choice. You got what you wanted. It's all you now, Fingle. You're a literary man, thanks to her. So come on. Let's hear you. Wow me. Hit me with an aperçu.'

Silence again. He looked like an enraged child. I wanted to tear that look off his face with my bare trembling hands. Lust wasn't the right word for it. When you want a woman you can wait, and savour the waiting. With Fingle I was having a hard time not lunging right now. So, from the look of it, was he.

'Did Skeats,' I went on, 'have any last words?'

No answer.

'I'm guessing he didn't.' I tried a smile myself, but it felt no more plausible than Fingle's. 'He wasn't the lapidary type. You didn't need to kill him, by the way. He knew nothing. Jade didn't tell him the important stuff. You prob-ably thought he'd turn up today and spoil your party. Well, he wouldn't have. Were you worried about that night on her driveway? Did you think he saw your face? He didn't. Of course he didn't. He looked but he didn't perceive. That was the story of *his* life. Tell me: were you wearing this get-up when he saw you – the Rick Danko threads? It wouldn't have mattered, even if you were. He *still* wouldn't have clocked you. He wasn't an observant man. He was probably looking at his phone. He was probably taking a selfie. You killed him for nothing.'

The twitching mania in his eyes had cooled to fury now. He could see that the end was not going to happen here. He had worked out that I didn't want that any more than he did.

'Say something, Fingle. Be deep. There's a girl over there looking right at us.'

'You're a dead man,' he said.

'Nice. Is that one of Dostoyevsky's, or did you come up with it yourself? Anyway, you might be right. One of us is a dead man. I'll give you that much. But we'll get to that. First let's talk about Jade. I know I'm not meant to ask about your private life, but let's live dangerously. She kept your draft, Fingle. She saved it for a rainy day.

I've seen it. Sweet Jesus. I thought the *published* version was scary. That thing should have been strangled at birth. And yet look at what she did with it.' I spread my hand at the waning junket – the silk banners, the literati flitting around the finger food like koi. 'All this is her, Fingle. Don't think any of it is you. This is as high as a marketer can fly. If only she'd lived to see it. A bubble of pure hype, and you're the puff of air inside. That was your job – to be nothing. To be a vacuum. To be *no good*. How did that conversation go – the one where she told you what she was up to? The one where you found out what you really were to her? A jumped-up, repulsive little Oswald. A lab rat who thought he was a PhD. It must have been a bad scene. Was that when you decided she had to go? Was the rest just being patient, waiting till she'd served her purpose? Waiting till the lie had its own momentum, so you could safely chuck her over the side?'

I watched his infinitely nasty face darken again with boiling blood. It struck me that this look, or something like it, must have been the last thing she'd seen on earth. I could think of no worse sight to go out on.

'What did she think she was doing,' I asked him, or myself, or her, or nobody, 'messing around inside a head like yours? She forgot you were real. Her imagination wasn't that vivid. She thought you'd be all hollow inside, like your book. She forgot you might have a few ideas of your own. Woeful ideas, like that feather in your hat. Like the hat itself. Poor things, but your own. She thought you'd be grateful for anything. She thought fifty per cent would do you. And why not? It was a hundred per cent more than you deserved. How did it feel, when you found out she was laughing behind your back? Or did she make the mistake of laughing into your face as well?'

Jill Tweedy rang her first chime. Five minutes left.

'I want you to come for me, Fingle. That's how this is going to end. You want me dead? Fine. Come and make it happen, tonight. You know where I live. The doors will be unlocked. I'll be waiting. Everyone else is dead already. I'm the last one left who knows anything. Do it, Fingle. Come for me. Let's close the circle tonight.'

He smiled. He said nothing.

'This is a one-time offer,' I told him. 'If I wake up tomorrow and one of us isn't dead, it's over. I walk down my drive and I hold my final press conference. But today – today is your lucky day. Today I have immortal longings in me. I want death. Preferably yours, but mine'll do. I'm tired. I've had it. Maybe it's time I made a half-graceful exit. This is your world, not mine. If books like yours are what people want, they can have them. If that's what they want to call literature, they can do that too. I'm sick of trying to stop them. I'm done. The one thing I still want out of life is a final chance to fuck you up. You scared it's a trap? I'm telling you exactly what it will be. You and me in a room. Just us two animals. The thumb drive will be in my pocket. Everything's on it. I'm the last one who knows. Kill me, take the drive, and all this will be yours.' I spread my hand again: the banners, the cameras, the lights, the women. 'You're close, Fingle. You're so close. You're like Gatsby. Know who he is? Your dream's right in front of your face. Don't let me snatch it away. Right now, as we speak, while you sit there like an op-shop dummy, Barrett Lodge is reviewing your book. And it's glowing, even by his standards. I've had a sneak peek. He will call you a stylist. He will call you the saviour of modern literature. Skeats won't be around to print it, thanks to you, but somebody like him will be. Maybe it'll be Lodge himself. You want to throw all that away? I doubt you do. Tonight, Fingle. Come for me. Do it. You've run out of other people to kill.'

Somewhere beyond the reach of the light, Jill Tweedy rang her final bell. We had a minute left. It hit me that I was probably having the last conversation of my life. And look at the man I was having it with. The destroyer of love, the wrecker of literature. If this was the way the world ended, I wouldn't miss it.

'We're talking now because we won't be talking then,' I told him. 'There will be no more dialogue. Understand? This is it. If you've got any final words, say them now. I've said mine.'

'You could have saved him,' Fingle said. 'You could have warned him. I knew you wouldn't. You're no better than I am.'

I shook my head. 'No, Fingle. No. Leave the philosophical stuff to me. You just turn up tonight, and do what you're good at.'

What Jill Tweedy did at the fifteen-minute mark I will never know, because I was already gone.

13

It was dark before I got home. On the last part of the steep twisting road my headlights raked up through the bush and ignited the big grey gums. Shreds of fog hung over the bitumen like dental nerves on an X-ray. Frogs and rats skittered out of my light and got reswallowed by the scrub. A feral dog bounded up out of the long grass and ran beside me for a while, this big pale freak of a hellhound loping along in the fog. There was something gimpy about his stride. His fur was a mess. He had just enough sense to avoid my wheels, but not enough to get out of my lights. He kept pace with me for a long time, lolloping along strangely like a bad old cartoon. His eyes looked shiny but dead. Finally he peeled away and faded back into the trees.

At the foot of my driveway I met a stranger omen. There was nobody there. No trucks, no vans. The whole carnival had packed up and moved on. All that waiting and they would miss the end. It spooked me, for half a minute. Then it shrivelled away and joined the list of things that no longer mattered: the fading things of the world. I was a ghost already. History had started to happen without me.

Inside I turned on no lights. I'm good at moving around the place in the dark. That much edge I would have on him. The air hadn't stopped reeking of sweet bad meat. I went to the sink and opened the little door under it. Somewhere in there was a claw hammer, standing inverted on its richly solid head. I felt around till I found it. I found a bottle too. It wasn't empty yet. That was one personal affair I could straighten out while I waited.

I shoved the armchair to the middle of the room and sat there in the dark with the hammer at one foot and the bottle at the other. Out in the sterile wind, the fronds of the big palm trees cracked like flags at a car yard. The big side window shuddered, as if a condemned man was shaking the bars of its uprights. One last animal act in the dark, then. That was how it had started: me and Jade, here in this room. A month ago, in calendar time. A bad month. Thinking about it would be a waste of my last few hours. But they were going to feel wasted anyway, whatever I did with them. I swigged from the bottle and put it back on the floor. How do you fill up your last night on the planet? There is no good answer. Nothing is quite up to the job. So you feel paralysed. Time curdles and goes sour on you. After a while I stopped returning the bottle to the floor between swigs. I wanted a thick bath of nectar between me and what was about to happen. Hammer on bone, the horror of terminal violence. Who wants to be fully there for that? Fingle, maybe. Not me.

Out in the wind, something plastic and hollow skittered across the dirt of the drive. That didn't bother me. Noises were okay. Silence was the thing to worry about. When he came, silence was the sound he would make. Stealth he could do. Suddenly he would just be here. But he would have a lot of floor to cross before he got to me. I weighed the hammer and I weighed the bottle. For the moment the bottle was heavier, and would make the bigger dent in his skull. But only for the moment. If the moment lasted much longer I would have to reassess.

The darkness was good. It was working for me. It was getting me back to my roots as an organism. With the lights on, in a room packed with fools, it's easy to be half in love with death. In the dark you feel less Keatsian. You rediscover your will to stick around. If it's either you or the other guy it might as well be you, especially if the other guy is Dallas Fingle. Also the booze was doing its work. It was starting to lubricate my limbs. They felt violence-primed, ripe for affray. The readiness hummed in them like static.

I got up and put on a record. Maybe the booze was working too well. I remember worrying about that, as I stood there in the glow of the amp's tubes. I looked for something quiet, something I would hear him coming over. I picked the Goldberg Variations: the preferred vinyl of the Hollywood psycho. I returned to the armchair and sat in the dark. Piano trills rippled fraily in the wind. They sounded better than I'd remembered, either because I was drunk or because I was about to die. You should have listened to things like this more often, I thought. You should have had that sort of life. You should have gone out to halls and listened to people play instruments. You shouldn't have shut yourself off from human contact. You should have tried harder to be somebody else. You had one life and you fucked it up. You should never have smashed your skull on that slab. Doing that was a bad move all round. When it happened, you should never have resurfaced. You should have taken the world's hint and stayed down there for good. From that day on, it was always going to be half a life. You should have chucked in writing when you were twenty, the way everybody else does. You should have been someone people needed. You should have been a fisherman, a shopkeeper. You should have spent less time alone. You should have fucked more and read less. There were people around you, once. You let them fall away. You put your head down and wrote things for people you didn't know. And when you came back up for air you were old, and everyone was gone. You put the world on hold, and it hung up on you. And the other people never read your stuff anyway. You should have fucked more, read less, and written nothing. You should have money, like everybody else. You should have stuff, like everybody else. You should have a wife and kids and a house and a dog like everybody else. There should be someone here with you now. It should be her. You should never have let her leave. What did you think it was all for, all those hours and months and years of pushing words around pages? It was for her. It was to get a girl like that to your door. She was the point of it all, the payoff. You should have seen that before it was too late. Her on the doorstep: that was the big moment. Everybody gets one. That was yours. How did you not see it? You should have dropped to your knees and hooped your arms around her and buried your face in the warm cove of her body and never let her go. You should have renounced everything else on the spot. You should have known you'd love her eventually and you should have started straight away, when it still might have made a difference.

The first side of the record ended. Down on the road a car went by. That had been my life: forty years of thinking things over when things *were* over. Forty years of seeing things clearly but too late. In his office, during the last two minutes we'd shared on the planet, Skeats had told me I'd wasted my life. He had been dead right, and now he was just dead. Those facts were not unconnected. There are some things you just don't get to say to another man, especially if they are true. Squandering your life is not a small deal. But it doesn't happen all at once. The bad news creeps up on you. When I was twenty, I thought the world would care about what I wrote, if I wrote it well enough. The evidence that it never would took a long time to turn irrefutable. By the time it did, it was too late to change my ways. I had less time left than I had heaped on the bad bet. All those hours at the keyboard. All those drafts. All those times in the dead of night when I turned on the light and scribbled down some phrase I thought someone might like in the non-existent future. I needn't have bothered. I could have stayed in bed all day and jerked off. I could have settled for being third-rate but solvent. It was all for nothing, all that time.

I got up and flipped the record. Back in the chair I closed my eyes. Maybe every life feels like a waste, when you look at it from the end. And shapeless, too: half-meant and half-accident. You could call my errors self-inflicted, but from the inside they didn't feel like that. A self I no longer was went off a garage roof one day, and the self I became kept leaping, kept seeking the concrete. I did those things, but it was hard to remember deciding to, or having much choice.

In the dark, waiting for Fingle, I recalled no day or moment when I could seriously have changed my fate. That original fall or jump: say I could rewind the tape beyond it, and play things forward again. Would I still go near the edge? How could I not, when I have never known why I did? If I made any deliberate choices up there, I forgot them at the moment of impact. But maybe I thought something like: This is art. Take the leap, and somehow the landing will work. Write, commit yourself, and something will break your fall. It's worked for others. There will be a public down there. They will catch you. They won't let you hit the ground. Well, I hit the ground then, and I never stopped hitting it, and I still didn't know if I chose the fall or the fall chose me. All I knew was that the difference didn't matter. Either way the result was the same.

I heard something from the bedroom, or thought I did. I waited to hear it again. Nothing. A trick of the ear. My eyes were still closed. Sleep was starting to want me. A rattling blast of wind. The power dipped out for a second. The record went sluggish then surged back up to speed. Another blast of wind. I sat up sharply. About five variations had gone by. I must have slept through them, because I hadn't been awake. I listened and heard nothing but more wind. I closed my eyes again. I fell into a dream that seemed to last no longer than two seconds. I was standing at my car, filling its tank from a jerry can. The fuel kept missing the hole and showering the earth. Fumes reared up into my nose and throat.

I opened my eyes. I was out of the dream and back in the dark room, but somehow the stink of petrol had followed me in. I was still working out what that meant when the night beyond the stippled glass of the front door erupted in a thump of yellow heat. For an instant I saw a vandal's silhouette through the door's haze, backlit by jittering flame. Then the shadow surged at the glass and the glass blew in and dropped like a curtain, the smash already half-drowned under the crackle of blazing timber. Here he came, riding into the room on this huge wave of light and noise and splintered glass, with the whole front deck a lake of orange fire behind him. The philosophical portion of the evening was over. Dallas Fingle had arrived, with a plan as barbarous as his prose.

Its first flaw, if you didn't count torching the house as a flaw, was that I saw him before he saw me. By the time he did, I had covered the boards between us and was arcing my bottle into his face like a nine iron. His crazed momentum doubled the heft of my swing, and my swing had been all heft to start with. The impact was magnificent. Both the bottle and his face exploded, and I took a lavish backspray of warm booze, warmer blood, spit, sweat, spume, glass, teeth. On the downside, the torn neck of the bottle did not remain in my hand. That turned out to matter a lot, because Fingle did not stop coming. My best shot had hardly given him pause. He slammed rampantly into me and rode me to the floor. His supercharged weight pinned me to the boards. I had forgotten how sinewy and furious he was in his proper element. He didn't even seem to have brought a weapon. So far he was doing fine without one. He had me fully on my back now, in the missionary pose. Hot fluids rained from his face onto mine. The open doorway behind him was a cataract of noon-bright heat. In the writhing light his rearing shadow crazily danced. His face flickered in monochrome,

like Nosferatu's, complete with fucked-up teeth. His hands
wanted my throat. I pushed back at his iron wrists. It was
equal to pushing back at some blind natural force, like time,
like erosion. Glenn Gould played on. Above me Fingle was
either smiling or grimacing. He had a beard of black slime.
This was as intimate as sex but only one of us was going
to like the ending. I doubted it would be me. I was starting
to feel my age down there. He was better at this than I was.
He was younger and stronger and madder. It was a bad time
to grasp how much these things mattered. I should have
challenged him to a prose contest instead. But I had, and
I'd lost that too. On the turntable the last variation stopped
and the coda began: the closing of the circle, the restatement
of the theme. I thought I might as well stay alive to hear it.
But after three bars I heard nothing but the roar of timber
becoming flame, like feral static, like thunderous applause.
The smoke alarm got the message and started pointlessly
bleating. Fingle's profane hands were six inches from
my throat. His knee was on my one good lung. I opened my
mouth to gulp air and tasted a salty rope of his blood and
oral slime. I spat and shook my head. The fire was all around
us now. We were inside it. It had gone from frightening to
fucking ridiculous. The iron roof of the porch groaned and
buckled as if being chewed. Rivets blew like rifle shots. Flame
doglegged through the open door and turned the curtains
into an inverted waterfall of fire. Fingle's goatee of blood
and drool went from monochrome to shocking red. Against
the front wall my pillars of unread books were going up like
effigies. Catullus, the guys like that, all those classics I had
saved for the rainy day that suddenly would never come.
Cinders spewed down on us like hot slag. It was hardly a

question, any more, of which one of us would die. We were both going to. It would be a miracle if we didn't. Was that what he wanted? Mutual extinction? I saw that it had been a radical error to leave the evening's finer points up to him. The fire was vintage Fingle: the epic gesture, void of sense. The halfwit's version of profundity. I owed it to the world to take this imbecile down with me. Surely that was the best I could now do: consign both of us to the flames, and hope it conflicted with his plans.

But a wilder option was still open to me. The armchair wasn't far behind us. The hammer was still on the floor beside it. If I released one of his wrists and reached back there, there was a fair chance I'd find it. But it would be my valedictory gamble. The moment I let go, he would have my throat. If all I found back there was empty floor, I'd be fucked. But I was getting fucked now anyway, pretty much literally. His quivering iron hands were two inches from my throat and his shirt was half off and his knee was on my balls and he was drooling blood into my eye. And his cock was on my belly, and it was rock-hard. Yes: the unforgivable little freak was hard. That settled it. It was high time one of us died. I let go and reached back. The dam broke and his hands came down on my throat: first one, then the other. If I'd known how bad it would feel I wouldn't have let it happen. A zeppelin exploded behind my ribs, and the flames had nowhere to go. My body wanted to cough and gag and breathe and scream and burst at the same time. When none of these things proved possible it tried harder. A riotous tingling filled my drifting distant limbs. I felt my eyeballs swell towards infinity, like Missy's. My vision went dark: I saw a night sky full of blooming flak, a deluge of paratroopers opening blotchy purple chutes. Flailing my flung-back hand, I hit and toppled the upright hammer. As I slid away from care, I found the fallen rubber handle and gripped it and swung the head lazily back into the fading world.

The steel glanced off something bony and skidded beyond it, the shaft twisting in my hand like a tennis racquet caught on the frame, the grip quivering with a sick electric buzz. The spillway to my lungs surged back open, and I raggedly gorged myself on air. Through a field of opening poppies I saw Fingle kneeling above me, with both hands pressed ardently to his upper face. Blood flowed through them like hose water through the cupped hands of a child. The hammer was still in my hand. The whole near side of his skull hung before me unprotected, proffered, floating there like a fruit, a sweat-matted coconut. Either time had frozen or he held this pose for an epoch, in eerie surrender, as if begging me to take the shot. I took it, with an exuberance I still half-regret. This time the hammer didn't bounce off. It sank right into his skull, like an axe into a wet log. I hadn't drunk nearly enough to make that sight forgettable. My own skull sizzled with tender horror in the same place, as if to confirm I was still human. Fingle no longer was, if he ever had been. He crawled away like a sprayed bug, vomiting. The hammer decoupled itself from his dented skull and flipped to the floor. With horrible zombie-like doggedness he struggled to his feet. He put a hand up and felt the wicked sinkhole in his head, then walked backwards in a stunned sort of way until he hit the flaming curtains and donned them like a cape. His sleeves went up fast. The poor dead stooge must have dappled them with splashback while laying down the fuel. When he reeled forward again he was clawing at his lapels, as if things could still be made right by the shedding of his jacket. He was wrong about that. A lot of him was on fire, including his hair. His arms were wings with flames for feathers. Like a great crippled bird he flapped them and staggered towards me. I backed away, not wanting to catch his disease. I retreated to the part of the house that was still part of a house. Soon I could retreat no further. I was up against the door that Missy Wilde was on the other side of. Fingle was up against that door too, in his lumbering symbolic way. He always had liked his metaphors crude. The tackler of the big themes was about to tackle the biggest theme of all. He was no longer a man on fire. He was fire in the rough shape of a man. He sank to his knees, uttering a burro's shriek that I doubt I will ever get out of my head. I heard it all too vividly, even over the roar of everything else. Then, briefly, he tried to crawl again. I decided that the rest had better happen in private. Watching it no longer felt right. I turned and took my leave through the bedroom door. The handle felt like the face of a hot iron: it flayed my fingers almost to the bone. The room behind it was a cube of mud-thick smog. I couldn't see the window but I knew where it was. I went straight for it. I didn't look back. If I'd had any prized possessions, I'd have died getting them. At the window I made the mistake of putting my hand briefly, very briefly, on the blistering sill. When I put the sole of my boot there instead I smelt frying rubber. I took a token last glance back at Missy but saw only a world of smoke. I launched myself out into the arctic air, and staggered to the top of the yard's slope, and fell down there and watched the rest of everything burn. It didn't take long.

14

Killing Fingle was a good career move, for one of us. Guess which one. Guess what getting exposed as a multiple murderer did for his bottom line. Guess how far into the black I sent him by toasting him alive. The marketers, Jade's heirs, worked fast. They refashioned the Fingle brand on the fly. Back when he was alive, and guilty of nothing except crimes against prose, they had positioned him as merely 'powerful'. Now they called him 'controversial'. They rush-released his novel with that word on the cover. That turned out to be controversial too, which was probably part of their plan. You don't sell the book, you sell the look. Did I make that phrase up, or did I get it from Jade? The cover is where the fiction starts. You can say whatever you like on it. If the contents turn out to be no good, that's the next book's problem, and that book will probably be no good anyway, and so will the next one, until finally, like the man who chopped down the last tree on Easter Island, you create one top-heavy idol too many, and there are no more books at all.

Did Jade say these things? Maybe she did, on that last night we spent together – that night I had and then lost before the fist of memory could close around it.

On the plus side, Fingle's corpse won no literary prizes. You don't get to kill that many people and still bag the major awards, no matter how morally okay you seem on the page. In the blogs and the book-chat columns, the pundits scratched their heads about his case. The contrast between his off-page evil and his on-page righteousness struck them as 'ironic'. It struck nobody that inoffensiveness must be a meaningless achievement, if a man like Fingle can pull it off. Instead they spoke of his complexity, his demons: the epic struggle between the regrettable life and the non-regrettable work. Nobody floated the radical thought that he was simply no good. That heresy wasn't conceivable. In that department Jade's work was done, and would never be undone. Fingle had *merit* – the notion had been grafted into the bible of received ideas. He was a touchstone. When people wanted to define quality now, they would think of Fingle's big creaking symbols on the harbour, blotting out the light of nuance, dropping their ponderous anchors into a cellophane sea.

Fingle smelled, when he burned, like cooking meat. I should have been ready for that. In a way I was. I knew he was just an animal. How could I not know that? But I wasn't ready for how *much* he would smell like meat. He didn't just smell a bit like it, or a lot like it. He smelt exactly like it. He *was* it.

Death is not as exotic as you think. It doesn't just happen to other people in other rooms. You start getting that message, once a certain number of corpses turn up in your house. Seneca was one old Roman I did happen to read, before all those classics of mine went up in smoke. You are wrong, he said somewhere, to think of death as something you haven't had yet. A lot of it has happened to you already. Look at all that life you've left behind, all those days you have already lost. So why worry about dying? Seneca said. Most of you is dead already. Apparently this struck Seneca as quite a feel-good observation. I'm fucked if I know why.

Skeats got replaced by Barrett Lodge. I had seen that coming. After a while, you get so good at reading the past that you can foresee the future. But by then there's not much of the future left. Lodge's first order of business was never to call on my services again. I'd seen that coming too. Finally we have found something Lodge doesn't like. He doesn't like me. There, as always, he is on impeccably safe turf.

Jill Tweedy rang me. She wasn't the only agent or publisher who did, but she was the only one I needed to see. She received me in the Bennett and Bennett conference room. There was a long table with a platter of fruit on it. Tweedy wasn't eating it, which evidently meant it was all for me. She was all smiles. Last time I'd seen her smile like that, the smiles had been aimed at Fingle, back when he was alive and still the blue-eyed boy. Now the A-game manners and the finger food were for me – the black-eyed boy, with fresh and legitimate bruises to go with my scars, and a thick glove of white bandage on my scorched right hand.

'I think we can start talking about deadlines now,' she told me. 'You've got your ending now, which you didn't before. That showdown in your house. A great reckoning in a little room. Get into that fruit, Ray, or I will. Also you're out of the woods legally, which is nice. Plus you've got a clear arc now, personally. It turns out you were the good guy all along. Before, people never really knew what to make of you.'

'They hated me,' I said.

More smiles, again not from me. You had to hand it to her. Before Fingle's body was cold, before it had even smouldered back to room temperature, Tweedy had shoved a hefty pre-emptive advance into my bank account. Strange, that: she had felt no such urgency when I was starving and suspect and not so heroically in the news. Nor, back then, had she been inclined to give me nearly so much money. But Fingle was dead now, and I had killed him. And here was Tweedy talking about deadlines, strategies, *pages*. She thought she had me snookered. Her literary ethics were not a big improvement on Fingle's. Oddly, she seemed to be betting that mine weren't even worse.

'There'll be a synergy here with *Tainted*,' she told me, interlacing her fingers. '*Tainted* will help your project, yours'll help it. I see us selling yours as sort of a non-fiction sequel. The candid story behind the big work.'

I had no wish to prolong the scene. I said, 'Here's something candid. Fingle was Jade's baby. She created him, out of some very primal clay. The moment she was out of the way, you started claiming the credit.'

She hadn't known I knew that. She threw out some flustered but irrelevant words of denial.

'Here's something else,' I said. 'Why *did* she pull Fingle out of that slush pile? Not because he was any good.'

'That's politics,' Tweedy said hastily. 'People don't want to read about that.'

'I see. Killing him's one thing, but saying he couldn't write would be letting down the side.' I waited, in case she wanted to register any more token protests. 'So you don't want me to be candid about *him*,' I said, when she didn't. 'Or her.' I waited. 'Or him *and* her.' I waited. 'Or her and Skeats.' I waited. 'Or the way the business works.' I waited. 'You're not looking for that much synergy.'

'That,' said Tweedy, 'isn't the book we want from you.'

'What a shame,' I said. 'But thanks for the money.'

She said nothing, which probably meant she had got my point already. In case she hadn't I said, 'You know what my story is. Either pay me to write it or pay me not to.'

She didn't have to think about it very hard.

So the rest is silence, paid for by Bennett and Bennett. I have moved up in the world. I have stopped being broke, for the moment. I am back to merely going broke. I am back to getting poor slow. Somehow that fall or leap I took all those years ago continues. I still haven't hit the ground. I have time on my hands. I am free to read Thucydides, Cicero, all those books that lie in ashes in the black and buckled frame of my home. I have time to think about Jade, which might not be the best thing for my health. Maybe I'd have been better off writing Tweedy's book. But if it's a choice between writing lies and writing nothing, I'm enough of a writer to write nothing. I have learned that much from all this, if no more.

I saw Ted Lewin last week. We met in a pub. I thought I was getting him drunk. Probably he thought the same about me. There were things we still wanted from each other. He already had the flash drive, and some idea of what it meant. He had Fingle's flambéed DNA. He had motive, if you wanted to call it that, for Jade, and Missy, and Skeats. But he wanted more. He was a completist. We talked way, way off the record. He told me some things he had known all along. On the night she died, my phone was with me in the car, spewing data as I drove. That whole sorry night, as I blundered towards her through the dark, I laid down digital spoor like a leaking sack of rice. Lewin showed me the printouts: the constellation of my missing hours, the spreadsheet of my innocence. Just before eleven I found her phone number online, and called her. The conversation went for six minutes. Then I got in the car. For about ninety minutes I laid down a trail going east, towards her house. I pinged towers. I triggered toll sensors. I tripped a speed camera or two. I took a few wrong turns. All of this meshed with my ragged memories. At twelve-twenty my phone hit one last tower and stopped moving. That meant I was at her house. And there the record went dark, in my skull and in Lewin's files. For nearly five hours I was off the grid. Whatever happened in that nook of time left no trace, except for a fading bite on my skin. And then at five-fifteen I existed again, according to the files. I was back out on the road, spilling data the other way. Just before six, when I was almost home, she rang me. Or somebody did, using her phone. The call lasted twelve seconds. Whatever got said made me turn round and go back, fast. I made it there in forty minutes. The rest I remembered, more or less. The sun rising before I got there. Her front door wide open. Walking inside and seeing what I saw.

So my ramshackle alibi (I wasn't there, except when I was; I did plenty, but I didn't do *that*) had been true all along, or at least not false. Lewin had always known that, but had never been able to believe it. And I had always believed it, but had never been able to know it. All along, Lewin had held his unbeatable cards: the irrefutable pings of the towers and tollgates. And all he was ever waiting for, in that slow-motion room of his, was the moment when I would outrage this data in some irreversible and fully damning way: the moment when I would commit myself, at last, to a coherent body of hard lies. And then he would have played his mighty hand, his lay down *misère*, and dared me to reply. (*Lay Down Misère*: a good title for the autobiography I will never write.) And no comeback would have been good enough, at that point, to prevent the sequel: the handcuffs, the cell, the confiscation of the belt and laces. Even the truth, or my tattered version of it, would not have worked. I would have been shovelling my words into a void. (My autobiography again.) So all along I had been one rash answer away from doom. Each week Lewin had waited, with his printouts posed. And each week I kept disappointing him, in more ways than I knew. I had such a hazy hold on the truth that I didn't even know when I was lying, or if I needed to. I had done my best, but my claims had lacked theme, pattern, structure. Whenever Lewin tried to close his hands around my story, he came up with nothing but air. I couldn't even get my lies straight, and that had saved me – if you wanted to call me saved.

And now Lewin needed saving too. He wanted closure. He didn't use the word. He was too grown-up for that. But he seemed to believe in the concept, which surprised me. You'd think he'd know better, even with a few beers in him. The case was closed. He knew enough, more than enough. But he couldn't stand not knowing the rest, and he was desperate enough to think he could get it from me. What happened in those uncharted five hours? What did we talk about? What made me leave? What made me go back? What got said in that twelve-second call? The satellites can't answer questions like that. Lewin thought I still could. He had never believed I could forget such things. He theorised that Fingle had been outside the house that night, watching us, waiting for me to leave. He wanted that theory verified by me. He thought I could remember sby an act of will. He still didn't get it. Hunched over his readout of her final hours, he begged me to repair its blind spots, its voids, its grey areas. This is all he's ever wanted from me – a story that is all light. And this is the last thing I am equipped to provide. Scan my brain and you will see shadows where the light will never go, smudges of dark matter as scrambled as Lewin's bad eye. The skull doctors can't fix me. They can only plot and image my failures, with white machines that look like streamlined coffins. And now Lewin thought he could restore me to health by waving a few scraps of data at me. This was touching but misguided. All he was giving me was more incompleteness, more fragments to shore against my ruins.

'You want to jog my memory?' I asked him. 'Jog it all the way. Where did you find my sample?'

He looked away from me, pretending not to know what that meant.

'You know what I'm asking,' I said. 'Tell me where it was. Exactly.'

He was disgusted, but this is what you get when you do these things in a pub.

'On her?' I said. 'In her? Where? On what? It's my sample. Tell me where I left it.'

It was not my finest moment. It got less fine. I started begging. 'Help me remember,' I said. 'Not just for you. For me.'

He knew the answer, but he wouldn't tell me. There was pity in his eyes, but not mercy. I sickened him. He sat there and watched me drown. I have never seen him again.

They have boarded up her little house, with its tangled gardens and its out-of-hand lawn. I am getting evicted from my past, one person and one venue at a time. They're winking out on me like lights: Jade, Skeats, Lewin, Lewin's room, the newspaper, my place, hers. I see now that I blew my best and only shot at salvation, that night I went back to toss her house. Raiding her panty drawer was a cheap short-term play. I should have pillaged her bookshelves instead. There, if anywhere, I would have found the real her. Did she own, for example, a copy of Ern Malley's *Complete Poems*? Did she fill its margins with notes? I have convinced myself that she studied his case: the bad poet invented by two good ones. This is Malley:

> *It is necessary to understand*
> *That a poet may not exist, that his writings*
> *Are the incomplete circle and straight drop*
> *Of a question mark*
> *And yet I know I shall be raised up*
> *On the vertical banners of praise.*

Not bad, for a man who never existed. Better than Fingle, who did. They don't make frauds like Ern Malley any more. I have convinced myself that his spirit hung over us as we lay twined on my bed. On good days I feel that her spirit was there too: not hovering or half-absent, but fully down there in her body, with me. But I will never know for sure. That case can never be closed. The question will have to hang forever: the incomplete circle, the straight drop.

If I had her back on the planet for just an hour, I would devote every minute of it to cross-examination. Sex is fleeting, and I have begun to hate fleeting things. Sex lasts for as long as it lasts for, and then it's gone. Unanswered questions never leave. They bloom and spread like tumours, and they kill you a lot more than once. I would have my questions ready for her, like a stalker. I would ask her the things Lewin asked me, and more. What made me leave her house that morning? Did she know Fingle was coming, or did he swing by uninvited, like me? Did she tell me again that Vagg was on the way? Was that how she got rid of me? Or did I break and tell her the truth and get kicked out because I had cost her fifteen grand? How many lies were there in the bed with us, that second time? As many as the first time, or even more? Or did we purify the air between us and go at it lie-free, like proper lovers? I would ask her about the distance I heard in her voice, that night on the phone. Was she falling away from me even then? Had I already served my purpose? I would ask these questions with shame, knowing she deserved better than to be pawed at by a Proustian maniac like me. But I would ask them anyway. I would ask her what her plans had been, post-Fingle. I would ask her point-blank if I was in them. I would ask her if I was ever inside her head, just a little bit. I would ask her if she had seen the same light in my eyes that I saw in hers. Recall that this is a fantasy, in which I would get the truth from her just by asking for it.

There are days when I half-forget that she is dead, or somehow manage to point my mind at other things. And then the huge fact of it just rears up out of nowhere and stuns me, like those big raw winds that sweep off the ocean and rattle your car on a coastal road. I blink and I sway on my feet, but I have to want the pain as much as it wants me. It means she still matters. The day it stops sideswiping me that hard will be the day she starts dying a second time.

There are days when I try to make that happen. I tell myself she used me and half-destroyed me. I tell myself she isn't yet done. I tell myself that one day soon the dead weight of her will drag the rest of me the rest of the way down, unless I cut the wire and let her drop. But I have never managed to believe these things yet, and probably never will. There are days when I tell myself I hardly knew her. I burnt my life down for a girl I met twice. It can't have been much of a life, if I was ready to do that. And maybe it wasn't. But maybe I'd have torched it for her anyway, even if I knew her better, and even if there had been more of it to burn. Maybe she was that much of a girl. If I could convince myself that she wasn't, would that make things better or worse? It doesn't matter. I am in no serious danger of believing it, or even of wanting to. She was worthy of the flame, and can still be saved from it. There are things about her that only I remember. Phrases, movements of the eyes, little gestures she threw out into the hurricane of passing time. If I don't hang on to those scraps of her, who will? I didn't kill her the first time, but if I let these last things fade she will die again, and this time it will be for good, and the culprit will finally be me.

I still think about her there on my doorstep, pressing her face against the flyscreen, shielding her little scrunched-up eyes against the afternoon sun. The moment slows, then freezes. The rolling film becomes a still photograph. Her body hangs there like fruit in the frame of the wire door. I feel I could reach back through the frame and seize her, and never let her go. Quick, now, before the lamp burns through the celluloid. But always I stay frozen there at the keyboard, stranded, clueless, paralysed in the act of writing something that no one will ever read. And then the film yaws back up to speed, and I have lost my shot again, and the scene plays out the way it always has and always will. There is no way of being ready for these moments. The bigness of the big half-hours is never clear until they're falling away from you, tumbling away in the rear-view: the lopped story that could have gone any way, the phantom limb that will never stop itching. The best luck you ever had, or the worst, or both. If I could have that moment back a hundred times, I would gladly live my way through every last one of its branching universes. I know I've lived the worst one already.

But she won't come back to me that way. The memory of that moment gets smaller all the time. It grows blurred and smudged with overuse. What I live for is the memory that will feel brand new, because I have never had it. The untouched memory of that lost final night: it's in there somewhere, in some walled-off cellar of my dusty head, unbreached, patiently waiting, pristine in its wrapper, like a gift I never opened and weirdly left behind. Lewin was wrong to think I can liberate those missing hours by force. I can't. I have tried. But maybe, if I stick around for long enough, they will return to me by accident. One day the frayed ends of my severed, wandering neurons might brush up against each other, and spark into service, and the dead memory will explode back into the light. And she will be here again, and I will meet her as if for the first time. She will be back, and her little eyes will be laughing again, and she will have no idea she is dead. Because she won't be, not yet, not then. It's a laughable little hope, but so are most hopes. I don't see why I shouldn't stick around and cling to it, for a while. There will be plenty of time for oblivion.